*"Alexa, I wanted
thought I should explain..."*

"Yes?" she prompted.

Ty cleared his throat. "I did a lot of talking when I was younger. I said I was going to prove something to everybody. That isn't why I'm back in town. That's not why I'm buying the mill."

"I'm disappointed. Aren't you trying to prove anything anymore? Or have you conquered everything you had targeted in your master plan?"

Ty grinned at the challenge in her words, and suddenly he was once again the cocky, hotheaded young rebel, ready to grab the world and shake it by the tail. Her taunting voice was the same one that had provoked the loading-dock worker to kiss the boss's daughter in the cool darkness of the warehouse.

The excitement kindled between them. Just as it had twelve years earlier...

Dear Reader,

Sophisticated but sensitive, savvy yet unabashedly sentimental—that's today's woman, today's romance reader—you! And Silhouette Special Editions are written expressly to reward your quest for substantial, emotionally involving love stories.

So take a leisurely stroll under the cover's lavender arch into a garden of romantic delights. Pick and choose among titles if you must—we hope you'll soon equate all six Special Editions each month with consistently gratifying romantic reading.

Watch for sparkling new stories from your Silhouette favorites—Nora Roberts, Tracy Sinclair, Ginna Gray, Lindsay McKenna, Curtiss Ann Matlock, among others—along with some exciting newcomers to Silhouette, such as Karen Keast and Patricia Coughlin. Be on the lookout, too, for the new Silhouette Classics, a distinctive collection of bestselling Special Editions and Silhouette Intimate Moments now brought back to the stands—two each month—by popular demand.

On behalf of all the authors and editors of Special Editions,
Warmest wishes,

Leslie Kazanjian
Senior Editor

CELESTE HAMILTON
Torn Asunder

Silhouette Special Edition

Published by Silhouette Books New York

America's Publisher of Contemporary Romance

For Leigh,
my partner, my teacher,
and above all, my *friend*

SILHOUETTE BOOKS
300 East 42nd St., New York, N.Y. 10017

Copyright © 1987 by Jan Hamilton Powell

ISBN: 0-373-09418-3

First Silhouette Books printing November 1987

America's Publisher of Contemporary Romance

Printed in the U.S.A.

CELESTE HAMILTON

began writing when she was ten years old, with the encouragement of parents who told her she could accomplish anything she set out to do and teachers who helped her refine her talents. Writing for the broadcast media captured her interest in high school, and she went on to graduate from the University of Tennessee with a B.S. in Communications. From there, she began writing and producing radio commercials at a top-rated Chattanooga, Tennessee, radio station. "Aside from a brief stint at an advertising agency," says Celeste, "I've stayed with radio, and I love it! I now work for Chattanooga's top country music station."

Celeste began writing romances in January 1985 and "never intends to stop." She's married to a policeman and likes nothing better than spending time at home with him and their two much-loved cats, although they also like to travel whenever their busy schedules allow it. Wherever they may go, however, "it's always nice to come home to East Tennessee—one of the most beautiful corners of the world." And Celeste used this setting she loves best in both *Torn Asunder* and her forthcoming *Silent Partner*.

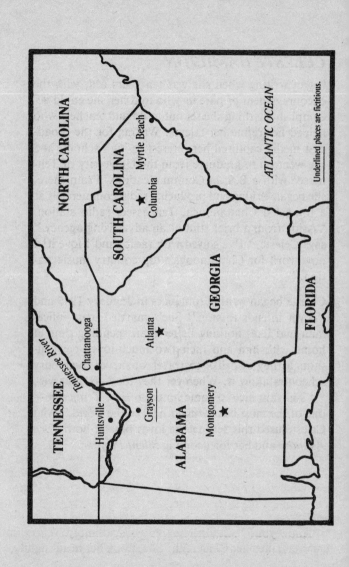

NORTH CAROLINA

TENNESSEE

Tennessee River

Huntsville •

Chattanooga •

Grayson •

ALABAMA

Montgomery ★

SOUTH CAROLINA

Columbia ★

Atlanta ★

GEORGIA

Myrtle Beach •

ATLANTIC OCEAN

FLORIDA

Underlined places are fictitious.

Chapter One

Hello, Cinderella."

Alexa Thorpe froze as the husky voice penetrated the surrounding restaurant noise and skipped along the edges of her memory. Disbelief turned slowly to recognition as she moved away from the salad bar and looked straight into the gray eyes of Tyler Duncan.

"Ty?" she asked, more to hear the spoken evidence of his presence than to ascertain it was really he. Although twelve years had passed, she would have known that voice, that unruly black hair and those irregular but handsome features anytime, anywhere.

"Lost any glass slippers lately?" His generous mouth curved into a lopsided grin. Ty could see Alex was having trouble believing her eyes. Well, after all this time perhaps she didn't want to remember him. "You know me, don't you?"

"Know you?" Alex echoed his words dumbly. Who else had ever called her Cinderella? She shook her head slightly, trying to dispel the faint feeling of unreality. "Of course I know you, Ty." She forced down the slight tremor in her voice. "What are you doing in Grayson?"

"Business." The answer was terse and dismissing, as if his reason for being in town was of no consequence to her. "I was having lunch with Walt Clemmer."

Alex followed the direction of Ty's nod to a corner table, where the president of one of the local banks sat. She frowned slightly. What business did Ty have with a local bank?

"Pardon me." A plump matron angled her way past them, headed for the salad bar. Shifting with murmurs of apology, Alex and Ty moved out of the mainstream of restaurant traffic. An awkward silence fell between them. Alex found herself studying the expensive Italian leather of Ty's shoes while she nervously smoothed the soft material of her red jersey sundress.

"You look almost the same," Ty murmured, his gray eyes silvery as he watched her intently. "But you cut your hair."

"Yes, well . . . it's been a long time. I've cut it several times." Alex's hand crept up to touch the point where her dark hair skimmed her shoulder.

"I guess you're right." Ty managed an awkward smile, and again the silence yawned, deep and uncomfortable, between them. "Well, I'd better get back to Walt. I saw you come in, and I just wanted to say hello."

"I'm glad you did." It was hard to speak around the sudden catch in her throat, but Alex tried to sound light and casual.

"Are you?" The intensity of his own question took Ty by surprise. *Damn! Why did I say that?* he thought.

"Of course I'm glad. It's always nice to see old friends." Alex hoped he caught the emphasis she put on the last word. After all, she had no hard feelings, did she? The pain had died long ago.

Alex responded automatically to Ty's goodbye and stood staring after him for a few moments. Winding his way through the crowded dining room, he looked tall, self-assured and successful. From all appearances, Ty Duncan had made something of himself. *I always knew he would,* she thought approvingly. *I always told him he could.*

She might have stood there by the salad bar gazing after his retreating back for several minutes if her best friend, Suzie Lewis, hadn't tapped her arm.

"Was that Ty Duncan?" Suzie said with a little squeal. "I can't believe it! What's he doing back in Grayson?"

"I don't know." Alex turned back to the salad bar and finished loading her chilled plate with food. The colorful array of vegetables and salads, so appetizing only minutes earlier, now seemed singularly unappealing.

"Didn't he say?" Suzie demanded.

"We barely had time to say hello. Good heavens, I don't care what he's doing here." With a small gesture of impatience, Alex returned to their booth, leaving Suzie to follow.

It was true. She didn't care what Ty Duncan was doing back in Grayson, Alabama. He might have left in a hurry twelve years ago, but that didn't mean he couldn't return. His mother and sister still lived here, as did other relatives. Perhaps he was seeing Walt Clemmer about some family business. Although why the bank president would be involved was beyond her, Alex decided that explanation was as good as any, and offered it to Suzie.

"Doesn't his mother still work at the high-school cafeteria?" Suzie asked, digging into her own salad.

"Yes, she does," Alex answered shortly. She saw Mrs. Duncan every lunch hour of every weekday during the school year. Something about the proud set of the woman's head reminded her of Ty, and she kept her distance.

Determinedly Alex shifted the conversation away from Ty Duncan and on to different, far safer, territory. "Now what was the big announcement you called me about this morning? At first I thought you were asking me to lunch because it's my birthday, but you said you had some good news. What is it?"

Suzie's dark blue eyes were alight with excitement. "Jason and I are going to have another baby."

"Suzie, that's wonderful!" Alex squeezed her friend's hand affectionately. "I'm so happy for you. I know you've been hoping for a brother or sister for Melanie for a long time."

The light in her friend's eyes faded a little. "And we've been disappointed too many times. That's why I've waited before making the announcement. But Dr. Maynard thinks things are going well, and we should have a new baby by Christmas."

"I can't think of a better Christmas gift—or a better birthday present, either! The only way to celebrate turning thirty is a toast to a new baby." Giggling like schoolgirls, the two friends lifted their iced-tea glasses to each other in a salute.

Suzie sent Alex a mischievous glance. "I wish we were celebrating something else, too—something like an engagement. Tom Jacobs has lasted longer than most of the men you've sent packing over the years. Do I hear wedding bells?"

"Tom's okay, I guess...." Alex faltered, searching for an exact description of what Tom represented in her life. Friendship. Security. Boredom. Unfortunately, bored was more and more how she felt when she was with him.

Her mother kept saying what a nice man Tom was. How successful his law practice had become. What a catch he'd be. On and on came the reasons why she should be engaged to him. However, none of them was compelling enough to allow Alex to accept his proposal.

Thankfully, Suzie didn't press her about Tom. Instead she chattered happily about her husband and daughter, the upcoming golf tournament at the club and her plans to redo the nursery. It was a pleasant conversation, not unlike thousands the two women had enjoyed throughout a friendship begun in the first grade.

But Alex couldn't keep her mind on any of the topics Suzie introduced. Instead she thought about Ty.

Seeing him again was definitely a shock. Whenever she'd allowed herself to think about Ty over the past years, it had been with the certainty that she'd never see him again. How and when she'd arrived at that conclusion lay buried somewhere in the pain of those twelve years. Now it seemed like a silly assumption to have made. Of course they were going to run into each other again with her still living in the same town as his family.

Alex instinctively made the correct responses to Suzie. Around them swirled the busy lunchtime activity of the Taylor Inn, Grayson's best restaurant. But Alex felt a peculiar distance, as if she were seated high above the room. She couldn't see the table where Ty sat. So, subtly, she kept an eye on the door, watching for his departure. He didn't leave. Eventually Alex and Suzie did.

Standing in the bright June sunshine after her friend had left, Alex experienced a familiar pull of disappointment. The tiny ball of hurt was the same she'd once felt in high school when the boy she'd liked hadn't said hello in the hall—a feeling she hadn't had in quite some time.

Crossing to the parking lot, she slid behind the wheel of her small blue Toyota. But she didn't leave. She rolled down the windows and sat watching the door—watching for Ty.

He was so casual, Alex thought. So carefree about coming up and speaking to her after all these years, after all that had happened.

Suddenly impatient with herself, she started her car and pulled out onto Main Street. "I'll forget I saw him," she said out loud. He had obviously forgotten what they'd meant to each other. Otherwise he'd have had something more to say than hello. Alex squashed her growing disappointment and resolutely headed for home.

Ty had watched Alex leave the restaurant with regret. For just a minute there, when she'd first recognized him, he thought he'd seen a flicker of pleasure in her brown eyes. He smiled cynically at the thought; he doubted Alexa Thorpe was pleased to see him. But still, after this long, surely she had forgiven him as he had forgiven her. She'd been pleasant enough, if a little surprised. But that was to be expected. It had been a long time.

"I don't anticipate any problems with the deal," Walt Clemmer said smoothly, drawing Ty's attention back to the business at hand. "This would certainly be a boost to the community. The closing of the mill really hurt the town."

"I know," Ty muttered grimly. His mother's letters in the last few years had been full of the hard times Grayson had been experiencing. His brother-in-law had gone without a job for two full years before a new tire factory had opened.

"I keep forgetting about Grayson being your home town." Clemmer studied Ty soberly for a moment. "You don't look much like the teenager I once threw out of my cabin up on the lake. You had quite a wild reputation back then."

Ty recognized the comment for what it was: a subtle yet pointed question about the present state of his reputation. In places all over the country, all over the world, a man could negotiate a business deal and his personal life wouldn't be mentioned. But not here. Not in Grayson, Alabama. Here men were judged by the side of town they were born in. And here the past could always come back to haunt you. God, no wonder he and Alex had never stood a chance.

He shifted easily in his chair and drawled, "You gonna hold something I did when I was sixteen against me now, Walt? As I recall, it was your nephew Charlie who threw that particular party at your cabin. I hear he's vice president of the bank now. Surely you've forgiven him his part in that little escapade."

Clemmer cleared his throat abruptly. "Yeah...well, I suppose you're right. That was a while ago. Obviously you've changed, just as Charlie did."

"Obviously," Ty said dryly. What wasn't said was something both men knew. After that wild party, Charlie Clemmer had been forbidden to spend any more time in Ty Duncan's company and had been packed off to an exclusive prep school. Charlie's current respectability was probably credited to his uncle's foresight in getting him away from Ty and his delinquent friends.

Clemmer took a last sip of coffee, then pushed the cup and saucer away. "As you know, the bank's board will need a while to go over your company's offer, and then, of course, I'm sure your board will have to finalize..."

"I'm authorized to make all the decisions about the mill property," Ty cut in, his voice hard with finality. "I'm a full partner in DunMar Carpets, and I'm completely in charge of this acquisition."

"I see." Clemmer hoisted his bulky frame up from the table. "Whatever the case, it will probably be a week. One of the board members is away, and we don't usually make decisions this large without a full representation." He handed Ty a set of keys. "In case you want to look around the mill further."

"Aren't you afraid I'll find something I don't like?"

Clemmer regarded him with a slight smile. "You look like a man who wouldn't have made an offer without being absolutely sure of what he was buying."

"You're right." Ty stood and took the keys, and the two men moved silently across the now almost empty restaurant. After paying the check, they went outside.

"I'll be in touch in a week," Clemmer said.

"Good. I'll be here in town, at my mother's."

After a quick handshake, the graying banker hurried across the street to the two-story red brick building from which he wielded his power.

Ty laughed at his mental description of Clemmer's duties. It was a carryover from his childhood, this thinking of the bank as an all-powerful, all-seeing entity. Standing here on Main Street in his home town, it was easy to remember his father going in that building to ask for a loan. How tall and proud Harris Duncan had looked walking into the bank. How beaten and old he'd looked walking out, the loan-denial papers clutched in his hand.

Shutting his eyes, Ty tried to block out the memory. But when he opened them there were a hundred more memories waiting for him on this street, in this town.

Leaving his crimson BMW parked in the inn's lot, he strolled down the street. Here in the downtown area not much had changed since he'd left. The brick courthouse, built in the late 1800s, still stood square in the middle of town. The shops and office buildings surrounding it still retained their 1930s and 1940s facades. Some, like the bank and the Inn, had been modernized a bit, but most had the sleepy feeling, the lazy ambience that Ty would always associate with small southern towns.

The rest of Grayson stretched out from this hub. To the north and east lay more shops and businesses and the wide, quiet streets of the affluent residential section. Ty knew well the feeling that could be found there—green, well-tended lawns, large cared-for homes, spreading trees providing welcome coolness on even the hottest days. That part of town belonged to Alexa Thorpe—or at least to her kind.

Ty stood facing north, picturing Alex's family's home, a pristine white house with neatly painted green shutters and boxwoods lining the front porch. It was an old house, mellowed by time, preserved by the power of generations of money.

Did they still live there? Ty wondered. He knew Alex's father was dead, knew the family's finances weren't what they once had been. After all, that was the reason he was back in town. The mill was for sale.

And what of Alex? What was she doing here? Perhaps she was married to some up-and-coming businessman. Ty thought of her deep brown eyes, wide and startled at the sight of him. No doubt she'd hoped never to see him again.

He wondered how she had felt, facing him after all these years. Her slightly friendly but certainly remote expression had given no clue. She's a lot like her family's house, Ty thought suddenly—a cool, pretty exterior with well-hidden secrets. The opportunity to discover those secrets was by invitation only, and Ty knew he'd never be on the guest list again.

Why had he gone over to her at the restaurant? It would have been just as easy to have pretended not to see her, to have stayed seated and simply watched her. But she'd looked so damn good. As always, he'd been drawn to her. Like a kid going for the forbidden candy, Ty thought with frustration. After all this time, he still wasn't immune to Alex's charms.

Shaking his head sadly, Ty walked back to the inn and got in his car. Pointing it south, he drove through the downtown area, past increasingly shabby buildings, across the railroad tracks and into his world. Or rather the world from which he'd come.

This was the industrial part of town. The now silent textile mill Ty hoped to buy rose like a sprawling giant on a cliff above the river. Other factories lined either side of the road. Gradually they gave way to houses.

Not for this part of town were there sweeping lawns and large homes. Here the lots were small, neatly defined squares. A tiny front yard, an economically planned two- or three-bedroom house and, in the back, another small patch of green. Here the houses were orderly and shabby by turns, depending entirely on the state of their owners' finances and their inclination to spend them. On this side of the tracks, food on the table was what you worried about, not a fresh coat of paint.

Ty pulled into the small driveway of his childhood home. The white frame house was, as always, tidier than either of its neighbors. Pink petunias spilled out of window boxes. Roses bloomed red and yellow in the hot summer sun, spreading their scent on the breeze. The gray concrete steps were freshly swept, and the green striped awning over the front porch was immaculately clean.

As Ty sat, drinking in the familiar peace of the scene, the front door opened. His mother came out on the porch, down the steps and across the yard, a wide, welcoming smile on her face.

Rose Duncan wasn't a small woman. Not heavy, she simply had the ample proportions of people who worked the land. Indeed, she'd been born and raised on a farm and had been set to marry a neighbor's son when Harris Duncan had come for a visit thirty-five years ago. Within two months they'd married and moved into Grayson, where Harris worked at the textile mill.

There had been good times and bad. They'd bought this house; Ty and Sally had been born. There were layoffs at the mill; another baby son had been buried a week after his birth. Money troubles, disappointment and hard work had stooped Harris's broad shoulders and dimmed the light in his gray eyes.

But Rose had borne all the trials with quiet dignity and an unshakable optimism. She'd been ambitious for her children, hopeful for her husband and unafraid to work. She'd gone to work in the school cafeteria to supplement the family's income. Vaguely she'd acknowledged Ty's shame that his mother dished up green beans and meat loaf, but she dismissed it as unimportant. They needed the money. What was the shame in hard work? This was the philosophy she'd imparted to her son, and that idea had paid off for him handsomely.

Ty uncoiled his long frame from the car and caught his mother in a warm embrace. As always, she smelled of lavender and baking, a pleasant, homey combination.

"Tyler," she said now, pulling back to look into his eyes and smooth the unruly curl of his black hair. "You look more like your father all the time." She tightened her arms around him again, tears sliding unashamedly down her face. "Oh, Tyler, welcome home."

Touching her softly curling graying brown hair, Ty blinked against the moisture collecting in his own eyes. "It's good to be home, Mama. Really good."

Much later, after a hearty reunion meal, mother and son relaxed on the front porch watching fireflies flicker dreamily across the lawn. From the house next door came the muted drone of the radio, and the scent of roses hung heavy in the hot, sultry air.

"Feels good to see you standing there," Rose said quietly as Ty crossed the porch and leaned against the railing.

He smiled at her gentle tone. "I know." He propped his back against one of the porch posts and enjoyed the peace of the moment.

In twelve years he'd been home only one other time—for his father's funeral. The visit had been painful, an unreal period of bereavement and shock. In the six years since, Ty had brought his mother and his sister and her family to visit him several times in Atlanta. He'd resisted coming back to Grayson until now.

"You think the deal for the mill will go through?" His mother left her cane-bottomed rocking chair and joined him.

"I don't see why not."

"The town needs it." She paused, clearly weighing her next words. "Would you be staying here if it does?"

Alex's face rose up suddenly in Ty's mind. He stared across the darkened lawn, willing her image to disappear even as he answered, "I don't know. Living here would be a big change. I've been gone a long time."

"We'd like to have you here."

"Oh, yeah?" Ty looped one of his arms across her shoulders. "Then maybe I could talk you into selling this place and letting me build you a new house. Maybe out in that new subdivision north of town. What do you say, huh?"

"I like my house," Rose answered defensively. "Save your money, or spend it on your sister. She needs it with those two kids and Keith out of a job for so long."

"Sally and Keith won't take a dime from me, and you know it. I've tried to help them before. Damn proud bunch, us Duncans."

"Yes, well, that's the way we raised you both—to take care of yourselves and what's yours." She hesitated a moment. "What you really need to do is find yourself a wife to spend some of your money on."

Grinning, Ty turned away and walked down the front steps, taking them two at a time, just as he'd done since he was ten years old. "I'm going for a ride, Mama."

"This time of night?" she asked plaintively.

Ty recognized the disapproving tone and chuckled. "Why do I feel like we just stepped back about fifteen years?"

"Oh, you..." Rose began, but then broke off her protest, laughing. "I guess old habits die hard, son. I always used to worry about you when you took off with that wild bunch of kids you ran with."

"Well, there's no wild kids waitin' for me tonight. I just want to look around town."

"All right. Just be careful."

"Sure, Mama." Flipping his hand in a casual wave, Ty hopped in his car, started the engine and drove away. A faint breeze stirred the hot air as he headed north toward Alex's side of town.

The warm breeze ruffled the starched priscilla curtains at her bedroom windows as Alex turned over for what seemed like the hundredth time that night. With a frustrated sigh she slipped out of bed and crossed the room to sit on the softly cushioned window seat.

The cloud-shrouded moon left deep shadows on the flower garden and pool in the backyard. Heat lightning danced on the horizon and thunder rumbled in the distance. The promise of rain floated on the breeze. I hope it rains, Alex thought. Maybe that will cool things off.

Of course, she could have switched on the air-conditioning, but her mother always complained that it made the house too cold. So they all put up with the heat until later in the summer, when even Lucia Thorpe welcomed the cooling air.

At the ocean there would be a refreshing breeze, Alex thought, closing her eyes. She could almost see the white-capped waves breaking on the sandy, moon-swept beach. *Why did I leave Florida?* she wondered. *What am I doing in Grayson again?*

Twisting a tendril of hair around her finger, she leaned against the window screen, supplying her own answers. Her father was dead. The business was gone. Her mother needed her. It wasn't fair for Grady and Gina to shoulder the entire burden of Mother's care.

Of course her brother, Grady, could handle the burden financially. He was a successful doctor, one of Grayson's busiest general practitioners. He had been able to save this house, their family home, buying it before it could be swept away in the bankruptcy that had taken the mill. Losing the family business had killed their father. If the house had gone, too, their mother would have given up.

Alex sighed, thinking back to that June three years ago when she had come home and watched her father die. Her sweet, impractical father, with his head full of poetry and dreams, had been no match for the real world, for the crumbling textile industry or the ravages of heart disease. How she had adored him. How it had hurt to see him in pain, to let him go.

After Sam Thorpe had died, his wife wouldn't hear of their daughter going back to Florida. She became hysterical at the mere mention of it. She said she wanted her family close; that she needed Alex's emotional support.

So Alex had stayed. She'd taught literature at her high-school alma mater for three years. She lived with her family in the house where she'd grown up. She traveled a little, dated some and indulged her mother.

Drawing her knees up under her chin, Alex frowned. Perhaps she'd indulged her mother too much. Some nights, like tonight, it felt as if she had no life of her own.

The whole family had gathered in the sitting room early in the evening for a birthday toast. Grady and his wife, Gina, were dressed for an evening at the country club. Their daughter, Carrie, had been impatient to leave for her Friday-night date. But Lucia had held them all until Tom Jacobs had arrived to take Alex to dinner.

Tom. Alex sighed sadly, thinking of him. He was so punctual, so considerate, so predictable. How could she even consider marrying someone so boring?

Her mother was immensely pleased that her daughter was seeing the tall blond lawyer. She'd laid it on thick tonight. Alex grimaced at the memory.

Lucia Thorpe had rolled her wheelchair forward, her elegant features arranged in a welcoming smile, when Alex's date had arrived. "Tom. We're so glad you're here. Now the family is complete. We were just about to offer a toast to Alexa's birthday."

Tom slipped a possessive arm around Alex's shoulders. "I'd be delighted to toast the most beautiful, charming woman in town."

"How gallant," Alex murmured, acknowledging the compliment. Why did it always sound as if Tom had rehearsed these little comments?

Their glasses clinked in a toast, and they drank to Alex's continued good health and happiness. Then Grady, Gina and Carrie left, leaving Tom and Alex alone with Lucia.

"Well, you two run along, too," the elderly woman said with a heavy sigh. "I'm just going to have a quiet dinner...alone...in this big, empty house."

Alex knew very well that Clarissa, her mother's maid and nurse, was within calling distance. Still, shooting Tom a hopeless glance, she sat down on the sofa. "Would you like to join us, Mother?"

Lucia touched her perfectly coiffed white hair with a hand that flashed diamonds. "Of course not. I wouldn't dream of imposing. You should just go have a nice dinner and not worry about me."

"All right." Suddenly impatient with her mother's theatrics, Alex stood, smoothing down the folds of her lilac skirt and reaching for the matching jacket.

"Tonight would be a good time for you to make some plans," Lucia commented casually.

"Plans?" Tom queried.

"Mother..." Alex warned.

Ignoring her daughter, Lucia zeroed in on Tom. "Well, it is Alexa's thirtieth birthday. High time someone swept her off her feet. You could be just the man, Tom."

Bending over to kiss her mother's cheek, Alex whispered, "You're driving me crazy. Stop this, please."

But Tom was pleased with the suggestion. "I'm not the one who's holding things up. You'll have to talk with your daughter, Mrs. Thorpe. Maybe you will succeed where I've failed."

"Why don't we drop this conversation and get me some dinner?" Alex interrupted.

Lucia's cornflower-blue eyes regarded Alex steadily for several moments. Her daughter's gaze didn't falter. "All right," she acquiesced gracefully. "But I'm sure Tom will pursue this topic at the first opportunity."

"Certainly." Tom grinned idiotically while Alex contemplated the various ways she'd like to wring his *and* her mother's necks.

The evening had gone downhill from that inauspicious beginning. Alex had tried to keep the conversation on general topics, but Tom had steered it back to marriage at every chance.

The same thing had been going on for almost four of the six months they had been seeing each other. Tom asked. Lucia pushed. Alex hedged. She was now searching for a way to let him down gently. After all, he was a nice man. She just didn't want to marry him, and she never would.

Tonight she'd pleaded a headache, convinced Tom to bring her home before ten-thirty and had gone straight to bed. She thanked her lucky stars her mother had retired for the evening.

But instead of sleeping, all Alex could do was think about Ty Duncan.

It had been very noble to think she could just push their meeting aside. Very noble and very unrealistic. Almost twelve years had passed since she'd last seen him, but that hadn't dimmed the unsettling feelings he could arouse with only a look.

"Damn!" Alex muttered. What was Ty doing here? She hoped he wasn't planning to stay.

A peal of laughter, hastily smothered, cut through the still summer night. Frowning, Alex leaned forward to scan the backyard. She couldn't see anyone, but another laugh rang out. She soon recognized the voice of her niece coming from the back veranda, directly underneath her window.

"Oh, Billy, don't be ridiculous. Mom and Dad aren't even home yet. Grandmother's room is around the side, and Aunt Alex is probably asleep."

The voice of Billy Rayburn, Carrie's current beau, was distinct as he answered. "I don't know, Carrie. I think we'll get caught."

"But I've always wanted to go skinny-dipping, Billy. This is the perfect chance."

"I don't care. I'm going to have your aunt for literature this year, and I don't want to face her if she catches us."

There was a moment of silence, and Alex could picture Carrie's pretty, pouting face. However, the girl gave up her idea, saying, "I guess you're right, Billy. I'd rather Dad catch us than Aunt Alex. She just wouldn't understand. I bet she's never done anything like that. She treats poor old Tom like ice. I don't think they even kiss. I wonder if she ever kissed anybody."

"But she's a fox!" Billy retorted.

"A lot of good it does her."

"I always wondered why she wasn't married."

"Mother says Aunt Alex isn't the marrying kind," Carrie said, her voice blunt with finality. She giggled, and her voice dropped so that Alex had to strain to hear. "As long as we've got a little time before my folks come home, let's not waste it talking."

Silence followed, and Alex drew back from the window, ashamed at having eavesdropped—and stung by her niece's words. Was that the way she appeared? Did she act like some kind of frustrated old hag who had never been kissed?

Sliding off the window seat, she went to her dresser, switched on a light and regarded her reflection in the mirror.

Her shoulder-length brown hair, normally curled in attractive waves, was mussed from her restless attempts at sleep. Her dark eyes were cast in shadow by the dimness of the room. She looked tired, yes. Maybe not as young as she'd once been, but hardly the stuff spinsters were made of. Hadn't Billy called her a "fox"? Grinning at the description, Alex flipped off the light and got back in bed.

Another hastily stifled giggle drifted in the window. Alex could imagine the scene. Carrie and Billy would neck on the glider until they heard her parents' car. Then they'd smooth their clothes, charge back into the house and announce that Billy was just leaving. The scene was one Alex had played out many times herself.

Contrary to what her niece thought, Alex had been kissed plenty of times. Kissed passionately. Kissed on the very glider where Carrie was now kissing Billy. Kissed by Ty Duncan.

Cinderella, he'd called her today. She could remember exactly when that particular game had started. They'd been at the beach up at the lake. The sky had clouded over; everyone else had been preparing to leave, and Alex had demanded that Ty take her home....

"Scared of a little rain, Miss Perfection?" he taunted.

"Of course not," Alex said, standing up to brush sand off her bright yellow bikini.

Ty's quicksilver gaze passed down her body, lingering on her breasts, stomach and thighs. She shivered a little under his bold perusal.

"Yeah, you're scared of storms. And Daddy's little girl doesn't have to put up with anything she's scared of."

"What do you mean?" Alex demanded.

"I'm saying everything is picture perfect in your little world, and you always get what you want."

"I don't see what that has to do with sitting out on the beach in a storm!"

"Everything," Ty returned. "You're afraid to do something you've never done before. Afraid to take any kind of a chance, Miss Alexa Thorpe." He pronounced each syllable of her name distinctly, making it sound haughty and snobbish.

"Oh, really?" Alex challenged. "Then why do you suppose I'm going out with you?"

The quickening wind caught a lock of Ty's longish, unruly hair, draping it across his eyes. He shoved it back and glared at Alex, not answering her question.

"What do you know about me, anyway, Tyler Duncan? Just because I live in a big house, do you think I don't have any problems? Are you the only one allowed to have a hard time? Things aren't always easy for me, either."

Ty rose to his feet, his defiance cooling to a teasing air in the face of her impassioned speech. "So you're just like Cinderella, huh? Imprisoned in that big house by your evil parents, working and slaving away, only allowed to go out and play once in a while with the local prince." He stepped closer, encircling Alex's bare waist with his muscular, tanned arms.

"Now you're claiming to be a prince?" Alex asked archly, leaning into his strength. The wind had whipped itself into a frenzy, and the sky had darkened ominously. Everyone else had fled for cover, leaving her and Ty alone on the beach.

"Of course I'm a prince. That's why it's necessary to kiss you like this." His lips touched hers softly, clinging to the full moistness of her mouth. Alex drew away before the kiss could deepen.

"Aren't you mixing up your fairy tales? The prince didn't have to kiss Cinderella; he just had to find her glass slipper."

"This is much nicer than kissing your feet," Ty murmured, and smothered her giggle under the questing pressure of his mouth. His tongue probed into her mouth, and Alex reciprocated, exploring his delicious, heady taste.

The wind drove the sand into swirls around them, thunder boomed and the first stinging drops of rain splattered their bare skin. But still their kiss continued. Ty had kissed Alex before, many times. But this was something different, a new dimension of sensation and reaction.

A tiny ache started in the pit of her stomach and spread deliciously, languidly downward. Ty's hands were warm against her back, electrifying her skin with his touch. One of his bare brown legs snaked in between her own, pushing against the thin material of her bikini bottom. Alex moaned against his mouth, pressed against his leg, giving in to needs she'd never recognized before.

When the rain was a steady, drenching downpour, Ty drew shakily away from her. His chest rose and fell as he struggled for control. His gray eyes, deepened to steely points of desire, stared down into the golden brown of hers.

His lopsided grin was wicked as he said finally, "Let's go home, Cinderella. Before it's too late."

They gathered up their wet things and stumbled, laughing and holding hands, through the rain to his car. They were young, carefree and caught in a web of first love and awakening passion....

Closer now, the thunder rumbled through the night and into Alex's bedroom. She lay staring at the ceiling, lost in her memory of desire. She could almost feel the touch of Ty's big, work-roughened hands on her skin. She could taste the salty gloss on his skin, smell the storm, see the yearning in his gray eyes. She shut her eyes to close out the sight.

Another laugh came from the porch, and Alex's eyes flew open. Perhaps she should have a talk with her niece. It was summer. The long hot days spread deliciously ahead. Desire touched off in the heat of an Alabama night wasn't always so easily cooled.

"I'll tell her what I know," Alex murmured, yawning. "I know all about summer love and how it can break your heart."

Ty stood beside his car, staring at Alex's family's house across the street. The mailbox still said Thorpe, but he didn't know if she still lived there. Probably not. Surely she had her own home. A husband. A family.

But somehow he always thought of her in this house, up in the pink-and-white room she'd snuck him into late one summer night. Ty lost himself in that particular memory.

"Lookin' for something, mister?"

Ty started at the voice and snapped around to stare directly into a policeman's face. While he'd gazed at Alex's childhood home, a patrol car had eased up behind his parked BMW.

"I was just out for a drive," he explained quickly. "I used to live here in Grayson, and I—"

"Ty?" the cop interrupted. "Is that you, Ty Duncan?"

"Yes," Ty answered hesitantly, peering through the darkness at the heavyset uniformed man.

"It's me, Tim... you know... Bubba Douglas!"

"Bubba? A policeman? Will you get a load of that," Ty said, laughing and shaking the man's hand.

"I know, I know. Everybody figured I'd end up on the other side of the law. But what are you doin' here? 'Specially on this side of town."

"I'm in Grayson on business, and I decided to take a little ride. You know, to see if the richies over here still live like richies."

"They do, believe me, they do." Bubba laughed and then snapped his fingers. "You got anywhere you need to be?"

"No, I'm staying at my mother's...."

"Well, then, come with me. It's time for the shift to change. I'm going to meet some buddies down at Pete's Place. Boy, there'll be some guys there who'd like to see you!"

"Well..." Ty hesitated.

"Aw, come on, Ty. I'll buy you a beer and then you can buy me one, just like the old days. I bet I can still drink you under the table."

Ty couldn't help laughing. If memory served him correctly, Bubba had been the one who always wound up under the table at their parties. "Just to prove you wrong, I'll come."

"Great! Pete's is where Nick's used to be."

The mention of Nick's name brought a wealth of other memories pouring through Ty's brain. He swallowed convulsively. "Same old dive with a new name, huh?" he said quickly.

"The very same. See you in about twenty minutes. I've got to file a report before I'm done for the night."

Ty waved goodbye and cast one more glance at Alex's house. She probably had dinner at the country club, he thought. And I'm headed for a couple of brews at Pete's. Nothing had changed. He and Alex might be in the same town again, but they were still in separate worlds.

Chapter Two

The sun was hot, but the air had the rain-washed freshness of the morning after a storm when Alex emerged onto the back veranda the next morning. Sparkling blue water beckoned from the swimming pool, but she ignored its inviting depths, walked across the yard and arranged a beach towel on a chaise lounge beside her niece's. Without saying a word, she reached for a bottle of suntan lotion. She felt the need to talk with Carrie but was unsure of how to begin.

Finally she plunged ahead, hoping her voice held the right balance of casualness and interest. "Did you and Billy have a good time last night?"

The sixteen-year-old cocked her sunglasses up and squinted at her aunt. "Sure. Why?"

"Just wondered. You see him a lot."

"Mom and Dad like him." There was just a trace of defensiveness in Carrie's voice as she settled her glasses back on her nose.

Alex smoothed lotion down her leg and covertly studied her niece. The slender young body was barely covered by the two strips of scarlet she called a bathing suit. Her hair, the same dark brown as Alex's, was pulled into a loose knot atop her head. Her eyes were still hidden by the glasses, but Alex could visualize them easily. They were just like Lucia Thorpe's, a deceptively innocent shade of cornflower blue.

Choosing her words carefully lest Carrie suspect their seriousness, Alex said, "Billy seems to like you a lot. Do you really like him?"

Carrie slid to a sitting position and looked at her aunt intently. "Okay, what's wrong?" She slipped off the sunglasses.

"Did I say something was wrong?"

"You didn't have to," Carrie answered, a frown tightening her delicately arched brows. "Anytime someone around here has a problem or wants to know something, they ask you everything but what they really want to know. Must be a family trait."

"Would you rather we didn't care what you did?" Alex met the girl's gaze straight on. This wasn't going as she'd planned, but she didn't want to back out now.

"Of course not. But what is it with Billy?" The younger girl was quiet for a moment, gazing thoughtfully at Alex. "I get it. You want to know if Billy and I are serious. Maybe if we're sleeping together, right?"

"I didn't say that...."

"You didn't have to." Carrie once more resumed her relaxed pose on the lounge chair.

"So, are you?" Alex asked pointedly when the girl didn't volunteer any further information. Carrie was so direct that it was best to be blunt with her.

"Aunt Alex..." she began warningly.

"I know. It's none of my business. But indulge your old spinster aunt. I just don't want you to get hurt or in trouble."

Carrie gave an exasperated sigh. "I'm not stupid. If I were sleeping with Billy... which I'm not... I wouldn't be dumb enough to get in trouble."

"That's a relief," Alex said dryly. When had her sweet young niece turned into such a knowing sophisticate?

"What's the deal?" Carrie pressed.

Alex smoothed lotion down her arms. She had been wrong to think Carrie needed any advice. Perhaps this conversation was more for her own benefit than for Carrie's.

She shrugged her shoulders and concentrated on rubbing the lotion across her nose. "I just wanted you to know that if Billy ever pressures you or you're confused about something, I'm available to talk."

Out of the corner of her eye, Alex could see Carrie's slightly irritated expression change to one of curiosity. Lord, she'd opened a can of worms now. The conversation she'd overheard last night had made it clear her niece didn't consider her aunt to have any worldly experience. Now here she was offering advice. Carrie's inquisitive nature was bound to take over.

Sure enough, the girl followed her customary forthright manner and asked, "Have you ever been in love, Aunt Alex?"

Alex didn't want to lie. "Yes, I have."

"Did you sleep with him?"

Again Alex didn't hedge. Carrie wasn't a child. And while Grady and Gina weren't exactly liberal, they didn't hide the varying life-styles and attitudes of others from their daughter. So now she told her niece the truth. "Yes, I did sleep with him. But I was older than you."

"Was it wonderful?" In Carrie's voice Alex heard the same wistful uncertainty she and her friends had expressed about sex when they were sixteen. That naiveté was somehow reassuring. Carrie wasn't as worldly as she'd sounded earlier.

Alex relaxed in her chair and smiled; it was a slow smile of remembrance "It *was* wonderful, Carrie, but in the end

I got hurt. That's why I asked you about Billy. I fell in love with someone, but we weren't ready for anything that serious. And when it was over, it was hard for me to deal with. I just don't want you to have to go through that, too."

"Are you sorry you made love with him?" Carrie asked softly.

Alex pondered the question. Was she sorry? Would it have been better to have never known the intensity of Ty's passion? Of course, if they had never made love, the chain of events that had pulled them apart might never have been set in motion. If they had waited, would things have been different? Somehow she didn't think so. And she had wanted the intimacy they had shared.

Even now she could remember the feel of Ty's body pressed against hers, the touch of his lips against the pulse at her throat, the sound of his voice, thick with passion. No, she thought sadly, no matter what it cost them, it was better to have known that sweetness.

She turned to intercept Carrie's steady, curious regard. "I'm not sorry," she whispered. The young girl's eyes filled with sympathy, and she touched her aunt's hand lightly.

"Listen to how maudlin we've become," Alex said brightly, breaking the serious mood. She stood and smoothed her navy maillot down over her hips. "Let's swim!" She walked to the edge of the pool and dove in. Laughing, her niece followed.

Later, Alex was drying her hair after a quick, reviving shower when Clarissa called her to the phone. The pleasant older woman had worked for the family since Alex was a baby. She'd moved in when Lucia had suffered the stroke that had left her confined to a wheelchair. She seemed more a member of the family than an employee.

"It's a man," she whispered now, rolling her eyes the same way she'd done when Alex was a teenager and boys called.

Alex was laughing when she took the phone and said a breathless hello.

"It sounds like you're having a good time."

The deep voice could belong to only one person. Ty.

"Hello, Ty." It was a struggle, but Alex kept her voice from quavering.

"I was wondering if we could get together for lunch."

"Why?" Alex couldn't stop the question. She had thought—no, she had prayed—that yesterday's meeting would be an isolated instance.

"There's something I'd like to discuss with you." He paused, and Alex heard him take a deep breath. "It's about the mill."

"I don't see what that has to do with me."

"There's something I want you to hear about."

Alex frowned. "Can't you tell me now?"

"I'd rather talk in person."

She waited to answer, mulling over the possibilities of this meeting. She'd lain awake half the night thinking of him after yesterday's brief encounter. To see him again would probably only bring further turmoil.

"Alex?" Ty's voice was hopeful.

She couldn't resist. "Okay, but not for lunch. I can meet you at the mill around one."

"The mill?"

"Sure. That's what you want to talk about, isn't it?"

"Yes, but . . ."

"Then I'll see you at one," Alex cut in smoothly and quickly said goodbye. The mill was the perfect place to see Ty again. It was run-down, dirty and decidedly unromantic. She could do without a cozy chat in a dimly lit restaurant.

Glancing at the clock, she saw she had a little less than an hour to get dressed and meet him. What does one wear to meet an old lover at a deserted factory? Alex mused, bounding up the stairs to her room.

Ty replaced the phone slowly. She hadn't wanted to see him. Her reluctance had been obvious. And now, faced with the fact that he would see her in less than an hour, his own trepidation was growing. But he knew the meeting was necessary. After last night, he couldn't avoid it.

With Bubba he'd enjoyed a boisterous reunion with a group of old friends. Pete's Place was a gathering spot for many of Ty's old schoolmates and fellow workers from the textile mill. Some were doing well, but others were suffering from the hard times the town had experienced over the last few years.

Clearly news of his company's plan to buy the mill had leaked. Bubba seemed to be the only person in the place who hadn't heard of the impending sale. The men were curious and anxious.

"What do you say, Ty? Plenty of jobs for your old friends?" The question, coming from Mike Pate, was light, but Ty caught the serious undertone. These men wanted jobs.

He assured them there would be job openings if and when the sale of the mill happened. "Not as many as I'd like, or as many as that place used to employ at first, but I won't forget my hardworking old friends."

"Let's buy the man a beer!" Bubba enthused, and the party began in earnest.

About two in the morning, Ty decided to call it a night. Truth was, the role of returning savior for the unemployed was an uncomfortable one. He couldn't miss the desperation in many of the men's faces. They all seemed to want to ingratiate themselves to him. It was stifling. He welcomed the rush of fresh air that greeted him outdoors when he left the overheated, crowded bar.

Mike Pate left with him. Years ago, Mike had been a good friend. When Ty had gone to work at the mill right out of high school, the tall, lanky redhead had been his partner on the loading dock. They had shared two years of backbreaking labor and hundreds of conversations laced with hopes and dreams. Mike had wanted to move up to a better-paying job at the mill. Ty had just wanted out.

"It must make you feel pretty good," Mike said, eyeing the sleek outline of Ty's BMW in the dim light of the parking lot.

"What's that?"

"You're doing it, man. Stickin' it to the richies."

Ty inserted his key in the lock, swung open the door and turned to look at Mike. "I don't know what you mean."

"Awww, come on, Ty. This is Mike, remember. All you ever used to talk about was showin' the stuck-up snobs of this town that you could do something more than load their trucks. For a while that summer I thought you were gonna do it by gettin' the boss's daughter...."

"Alex." Ty breathed her name.

"Yeah. Alexa Thorpé. Things were pretty tight with you two, if I remember right."

"Not so tight," Ty answered, a painful wrench of remembrance in his gut.

"Well, when you left all of a sudden, I figured her old man had finally put a stop to it."

Anger charged through Ty. He'd tried not to think too much about Sam Thorpe since he'd driven over the county line. There was no use wasting his time on hate.

"Yeah," Mike continued. "I've gotta admit, this is better. Much better. I mean, you're buying the factory that her old man lost. And you're buying it from Clemmer's bank!"

"What does Clemmer have to do with it?"

Mike chuckled. "You gotta be puttin' me on. You told me all about how your old man went to Clemmer for a loan to start that business. But the bank turned it down on account of that time you and his nephew busted up Clemmer's lake house havin' a party."

"Yeah." Ty's voice was flat. He'd certainly shot off his mouth to Mike a lot in those two years they'd shared on that dock.

"Boy, oh, boy, Ty. This has got to be sweet revenge—you ridin' into town on top of the world and buyin' that mill."

"Sweet?" The bitter taste in Ty's mouth belied the word.

"Yeah, sweet." Chuckling softly, Mike clapped Ty on the back and walked away.

The man's remarks had echoed in Ty's mind for the remainder of the night and the morning. The more he thought about it, the surer he was that other people would share Mike's view. He'd been full of talk and plans about how he was going to set the world on fire before he'd left this town. He'd told anyone who had the time to listen. He'd bragged that you didn't have to be born on the north side of the tracks to make a lot of money.

Now he was back. He was successful. He was buying the mill and would soon be an important member of the business community. It must look as if his plans had been achieved.

However, Ty hadn't really thought about all of that in years. The swaggering boy had long ago turned into a sharp-minded man who recognized good business opportunities. And that was exactly what the empty mill building had represented—a good deal. His company, DunMar Carpets, was expanding into a commercial line. They needed a facility large enough to produce their own yarn, just as they did at their residential-carpet factory in Georgia. The old mill in his home town had seemed like a bargain. The team of experts he'd sent to check it out had agreed. He'd looked over the place with Walt yesterday morning. It was a bargain. The bank was desperate to sell.

But now Ty wondered if there'd been something more in his motivations. Was Mike right? Maybe buried somewhere beneath the suave veneer he'd cloaked himself in there remained a hint of the boasts Mike had made him remember. Maybe he really did want to show the Walt Clemmers and Alexa Thorpes of this town that he was their equal.

The idea disturbed Ty. He didn't want to feel that way. More importantly, he didn't want Alex to think he had come back to gloat over her family's misfortune. He'd called her, hoping no one else had told her of the impending sale.

Dialing her parents' old number had been a shot in the dark. During the night he'd built up a very real picture of her ensconced in her own two-story colonial with a smiling, successful husband and two cherubic children. He'd expected a maid to answer and tell him Alex no longer lived there. He'd even had a story worked out for getting her number—he'd be a high-school acquaintance in town for the weekend to renew old ties. He'd been shocked when Alex had been called to the phone.

Ty looked around his mother's small, spotless kitchen and thought about seeing Alex again. A feeling of dread mixed with eagerness filled him as he got his car keys and headed out the door. One thing was certain—twelve years could change a lot of things, but he hadn't kicked the Alex Thorpe habit.

"God, what are we going to say to each other?" he muttered, getting in his car, feeling somewhat like a schoolboy on his way to his first date.

Turning off the main road, Alex spotted the crimson car before she saw Ty. The glossy finish stood out in vivid contrast to the drab wire-mesh fence surrounding the mill property.

She pulled her car in beside his and watched while he ambled forward from where he lounged against the fence. In faded jeans and a yellow polo shirt, he looked more like the Ty she remembered than had the elegantly attired man in the restaurant yesterday.

Shoving her sunglasses firmly up her nose, Alex got out of her car. "Have you been waiting long? I hope I'm not late."

"No, not at all." Ty stopped at the hood of her car and regarded her with searching eyes.

She hadn't really changed, just as he'd said yesterday. The hair was shorter, but it was still a soft, dark cloud, glinting in the sunlight with traces of auburn. He knew how it would feel tangled like silken threads in his hand. Her brows were the same delicate arches. Her cheek had the same sweetly rounded curve he'd caressed with his hand, touched with his lips. And her figure . . . the younger Alex had been boyishly slim. With male appreciation he took in her full, thoroughly feminine silhouette, and the old feeling stirred within him.

Alex nervously tucked her blue-and-white print blouse into the waistband of her crisp navy slacks. Ty's bold, appraising glance was one she knew well. He'd always looked at her this way—in a manner that made her feel warm all over. From the first time their eyes had met in high school— till the last time they'd made love.

Tearing her eyes away from his knowing silvery gaze, she strode toward the fence. "What did you want to discuss about the mill? You know we don't own it any longer, don't you?"

"Yes." His answer was quiet as he came and stood beside her, drawing the keys Walt Clemmer had given him out of his pocket. "My company has made an offer to buy it."

Alex's head snapped around, and she stared at him, openmouthed. Ty fought the urge to tear off her sunglasses so he could see the expression in her gold-kissed brown eyes.

"I wanted to tell you myself," he continued. "I didn't want you or your family to read about it in the paper. I know how much this company meant to your mother." The metal gate scraped against the asphalt of the drive as Ty pulled it open. He gestured for Alex to precede him as they walked up the hill toward the rambling group of buildings.

Moving silently beside him, Alex stared at the weatherbeaten exterior of the abandoned factory. To say the mill had meant a lot to her mother was an understatement. For Lucia Nelson Thorpe, and for her family before her, Nelson Textiles had been everything.

Lucia's grandfather, Alexander Nelson, had started the textile mill in the late 1800s. A smart and savvy young man, he'd quickly seen the potential for a factory of this nature in Grayson. The Civil War and Reconstruction had brought sweeping changes to the region. Once-proud plantations had been divided into small farms. Many men, discouraged by the returns brought by these tiny plots of land, had been packing up and heading for the industrial opportunities of the cities.

Spurred on by a northern investor, Alexander built the mill and turned it into a thriving operation, providing jobs for many men, women and children. Other men followed his lead and other companies moved into town. The mill changed the economic structure of the town.

The fortune Nelson Textiles made built the big house in town, paid for trips to Europe, for good educations for Alexander's son and daughter, for clothes, automobiles and opportunities. In time, his son Marshall took over. The company continued to thrive. Through wars, economic changes and unions, Marshall proved to be an innovative, resourceful manager.

Marshall Nelson had only one child, Lucia. After leading her parents and a long line of suitors on a merry chase for twenty-five years, Lucia finally married Sam Thorpe, a sensitive, quiet young man. Rather doubtfully, Marshall groomed Sam as his successor at the mill.

As it turned out, his doubts were well-founded. Cautious by nature, Sam didn't have the strong hand needed to guide the company through the onslaught of foreign competition throughout the 1960s and 1970s. Alex doubted anyone could have saved the mill, but it was her studious, dreamy father who shouldered the blame when Nelson Textiles joined many other such companies across the South in bankruptcy and foreclosure.

The history of the place flooded through Alex now as she stood outside the main building with Ty. "What are your plans?" she asked dully.

"To produce commercial carpets for DunMar."

"You work for DunMar Carpets?"

"No. I own half of it." He turned to unlock the door and led the way into the dim interior.

Alex digested the news quietly. DunMar was a well-known name in carpets. Their ads were splashed throughout the decorating magazines her sister-in-law brought home. Alex hadn't known Ty had anything to do with them. Somewhere along the line the local newspapers must have done a local-boy-makes-good story about him. Why had she missed it?

They walked without speaking through the empty front offices. The furniture and fixtures had been auctioned off. Beyond the offices, the floor of the factory was bare also, its machinery sold to other, still-operating mills.

Ty pushed open the door, and they stood on a platform above what had been the main production floor. Where once the noise of equipment and the shouts of workers had been overwhelming, silence now coated the concrete floor with a blanketing hush. They walked down the stairs and across the room, their footsteps echoing hollowly off the walls.

The only light filtered in through a bank of grimy windows. Alex slipped off her sunglasses and looked around. "Doesn't seem like the same place, does it?"

"No, not at all." Ty glanced about him, easily visualizing the factory as it had been—the rows of machinery, the perspiration rolling off the men and women operating it. He'd promised himself he would get out. He'd vowed Tyler Duncan would do more than operate a machine day in and day out. And he'd kept his promise. For the first time since coming back to town, a wave of exhilaration washed over him.

"Is the deal final?" Alex spoke softly, snapping Ty out of his reflections.

"Almost. That's what I was seeing Walt about yesterday."

"I wondered." She walked over to the windows and rubbed away some of the dirt. From this vantage point, high on a cliff, she could see the lazy flow of the Tennessee River. The river's proximity had been one of the main reasons Alexander Nelson had chosen this site. Down the hill, the docks where boats had been loaded still stood. The cargo had been shipped up to Chattanooga, a scant sixty miles away by river.

What would her ancestor think about the new plans for these buildings his family had built? He'd be pleased, Alex decided suddenly. Better this than standing empty.

Alex felt, rather than saw, Ty move closer. In the stifling warmth of the closed building, heat radiated off his tall, broad body.

"Alex, I wanted you to know...I thought I should explain..." He faltered when she didn't turn around.

"Yes?" she murmured.

He cleared his throat. "I did a lot of talking when I was younger. I said I was gonna prove something to everybody. That isn't why I'm back in town. That's not why I'm buying this property. This is a sound business investment, nothing more."

"I'm disappointed," Alex said, turning to face him at last. "Aren't you trying to prove anything anymore? Or have you conquered everything you had targeted in your master plan?"

Ty grinned at the challenge in her words. And with that one movement of his facial features he was once again the cocky, hotheaded young rebel, ready to grab the world and shake it by its tail. Her taunting voice was the same one that had provoked the loading-dock worker to kiss the boss's daughter in the cool darkness of the storage warehouse. Moments passed, and the excitement kindled between them just as it had twelve years earlier. Just like before, it was Alex who turned away first.

She looked out the window again. "Will you be staying here in Grayson, then?"

"For a while." The words hung between them, suspended in the hot, still air.

Shutting her eyes, Alex leaned against the metal window frame. Ty would be here. How then could she stay? For the first time she acknowledged her fears. She'd never forgotten Ty, never gotten over him. For twelve years she'd been asking herself why he had gone. Why had he left her alone to face...

She whirled around, the question poised on her lips, only to falter under the steady regard of those unnervingly direct gray eyes.

"Does it bother you that I'll be here?" he asked.

Bother her? Alex wanted to laugh. It was more than a bother. It was more like drowning in a tide of cashed-in dreams and fruitless plans. Had he really not cared? She should tell him now how he'd made her suffer, how lost she'd been. She wanted him to know the same white-hot pain she had experienced.

God, she'd thought this was behind her. She'd thought these feelings were put away, packed somewhere in the attic along with her high-school mementos, to be forgotten like some faded movie pass.

She opened her mouth to tell him how she felt. But she couldn't do it. She couldn't tell him about the sleepless, tear-filled nights, about the anger and the fear. To tell him would be to admit she still cared. And Alex's pride wouldn't let her do it. Instead she smiled and said, "No, your being here doesn't bother me at all."

Ty grinned again. Strange the way his smile still has the same hypnotizing power, Alex mused. Strange and decidedly dangerous.

"Good. I just wanted you to hear from me why I was buying the mill. I thought you should know. I figured you'd want to tell your mother."

"I appreciate that, Ty. I'll tell her this afternoon." Alex fell into step beside him as they crossed the large, echoing room again. Stealing a glance at his strong profile, she wondered what had happened to turn her misfit into such a success. On impulse she said, "Tell me how you got into the carpet business."

"Luck."

"Surely it took more than that." They paused while Ty locked the door. The slight afternoon breeze was a welcome relief after the heat inside. Alex felt a trickle of perspiration run down her spine as they walked toward their cars.

"I started out working in a carpet mill. The work wasn't too different from here. One loading dock pretty much works like any other." He laughed shortly. "I spent almost a year working there before the boss offered me a chance to try sales."

"Sales?" Alex queried, surprised.

"Yeah. I was surprised, too. But he thought I was just cocky enough to make it. So I bought a suit and tie and hit the road. The boss was right. In three years I was their top salesman. I busted my butt, and it paid off. About that time Chuck Martin, a friend of mine, decided he wanted to branch out on his own. We pooled our savings, borrowed a bundle and bought some property a lot like this for next to nothing. The rest, as they say, is history."

"DunMar Carpets," Alex completed.

"We've worked hard. It's a tough business."

They reached the gate, and Alex almost said goodbye. But she didn't. Ty stood there, the sunlight glinting off the blue-black curl of his hair, and she knew the last thing she wanted was to leave. Ignoring the danger bells that trilled in her head, she turned to him with a smile.

"Tell me, do you still like double chocolate shakes?"

"Double chocolate?" A tiny frown creased his brow. "I don't . . ." He smiled as realization struck. "You mean the kind of shakes Mr. Carson always made at the drive-in? Don't tell me he's still making them."

"To this day," Alex answered with a laugh. "I'll buy you one if you want."

"Okay. But I'll drive. I'll bring you back for your car."

He opened the passenger door, and Alex slid across the plush black leather seat. "Nice," she commented, touching the leather with a caressing hand.

"The trappings of success," Ty said mockingly, pulling on narrow, dark sunglasses. He started the car and headed toward town.

The car was fancier than the beat-up Mustang he'd had in the old days, but Ty drove it the same way. Fast. Aggressive. Bordering on reckless. Alex was breathless by the time they pulled into a slot at the drive-in restaurant.

He pressed the speaker button and ordered. "Two double chocolate shakes and—" he paused to flash a wicked grin at Alex "—two orders of onion rings."

"I can't believe you remembered!" She giggled. "I haven't had that combination in years. I'll have to diet for a week."

"I doubt that," Ty said, eyeing her trim figure. "You never had to diet, and we ate junk like this all summer long."

"I was eighteen. A thirty-year-old body burns up fewer calories."

"Well, we did find plenty of ways to burn off the junk food." Ty tucked his glasses into the sun visor.

Alex stared at her hands. It was easy to remember all the ways they'd found to work off their excess energy. It hadn't seemed to matter that Ty was working full-time at the mill every day. He never seemed tired, never grew tired of making love with her. She felt as if the air had been sucked from her lungs as she remembered making love with him.

"Alex . . ." he whispered now.

"Here's your food, sir." A gum-chewing teenage waitress was hooking the tray to Ty's window. He handed her some money and waved her away.

Alex took advantage of the interruption to quiet her nerves. Settling her carton of onion rings on the dashboard, she took a long sip of the creamy mixture in the paper cup. "This is heaven."

"The best shakes in the world." Ty shifted around in his seat until he lounged against the door, facing Alex. "Why are you still in Grayson?"

Dipping an onion ring in ketchup, Alex was tempted to lie. She wanted to tell him being here was her own choice. Ty had always thought she let her parents run her life. She didn't want to admit her mother had kept her here.

"Well?" he prompted.

The subterfuge seemed suddenly pointless. "I went to college in Florida and stayed on there to teach. Three years ago, Father died. I came back to be with him at the last. Then Mother needed me. Grady and Gina had bought the house. Mother wanted us all together. They said they wanted me to stay. So I did." It all seemed so simple when she said it like that.

"I bet it hurt your dad... letting go of the mill."

"It killed him," Alex said without thinking, and looked sharply at Ty. Instead of sympathy, his expression showed hardness and bitterness. He had never had any respect for Sam Thorpe—the cause of several arguments between her and Ty. He had always said her father wasn't aggressive enough in marketing the mill's products. Alex, who loved her father blindly, had always defended his actions. Not anxious to precipitate a disagreement now, she nevertheless hastened to explain her statement to Ty.

"I don't mean the mill killed him. He was sick; he knew neither Grady nor I had any real interest in the company. He got tired of fighting a losing battle."

"He might have won." Ty's jaw was set in a stubborn line.

"No, he couldn't have," Alex said firmly. "And it doesn't matter now."

"How did your mother take it?"

Alex took another long sip of her shake. "Mother had a stroke about eight years ago. She's been confined to a wheelchair ever since. When the mill closed, she just didn't accept it at first. It was like she had already lost touch with so much of the world, losing the business was almost more than she could accept. Do you understand what I mean?"

"I guess." Ty stirred the slushy contents of his cup thoughtfully. It was hard to imagine Lucia Thorpe in a wheelchair. She'd been such a strong woman, a vibrant, powerful woman.

"Sometimes I think she still doesn't believe it. I think she expects Grady or me to muster enough money together to buy it all back and start again." Alex shook her head sadly.

"Do you miss Florida?"

Glad of the change of subject, Alex sat back in her seat. "Yes, I do. I had lots of friends, and the school where I taught was very progressive. Here in Grayson..."

"It's like being caught in a time warp," Ty finished for her.

"Sort of. Traditions die hard here. In some ways that's not a bad thing. But in others—well, they still don't allow *Lady Chatterley's Lover* in the library. Kids can see much worse on their favorite soap opera, but a classic love story is too sensuous for their eyes."

Ty laughed. "I bet old Miss MacGruder is head of the committee to ban the steamy sex novels."

"You guessed it!"

"Is she ever going to retire?"

"After next year, God and the school board willing. If she does, I'm in line for assistant department head. Jake Lowery will probably be in the top spot. He and I will make some changes."

"So you intend to stay." The way Ty said it, the words weren't a question but a simple statement of fact.

It wasn't one Alex had given a lot of consideration to. For three years she'd felt as if she were constantly poised for flight. She frowned at the thought. "I don't know if I'll stay or not. I haven't decided."

"Why is that?"

She shook her head and grinned. "You ask too many questions, Ty. You didn't use to be so inquisitive."

He gave her a quietly considering glance before answering. "It's been a long time. I guess I want to find out if you've really changed. That's all."

"I've changed a lot," she told him, meeting his eyes directly.

"How? What's the most important way in which you're different?"

She thought for a moment. "I'm much more independent."

"Is that why you're not married?"

Alex leaned back against the headrest. "I thought we were through with the inquisition."

"Then you ask me a question."

"All right." She stole a glance at him. "Are you married?" That thought had nibbled at the back of her mind ever since they'd left the mill.

"No."

"Ever?"

"Never."

"Why?" She couldn't help asking.

"That was three questions, and your time is up, Miss Thorpe." Ty hit his horn, and the young waitress came to take the tray away. They drove back to the mill in virtual silence.

Her hand on the doorhandle, Alex said, "I enjoyed the shake, and I appreciate your letting me know what you plan to do with the mill."

"Wait a minute." Ty ran his hands over the steering wheel, trying to decide on his next move. Suddenly it was imperative that he see her again—soon. He didn't want her to leave without making future plans. Once before he'd watched her drive away, and they'd lost each other. It couldn't happen again. "Could we have dinner?" he asked hastily.

"When?" she returned, trying not to sound too eager.

"Tonight?"

She smiled with pleasure. "Fine."

His next words seemed to come out in a rush. "Alex, I want you to know. Twelve years ago, I . . ."

"Don't, Ty." The smile faded from her face.

"Don't what?"

"Don't try to change the past. You can't."

"But I want you to understand what happened. I think we have to talk about it, so we'll both know . . ."

Alex interrupted him with an angry flood of words. "I don't think it would do either of us any good to rehash ancient history. I don't want to know why you left. We can't change it now. It wouldn't make any difference. . . ."

"How do you know?"

"I know," she answered sadly. "Just let it be."

"But what about now?" His heart stopped, then seemed to turn over at the flicker of hope he read in her golden-brown eyes.

"You think we can take it from here?"

"Don't you?" Ty reached out and captured her hand, drawing it up to his lips. It was such a small hand, small and neat, with delicately rounded nails and soft, delicate skin. Her fingers traced the outline of his mouth, and he closed his eyes at the joy the simple touch could bring. When he opened them again, his gray eyes were stormy and they locked with hers.

"There's still something between us, isn't there?" she said hesitantly. "Something that doesn't need the past?"

He pressed a kiss in her soft palm and held on to her hand as he studied her earnest, flushed features. Maybe she was right. Maybe the here and now was all that mattered.

Alex returned Ty's gaze without wavering. She was being truthful; she didn't want to know why he'd left. She didn't want to go over the reasons why they'd ended up apart. There seemed no reason to relive the pain. The hurt could destroy any chance for them in the future. And she did want that chance. She decided that quickly, in the moment it took for his fingers to tighten around hers.

"Okay," he agreed finally. "The past is a taboo subject. You and I just met, Miss Thorpe." His smile was impish. "Have I told you how much you intrigue me?"

"No, you haven't." His easy, familiar charm relaxed Alex in the way it always had.

"Then we'll discuss it over dinner. Shall I pick you up around seven?"

"Perfect."

He relinquished his hold on her hand with obvious reluctance and watched as she got out of his car and into hers and drove away.

Ty didn't remember the drive from the mill. One minute he was staring after Alex's car, the next he was in the driveway of his mother's house. He raced up the front steps, whistling a happy tune.

"I'm home, Mama," he called cheerfully in the direction of the kitchen. Upon entering the room, he saw that his sister was seated at the small round table. "Sally," he said with pleasure, patting her shoulder affectionately.

Sally's gray eyes, so like her brother's, crinkled as she smiled. "It's good to see you, Ty. We were beginning to think you'd taken off back to Atlanta."

"Not yet. Where are Keith and the kids?" Ty sat down in the chair opposite hers.

"At the movies. Cody's been begging to see some new kids' movie. I think Keith finally got tired of hearing about it and decided to take him. I'm kind of glad to have a Saturday afternoon to myself."

Ty studied his sister intently. Sally Craig was tall and big-boned, with her mother's light brown hair and soft features. Never a beauty, she was nonetheless attractive in a quiet, serious way. The problem was that she always looked tired. With two growing children, a full-time job at a packing plant and the worry she'd been through with her husband so long out of work, Sally rarely relaxed. Even as she sat beside her brother, her hands were busy stringing and snapping green beans.

Reaching out, Ty stilled her fluttery movements with his hand. "Slow down, sis. Take it easy."

She leaned back in the chair with a tired sigh. "There's just so much to do."

"So much for an afternoon to yourself."

She actually laughed. "I guess you're right." But she reached for the tray of beans once more, and Ty merely shook his head.

Their mother bustled into the room. "I thought I heard you, Ty." She crossed to the refrigerator. "How about some lemonade?"

"Sounds good." Ty couldn't help but smile; his mother didn't think you were complete unless you were eating or drinking something.

"Mama says you got in late yesterday afternoon," Sally said.

"And he stayed out half the night." Rose Duncan set three glasses of lemonade down on the Formica tabletop and settled in a chair.

"It wasn't that late, Mama. I ran into some old friends." Ty sipped the tart, refreshing drink.

"I saw Myra Douglas at the grocery store this morning. She said Bubba had met you at Pete's Place after he got off from work," Sally added.

"You'd think people would stop calling him Bubba now that he's a policeman." Rose brushed a tired hand through her graying hair.

"How was the yard sale at the church?" Ty asked her, changing the subject.

"We raised quite a bit of money toward the new choir robes. Still isn't enough, though. The way things cost nowadays." Rose clucked disapprovingly.

"Let me make a donation, Mama." Ty automatically reached for his wallet.

"You just save your money for tomorrow when you come to church with me," she answered smartly.

Sally giggled. "She's trapped you again, Ty. Mama always found a way to get you into church."

Rose sniffed. "I raised you both to go to church. Besides, I want to show off my good-looking son." Her eyes twinkled merrily. "Of course, everyone in town has probably seen you by now. Where'd you go this afternoon?"

"Out and about." Ty was reluctant to tell them he'd spent the entire afternoon with Alex.

"Keith and the kids are coming over after the movie, and we're going to grill some hamburgers."

"Laura and Cody are anxious to see if you brought them any presents," Sally added.

"Well, maybe I can see them before I leave."

"Leave?" both women questioned at once.

"I have a date for dinner."

Sally laughed heartily. "My brother! Back in town for less than twenty-four hours and he already has a date. Who with?"

Ty took a deep breath. He couldn't lie. In Grayson the truth would reach them eventually. Besides, there was really nothing to hide. "Alex Thorpe," he supplied finally.

"Ty!" Rose exclaimed, her eyes wide with disbelief.

"Why in the world?" his sister cried.

Holding up a beseeching hand, Ty protested, "What's the big deal? We ran into each other yesterday."

"You know perfectly well what the big deal is," Sally said crossly. "You'd think you had learned better."

"That was a long time ago, sis."

"Didn't she cause you and Mama and Dad enough heartache twelve years ago?" Sally got up and stalked across the kitchen, slamming her empty glass into the sink. "It won't be any different now, you know." She turned to stare at Ty with narrowed gray eyes. "Is this why you're back in town trying to buy the mill? Are you trying to get that rich little spoiled brat to notice you again?"

"Don't be ridiculous." Ty bit out the words tersely. "Do you think I built a successful business by acting on crazy impulses like that? I'm buying that property because it's a good deal. It has nothing to do with Alex."

"I hope not," Sally said icily. "For your sake, I hope not." She turned to her mother. "Save the hamburger, Mama. When Keith gets here, send him home. We'll be here for Sunday dinner tomorrow. Maybe after a night with Miss Alexa Thorpe, Ty will see the error of his ways and will come back down to earth with us commoners."

"Sally—" Ty began.

"It's no use, Ty. She's poison, and I don't want to see you hurt again." Sally turned on her heel and walked out, closing the back door with a bang.

"What's it to her?" Ty asked, turning to his mother.

"Do you really have to ask?" Rose pushed away from the table firmly and started out of the room. "You always have to learn things the hard way, don't you?"

After she was gone, he sat in the quiet kitchen, replaying the scene in his head. His mother and sister thought Alex was big trouble. They're wrong, he thought with grim determination. Dead wrong.

At her home, Alex started up the curving, graceful stairway in the central foyer just as her mother wheeled out of the living room. "Tom called, Alexa."

"Damn!" Alex said guiltily. She hadn't spared Tom a thought since last night.

"Alexa!" Lucia admonished.

"I'm sorry."

"He said he'd call back. He wants to see a movie or something tonight."

"I have other plans."

"Really?" Lucia's bright blue eyes narrowed. "I was hoping you'd be here for dinner."

"Why?"

"To talk with Grady and me about what we're going to do about the mill."

"The mill?" Alex stepped back down the stairs. "What about it?"

Lucia's hands twisted in her lap. "That awful Tyler Duncan has come back to Grayson, and he's planning to buy the mill property."

Alex ran her hand across the gleaming oak finish of the stair railing, avoiding her mother's eyes. "I know," she said at last.

"You know? You know!" Lucia sat up indignantly in her wheelchair. "Then why didn't you tell me?"

"Because I just found out."

"How?"

Alex bit her lip. For the second time that day, she was tempted to lie. But she was tired, sick to death of shielding her mother from life's little unpleasantnesses. Lucia would know the truth around seven, anyway. Maybe it was best to warn her.

"I know because I spent the afternoon with Ty."

With a shocked gasp, Lucia said, "You didn't! Alexa, how could you have anything to do with that man after he ran out on you? I suppose he had some sort of explanation for his behavior?"

"No, I didn't want an explanation." Alex turned away and started back up the stairs.

Lucia wheeled herself to the very foot of the staircase. "Did he tell you what he's going to do with the mill?"

"He owns a carpet company. They're going to open a new plant here in Grayson."

"And he didn't tell you why he left?"

To Alex, her mother's voice sounded almost relieved. She turned to look down at her. "No. I told you I'm not interested."

Lucia sighed heavily. "It's revenge," she muttered, almost under her breath.

Alex frowned. "Revenge for what?"

Her mother seemed to fumble for words. "Revenge for . . . for . . . for being born poor, for having to work in the mill."

"Don't be melodramatic," Alex snapped.

"Well, is he going to stay here?"

"You can ask him that yourself." Alex continued up the stairs. She couldn't stop her lips from curving into a tiny smile.

"Ask him?" Lucia sputtered. "When would I ask him?"

"When he comes to pick me up tonight," Alex answered just as she turned the curve of the staircase. It was nearly impossible to contain her laughter as she pictured her mother's stricken face.

This is going to be interesting, she thought, very interesting indeed.

Chapter Three

An impatient knock sounded at Alex's bedroom door, and before she could answer, Carrie burst inside.

"This is him, isn't it?"

"Him, who?" Alex twisted around in her seat at the dressing table to look at her niece.

"Tyler Duncan is the guy you were in love with, isn't he?"

Alex turned back around, laid down her hairbrush and picked up a palette of eye shadow. Reflected in the mirror she could see her niece lounging across the mauve silk bedspread, an expectant look on her face. Her expression demanded an answer. "Yes, Ty and I were pretty serious the summer after I graduated from high school."

"I knew it!" Carrie exclaimed, sitting up on the bed. "Grandmother is in a tizzy, so I asked Clarissa what the big deal about this guy was. She told me you and he were pretty heavy."

Alex smiled. "I guess heavy is as good a description as any." She continued shadowing her eyes with delicate color.

"But he's the guy you told me about this morning, isn't he?"

"I said so, didn't I?" Alex retorted. Lord, why in the world had she bared her soul to Carrie this morning? The girl was bound to think this was some sort of fairy tale. And that hadn't been her intention in telling her about Ty. She didn't want Carrie to make the same mistakes she had. "Carrie—" she began, but her niece's enthusiasm stopped her.

"This is so romantic I could just die!" Carrie catapulted off the bed and tugged open the folding door of her aunt's closet. "What are you going to wear?"

Alex laid down the makeup and turned around. "Carrie, I don't want you to think Ty and I are going to ride off into the sunset together for some kind of happily-ever-after. We're just going to dinner. After that, I don't know. He hurt me very badly once, and I don't want you..."

"You don't want me to think this a reason to get real involved with Billy, right?" Carrie finished for her as she flipped through the clothes hanging in the closet. "Don't worry, Aunt Alex. I'm not getting serious about anyone for a long time. There's too much I want to do."

With a gentle smile, Alex sat watching the young girl. Had she ever sounded so wise and confident at that age? Carrie seemed to know exactly what she wanted: college, a career, maybe a family. *I hope nothing stops her,* Alex thought with a swell of emotion. *I hope she gets to have everything she wants.*

"Come on, what are you going to wear?" Carrie implored, breaking into Alex's thoughts. "You have to look really great. He has to regret breaking your heart."

"Oh, Carrie," Alex said, finding it impossible to suppress a giggle. She might as well give up and let herself be swept away by her niece's romantic enthusiasm. After all, she was doing the unbelievable—seeing Ty again.

"How about this?" Carrie pulled a bright yellow dress out of the closet. The back was cut deeply away and the neckline was daringly low, held up by two tiny spaghetti straps. The skirt flared full and feminine from the fitted waist.

"Do you think so?" Alex said doubtfully. The last time she and Ty had seen each other, twelve years ago, she'd been wearing a yellow dress. She didn't want to be reminded of that disastrous evening.

"Believe me, this is perfect. You look great in yellow." Carrie pulled Alex in front of the full-length mirror and held the dress in front of her. The color was just the right foil for Alex's dark hair and eyes.

"I guess you're right," Alex agreed as she pulled silky underwear out of her dresser drawer.

While her aunt finished dressing, Carrie kept up a continuous line of chatter about Ty and how angry Lucia was. "She told Clarissa she'd be in her room until dinner."

"I doubt that," Alex said dryly. "Your grandmother never backs away from a confrontation."

"Why didn't she like Ty, anyhow?"

Alex raised her eyebrows at the girl's innocent tone. "I imagine Clarissa has already filled you in on most of the details. Not much has happened in this house that has gotten past that woman. I don't think you need any further information." Stepping in front of the mirror, she surveyed her reflection with some satisfaction. The dress flattered her tan, and the white strappy sandals she'd chosen gave the outfit a dressed-up look.

Carrie stepped forward and fluffed the ends of Alex's hair with a brush. "Is he really buying the mill?"

Turning away, Alex began transferring the contents of her casual straw purse to a small white clutch. "Yes, he is. It'll be good for the town."

"Grandmother didn't really think Dad would be able to buy the mill back and start it up again, did she?" Carrie said thoughtfully, following her aunt out of the bedroom.

Alex switched off the light and closed the door. "I don't know, honey. Sometimes your grandmother slips into the past a little, especially when something in the present doesn't please her.''

They started down the wide staircase, and the doorbell rang, echoing through the house. "I'll get it!" Carrie yelled, flying down the stairs and narrowly missing a collision with her father at the bottom.

"Sorry, Dad." She tugged open the door and gave Ty her usual boisterous welcome. "Hello, I'm Carrie. Come on in."

In taupe slacks, cream shirt and a tan raw-silk jacket, Ty managed to look both masculine and appealing. "Now I really feel old," he told Carrie. "You were about three when I first met you. You've grown up." The glance and smile he gave Carrie had melted the defenses of older, far more worldly women. From her vantage point halfway up the stairs, Alex could see he'd won over her niece.

"Hello, Ty." Grady stepped forward, extending his hand in welcome, smiling pleasantly.

Alex joined them and sent her brother a grateful look. She could always count on Grady's calm, stabilizing presence. He had inherited their father's quiet intelligence and their mother's determination. Alex respected him immensely. For some reason she was glad her brother was standing beside her as she turned to greet Ty. It helped keep her feet on the ground.

"Hi," she said, trying to keep the nervous tremor out of her voice.

"Alex." On Ty's lips, her name was an endearment. "You look beautiful."

"Thank you." Warmth danced along her veins.

With a sense of wonder, Ty watched the color come to her cheeks. Alex wasn't merely beautiful tonight; she was luminous. Her hair shone in the muted light, and her dark eyes sparkled. Was the excitement he saw in her features really for him? Perhaps this afternoon hadn't been just a temporary puff of magic, as he'd feared.

Grady cleared his throat, and Ty realized he and Alex had just been standing, silently staring at each other. Carrie was eyeing them with obvious interest, and Alex sent her a tiny frown. The teenager only grinned.

"How about a drink?" Grady asked smoothly.

Mindful of her mother's attitude toward Ty, Alex started to protest, but Ty overruled her. "I'd love to."

The men followed Alex and Carrie down the foyer and through an arched doorway. Ty glanced about with interest. He hadn't spent too much time in Alex's home twelve summers ago, but he could still remember the feeling of quiet elegance. That feeling remained. The wood floor gleamed with the sheen of countless waxings and years of care. The gold flocked wallpaper, though obviously new, fit the atmosphere of old money. There were oil paintings on the wall and thick Oriental rugs under their feet as the group turned the corner and went into the sitting room.

Grady's wife, Gina, was waiting for them, sipping a glass of white wine. The subdued grays and misty blues of the decor were the perfect setting for her ash-blond beauty. In cream linen slacks and a lilac silk tunic, she was, as always, the epitome of style and elegance. She touched a well-manicured hand to her hair as she rose to greet Ty. But Alex noticed her smile didn't quite reach her blue eyes.

"Beautiful room," Ty commented, accepting a Scotch-and-water from Grady. "You've redecorated since I was here."

"Yes," Gina said. "I think it's comfortable. We spend a lot of time here—family tradition."

Ty raised a quizzical brow, and Alex hastened to answer, "My great-grandfather, Alexander Thorpe, used to insist that his family meet here before dinner to discuss the day's events. Mother and Father did the same. Now Grady and Gina are following the custom."

"Although we don't insist on it, of course," Grady added. "We just think it's a pleasant way for a family to touch base at the end of the day."

Ty nodded, but before he could make another comment Lucia's wheelchair glided almost noiselessly into the room. "I'll have a sherry," she said, nodding at her son as she maneuvered her chair beside the blue velvet couch where Gina sat. "Hello, Tyler." Her voice was faultlessly polite, but cold.

"Mrs. Thorpe," Ty answered, a little stiffly. "You're looking well."

"Thank you."

Grady presented his mother with her drink and sat down in the chair next to Ty's. Carrie perched on another, and an uncomfortable silence fell over the room. Alex stood next to the bar and watched the two camps. This must be what it feels like before a battle, she thought—two opposing sides waiting for the opening shot. Her family had clearly chosen sides. Grady and Carrie were firmly aligned with Ty, while Gina and Lucia glared at them challengingly from across the room.

"Will you be in Grayson long?" Grady finally asked Ty, breaking the overpowering quiet.

"I haven't decided." He glanced at Lucia. "If the deal I'm working on goes through..."

"It will," Lucia interrupted in a hard, brittle voice. "The bank needs to sell that property, and the town needs the jobs. You won't have any problems."

Their eyes locked, and Ty realized with a start that, wheelchair or not, this was still a woman to be reckoned with. He didn't allow himself to look away. "I've learned not to count on anything before I've signed on the dotted line."

"A smart policy." Lucia glanced archly from Ty to Alex, her meaning clear.

Gina frowned. "Why don't you go help Clarissa finish dinner, Carrie?" It was obvious she wanted her daughter out of the room in case an argument ensued.

"But, Mom..." the girl protested.

Ty rose from his chair and turned to Alex. "Don't you think we should be on our way?"

"Yes." Hastily draining her drink, Alex gathered up her purse. She was relieved Ty had chosen not to pursue the conversation with her mother. She was afraid things could get very, very ugly. Stooping to kiss her mother's cheek, she whispered, "Good night."

"Good night, Alexa." Lucia avoided her daughter's eyes.

In a matter of moments Alex and Ty were crossing the deep, shadowed front veranda. "Why do I feel I should check to see if my tires have been slashed?" Ty paused beside his car to open the passenger door for Alex.

"You didn't expect it to be easy, did you?"

"No, but I hoped she would have mellowed with time."

The door closed and Alex waited until Ty slid into the driver's seat before continuing, "Mother doesn't mellow. She doesn't even change. She'll always act as if this were 1940, and she's the rich debutante daughter of Marshall Nelson. She steamrolls over everyone."

"Not me," Ty said bluntly. He started the car and headed for the Taylor Inn.

The strained beginning to their evening seemed to have put a damper on Ty's good spirits. He was very quiet as they made their selections from the menu.

The restaurant was filled to capacity. Many of the diners were people Alex knew, and she didn't miss the looks they sent her way. She could see the wheels turning in the women's brains as Ty was identified. There'd be talk.

Determined to ignore their curious onlookers, Alex cast about for a safe topic of conversation. They couldn't talk about their common past or their families. That left Ty.

"Tell me where you live," she said.

"I have a condominium just outside of Atlanta. Our mill is in a smaller town just north of there. I travel a lot, and it helps to live close to the airport. It's a comfortable place. Not too fancy."

Nonetheless, Alex conjured up an expensive bachelor pad in her mind, visualizing Ty entertaining a series of beautiful women. She blinked to dispel the image, saying instead, "Living in Grayson would be a big change."

"The voice of experience talking?" He laughed slightly.

Alex took a long sip from her glass of iced tea. "Well, you can't say the old home town is the most cosmopolitan spot on earth. You'll have to make a cultural adjustment. I mean, the only place you can even order a drink other than beer is at the country club."

"What do you do for fun, Alex?"

"Fun?" Alex thought suddenly of Tom Jacobs. Yes, they'd had some good times together. He was probably wondering why she hadn't returned his call. She swallowed a little guiltily. He'd soon know. The news would spread fast, judging from the looks being sent her way now.

"Alex?" Ty prompted.

"Huh?" She stared at him, momentarily confused.

"I asked what you did for fun."

"Well, during the school year I stay pretty busy. I swim and play golf and tennis. . . ."

"No dates?"

She almost gulped. Was he reading her mind, just like in the old days? Looking down at her hands, she said, "I date, yes."

"But not one special guy?" Ty pressed, an oddly intent look in his eyes.

"Well, there is . . ." she began, almost nervous.

"Alex!"

Turning, Alex saw Suzie and her husband, Jason, weaving their way across the crowded room. She groaned; she'd hoped to avoid anyone who might actually try to strike up a conversation with them.

"We saw you just as we were leaving," Suzie said, coming to a stop beside the table. The look she gave Alex was full of questions.

"Ty, I'm sure you remember Suzie and Jason Lewis," Alex said.

"Of course." Ty stood and shook Jason's hand.

"I heard you were back in town," Jason said.

"And that you're buying the mill," Suzie added.

"My company has made an offer, yes," Ty answered guardedly.

"I hope it works out," the shorter, stocky man said with sincerity.

"I appreciate that."

Jason took his wife's elbow and began edging her away. "Very nice to see you again."

"Yes, maybe we can all get together," Suzie chimed in, giving Alex a sly grin.

The waiter arrived with their dinner just as the other couple left, and Alex tried to hide her laughter.

"What's so funny?" Ty asked after the young man was gone.

"Suzie suggesting we all get together," she answered. "You do remember what happened the one and only time we double-dated with them, don't you?"

"You mean the night we took them to Nick's?" Ty joined her in laughter, remembering.

"Nick's wasn't exactly their style. I doubt either of them had ever been in a bar that served beer in cans and had a room in the back for gambling." Alex buttered a roll and grinned, thinking back to her friends' shocked expressions when she and Ty had led them into the ramshackle bar.

Mischief danced in Ty's eyes. "It seems to me one of the regulars took exception to the color of Jason's shirt."

"It was pink," Alex supplied.

Ty leaned back in his chair. "I kept him out of that fight, and then another guy started hitting on Suzie. Man, I thought Jason was going to explode."

"Suzie was scared to death. She couldn't understand why I loved that place."

Fixing her with a suddenly serious gaze, Ty asked, "Why weren't you scared?"

"I was with you." There was simple truth in the words. She and Ty had done some wild things that summer, things Alex would never have dreamed of doing otherwise. But as long as Ty had been near, she'd never been nervous.

Leaning her arms on the table, she cupped her chin against the palm of one hand, her brown eyes dreamy. "Remember that song Nick used to play over and over?"

"Yeah, 'Crazy' by Patsy Cline."

Alex sighed sadly. "Nick would play it again and again on that jukebox. And then he'd tell us all about his wife."

"Who ran off to Nashville to try and become a country singer," Ty finished, leaning forward too, caught up in his own memories. "He said she promised to come back...."

"But she never did."

"And she never became a star, either. Poor old Nick just stayed here, running a bar, listening to that sad old song and trying to drink his loneliness away."

"I liked Nick," Alex murmured. "I liked going there with you."

"Yeah." Ty looked away from the stars in her dreamy brown eyes. He could remember those nights at Nick's too well. The big, burly bar owner had a heart of gold, and he'd taken a shine to Alex. He had always cautioned Ty to take good care of her, to never let her go. God only knew why Ty had taken her there in the first place. Maybe he'd been trying to shock the poor little rich girl. It hadn't worked. She'd been thrilled with the place.

"I wonder if that story was really true?" Alex said softly.

"You never used to doubt it back then, Cinderella." Ty slipped easily into calling her by the old nickname as he remembered being with her at Nick's. He could almost smell the smoky heat of that crowded room, hear the melancholy strains of that old song and feel the softness of Alex's body as they'd swayed together on the tiny dance floor.

"It was romantic. I wanted to believe it then." Alex sliced into her steak, determined to block out the memories now that they were flowing back.

"Don't you still believe in romance?"

"Let's just say I'm more of a realist." Alex smiled tightly. "You can't live in a fairy tale forever."

"Cinderella would never let reality intrude too much."

Alex stared across the table into the turbulent gray of his eyes. It's like being drawn into the heart of a storm, she thought, forcing herself to look away. "I'm not Cinderella. I never was."

"No more than I was your Prince Charming." Ty's words were harsh, his face an unreadable mask as he began his own meal. They ate in uncomfortable silence for a few minutes.

"I wonder whatever happened to Nick," Ty said at last.

"He died about two years ago."

Ty gazed at her in surprise. "How do you know?"

"I saw it in the obituaries, so I went to the funeral." She frowned slightly. "Nick always talked like he had nobody in the world, but that church was packed to the rafters."

"He helped a lot of people." Ty picked up his water goblet and stared intently at the clear contents. *I should have been at that funeral,* he thought with shame. It had been Nick who had given him money and found him a job when Ty had left town. Without his help, Ty's life might have turned out very differently.

He looked up at Alex and continued, "Maybe Nick always seemed lonely because he had lost the person who meant the most to him. Without her, he was...incomplete."

Alex concentrated on her plate, not daring to look at Ty. "It's hard being alone," she murmured after several long moments.

"Yes, it is," Ty agreed. But we don't have to be, he wanted to add. We have the second chance Nick never got. But he couldn't say that to Alex. Not yet. This wasn't the time to get serious. They needed to laugh together, to talk, to get to know each other all over again.

So Ty smiled. It was the devil-may-care look which Alex remembered so well, and she couldn't help smiling back. "You know we've broken all the rules tonight, don't you, Miss Thorpe?" he said.

"What rules?"

"Don't you remember? We said no talking about the past, no dwelling on things we can't change."

"You're right," she said, warming to his teasing air. "We need to do something about that."

"Exactly. Tell me about teaching high school. Do you have any students who are as disruptive as I used to be?"

They began to talk, and the words almost overflowed from both of them. They talked about Alex's work and Ty's travels. About movies, books and music. About politics, food and fashion. They dawdled over dinner, drew out the conversation over dessert and lingered over a last cup of coffee.

There seemed no end to the things Alex wanted to tell Ty. About Florida sunsets, college pranks and her reactions to the major events of the past twelve years. It was as if they had only a few hours to fill in the missing pieces of each other's lives. As always, they had more to say than they could hope to cover in one evening.

Just like the old days, Alex thought, listening to Ty tell her what he'd thought of the latest Woody Allen film. Most people had believed Tyler Duncan had nothing in his head but plans for big trouble. However, she'd known better. Appearances to the contrary, Ty had been intelligent and introspective. She'd been able to draw that out of him. The qualities she'd recognized in the boy had matured in the man. She still found him fascinating.

It was after ten when they rose to leave. Main Street was virtually deserted, the streetlights casting pools of golden brilliance on the darkened buildings.

"Let's walk awhile," Alex suggested, taking a deep breath of the warm summer air.

"I had forgotten how quiet it can be here." Ty took her arm as they strolled down the street.

"Especially in the summer," she agreed. "I think the heat acts like cotton, muffling the noises and softening all the hard edges. In the winter the cooler air sharpens everything again."

He nodded his head, appreciating her analogy, and they walked along, pausing now and again to look in a shop window or comment on something that came to mind. Their silence was easy and companionable, and quite naturally Ty's arm slipped loosely around Alex's shoulders. Just as naturally, he drew her into the darkened doorway of a shop and kissed her.

On his lips there was the taste of the old Ty. Impatient. Demanding. He'd always asked things of Alex that she wasn't quite ready to give. He'd always been in the lead, setting the pace, leaving her to catch up.

Tonight it was different. For every demand his mouth and tongue made, Alex made one of her own. His hands caressed the skin left bare by the deeply cut back of her dress. Her hands slid under his jacket and crept up his lean, muscled torso. When her breath was coming in deep, ragged gulps and her legs felt ready to give way, Ty released her. But she pulled him back with a soft moan and the quiet insistence of her mouth.

They leaned against the plate glass of the store's front door, their bodies straining for an impossible intimacy. Only when a stream of cars swept by did they pull apart, jumping guiltily in the sudden beam of the headlights.

Alex turned and pressed her flushed face against the welcome coolness of the metal and glass. God, it was still the same. A touch of his hands and she was spiraling out of control. Heaven help her if he asked for more than a kiss, because surely she would give him anything he demanded, right here on Main Street.

Ty's body curved around hers, shielding her from the unwelcome intrusion of light. He was shaking from head to

toe, his senses bowled over by the swift ascent to full
arousal. She was more than he remembered, and he yearned
to satisfy the ache she had started.

The cars passed, and Ty turned Alex gently in his arms,
pressing his cheek against her silky, sweetly scented hair.
Brushing a soft kiss against his neck, she sent up a small
prayer of thankfulness. Being in his arms again felt so right;
this had to be the answer to twelve years of hopes and
dreams.

"Come on," he said roughly. "I'll take you home."

"But I don't want to go home!" Alex broke away from
him, her brow furrowing.

Grasping the soft skin of her upper arms firmly, Ty stared
down at her. "Where do you want to go, Alex? To the lake,
like we did when we were kids? To a motel? I don't want it
to be that way, do you?"

"I don't care. I just want *you*." The words were an urgent plea torn from somewhere deep inside her.

"You do now, while my kiss burns on your mouth. That
always convinced you. But what about tomorrow? What
about when you forget this?" He pulled her close for a hard,
almost brutal kiss. Thrusting her away, he turned sharply,
heading back down the street.

Watching him stride away, Alex was struck by the rever-
sal of their roles. Before, she had always been the one who
stressed patience, who'd urged him to think of more than
just the night and the swift assuagement of desire. He had
never listened to her then. He'd just swept her away in a
storm of lovemaking. Now he was holding back. She hurried after him, grabbing his arm and forcing him to look at
her in the dim glow of a streetlight.

"I know you want me as much as I want you."

Ty shook his head. "That isn't the issue."

"Then what is? God, Ty, don't make me beg you." The
last sentence was almost a sob.

Unable to resist her tear-drenched eyes and trembling lips, Ty caught her to him again. "It isn't a question of wanting you, Alex. I just want it to be right this time."

"Then let's go away. Surely you don't have to be back here in Grayson until Monday."

"And when we got home, your family would be lined up on the front veranda, looking at me as if I'd violated you again."

Her mother's face, harsh with disapproval, loomed in Alex's mind. He was right. It was impossible. "Oh, Ty," she breathed. "I just don't want to lose you again."

The words sent hope soaring through him. But he couldn't get carried away. They had to take it slowly. That was the only way they had a chance at anything lasting and solid—slow and steady.

It was easy to think that. Harder to make it happen when steady was anything but the way she made him feel. Ty spoke carefully, "Let's do it the right way this time. We're not kids who think the world's gonna end tomorrow. Let's be patient. We can take it slowly."

"But we've lost so much time already!"

"Maybe that's why it seems so urgent tonight. But it isn't. We have time." He lifted her chin with a firm hand and gazed into her eyes. "I want to be more than just your lover, Alex."

Her heart racing, a thousand questions tumbled through Alex. She couldn't allow herself to dwell on what he meant by those words. If her hopes were built up too high, they only had farther to fall. Nodding silently, she walked beside him back to the car.

At her home he pulled to a stop at the veranda and left the motor running as he escorted her to the front door.

"When will I see you again?" she dared to ask.

"I'll call you tomorrow." He pressed a swift, hard kiss on her lips and left.

She stood in the doorway and watched his car pull away. Long after the taillights had disappeared down the circular drive she still leaned against the door, her hand on the lips he had so recently kissed. She was afraid if she went inside, away from the magic of the summer night, the events of the evening might fade away like some sweet, impossible dream.

The scent of honeysuckle swam in the breeze, and crickets sang their summer song in the deep shrubbery lining the porch. It could have been any June night, so similar was it to a thousand she'd known before. But I pray the morning is different, Alex thought. I pray Ty is back in my life to stay.

Ty drove home, his hands tight on the wheel as the familiar feelings washed over him. Many evenings he had deposited Alex safely at home, then driven away, aching with the need of her. But in those days the decision to leave hadn't been his. Tonight, leaving had been his only choice.

He would have been lying if he hadn't admitted pleasure in the fact that she desired him. A feeling of power, raw and elemental, had surged through him when she'd pulled him into her arms. She had changed. Instead of a girl playing with adult emotions, Alex was now a woman, unafraid to express her passion. It made him wonder if she'd had many lovers over the years. Maybe not here in Grayson, but surely in Florida there'd been someone....

Firmly Ty closed his mind to that train of thought. What Alex had done in the past twelve years was none of his business. He'd given up the right to ask. Certainly he hadn't been celibate himself. What mattered most was now. He'd meant what he'd said; this time it would be right between them. Ty intended to woo Alex as if they had never met, as if they'd never shared a sweet, tragic summer.

Ty felt oddly confident about the present and the future. It was the past that caused him to waver. Many of the events that had torn him and Alex apart were still a mystery to him. And there was one question that tantalized him at all times—one question he was afraid to ask. Alex had made it clear she didn't want to explore that aspect of their relationship, and he had to obey her wishes. There was pain in her eyes every time they even started to talk about that summer. Ty never wanted to hurt her again. Indeed, the feelings growing between them were so delicate that that long-ago hurt might snuff out any hope for the future. And God, how he needed that hope.

Alex is right, Ty thought as he arrived at his mother's house. *Looking ahead was better.*

As he swiftly mounted the front steps, a slight movement in the darkened recesses of the porch caught his attention. He was startled until his mother spoke. "You're pretty early, son."

"We had dinner and talked. There's not too much else to do in Grayson." He sat down in the rocker beside hers, reminded poignantly of other nights when his mother would wait for him here, anxious for him to be safely home. Even for the rowdy, troubled boy Ty had been, that sense of homecoming and security had been welcome.

"I'm sorry about Sally and me getting angry with you earlier." Rose spoke stiffly, as if the words had been carefully rehearsed.

"That's okay. Alex and I don't exactly have the best history."

They sat silently, the quiet creak of the rockers the only sound in the hushed evening air. It was Rose who spoke first. "Have you and Alex talked about what happened that summer?"

"No. She doesn't want to."

Rose sighed. "I guess that's understandable."

"Maybe." All of Ty's uncertainties came through in that one word.

"Your father would say to let it be."

"Dad would say let *her* be," Ty corrected.

"He always did." The movement of her rocker ceased, and Rose stood. "Your father wasn't always right. Much as I loved him, I could see his faults. I often disagreed with his methods. But about Alex Thorpe, he knew what he was talking about." She laid a gentle hand against Ty's cheek. "Be careful, son."

Reaching up, Ty covered her work-roughened hand with his own. "I'll try."

"Good night." She turned and walked inside the house, the screen door closing softly behind her.

The mention of his father settled a fog of gloom over Ty. Harris Duncan had not only disapproved of his son seeing the mill-owner's daughter, he had gone so far as to forbid it. His command had prompted an ugly, bitter argument Ty could remember well....

"You'll never be what she needs." The tall, powerfully built man had fixed Ty with the steely gray eyes he'd passed on to both his children.

"I think that's none of your business." Ty was furious, unwilling to accept advice about Alex from his father.

Harris stood, towering over his seated son, and jabbed a finger into Ty's chest. "Don't you understand, boy? Right now you're just like a forbidden piece of candy for that young lady—a little something different to spend her summer vacation with."

"Alex isn't like that," Ty answered stubbornly.

"You've got it bad, don't you? With all your highfalutin talk about goin' somewhere and makin' a lot of money, you think that fancy piece of—"

"Shut up!" Ty jumped to his feet, grabbing his father's shirtfront. "Don't talk about Alex like that!" His balled fist knotted the material as he jerked his father forward.

"Do you think she loves you? Did she tell you so?" Harris laughed derisively in his son's face. "I thought you were smarter than that. I didn't realize I'd raised such a fool, to be hoodwinked by a rich, scheming bitch."

Blind with rage, Ty pushed his father across the tiny kitchen, sending him sprawling across the table. Just as quickly the older man came back at him, grasping his son by the shoulders, shaking him until the room spun round in circles.

"I want you to stop it!" Harris shouted. "I don't want you to see her again. I don't want my son chasin' after something he'll never have. Wastin' his time on somebody who will never, ever think he's good enough for her. Don't waste your life on a dream. I know what it's like. I know how it sucks the life out of you. Now stay away from her!"

He flung his son away from him and stomped out of the kitchen, but not before Ty saw the dull look of defeat in his silvery eyes. Both men knew it was too late, that Ty would follow his attraction to Alex until the end.

If anything, Harris pushed his son further into involvement with the girl. Ty was intent on proving his father wrong, on showing him Alex was the opposite of all he'd accused her of being. He brought her home, even took her to church. But Harris maintained his distance, and the rest of the family followed his lead. Ty was twenty years old that summer, and short of throwing him out of the house there was nothing Harris could do about his relationship with Alex. Rose would never stand for putting their son out, so his father kept silent and watched the two young people act out their parts in a summer of tremendous highs and unspeakable lows. And he was there for his son in the end.

The screen door banged behind him as Ty went into the house, toward his room, seeking escape from the memories of his father. But Harris's face smiled from a framed snapshot beside the bed. A faded ribbon they'd won in a father-son sack race at a mill picnic hung limply on the old bulletin board above a chest of drawers. The feel of his father still permeated the entire house. Ty lay in the silence, remembering, until he drifted off into an uneasy sleep.

The next morning dawned humid and overcast, but the gloom of the skies couldn't dampen Alex's spirits. Ty Duncan was back. She hummed a little tune of happiness as she went downstairs to the kitchen.

Sunday was Clarissa's day off, and the family usually fixed breakfast together. More often than not Grady would descend on the kitchen first and mix up a batch of pancakes. Today was no exception. Her brother was presiding over the griddle while Carrie poured orange juice when Alex entered the cheerful blue-and-white room.

Gina and Lucia were at the round table by the big bay window, sipping coffee and looking at the Sunday newspaper.

"You're up early, Mother. Did Clarissa give you a hand before she left?" Alex kissed her mother's cheek before taking the seat beside hers. Lucia usually slept late on Sunday morning and allowed her daughter or Gina to help her get dressed, although she hated to admit her helplessness.

"Carrie came down and helped me this morning." Lucia's blue eyes narrowed as she glanced at her daughter. "I thought you probably had a late night and would be sleeping in."

"Not too late," Alex answered blithely, refusing to rise to the bait and discuss Ty with her mother. She wanted nothing to interfere with this delicious feeling of happiness.

"Tom called last night." Carrie placed the glasses of juice in front of her grandmother and aunt. "Twice. I told him you were out with an old friend." She winked at Alex conspiratorially.

"I'll call him today." Reaching for the coffeepot, Alex poured a full cup of the rich brew. "Are you going to church this morning?" she asked her sister-in-law.

Gina yawned. "I don't think so. I didn't sleep well."

"I did." Alex stretched languidly. "I feel wonderful."

Four pair of eyes were instantly fixed upon her. Grady's were speculative. Carrie's were approving. Lucia's were cold and Gina's were hostile. It was her sister-in-law's reaction that puzzled Alex. The others were behaving just as she'd expected, but why was Gina so opposed to Ty? She'd never seemed to take more than a cursory interest in anything Alex did. The two women had little in common.

"Breakfast is served," Grady announced, placing a stack of pancakes in front of each of them. The subject of Alex and why she felt so wonderful this morning was momentarily dropped as the family enjoyed the hearty meal.

After they had eaten, Alex stacked the dishes in the dishwasher and busied herself straightening the kitchen. Carrie accompanied her grandmother outside. Though Lucia spent most of her time indoors, she enjoyed pruning the rosebushes that lined the stone patio beside the pool. Her granddaughter usually helped, reaching the blooms her grandmother couldn't from the wheelchair.

"I thought you were going to church?" Alex said, glancing at the jacket that hung on the back of Grady's chair.

"Just to the service, not Sunday school," he answered vaguely, intent on an item in the newspaper.

"Why are you seeing Ty Duncan?" The hostile question was like a shot in the quiet room, and both Alex and Grady stared at Gina after she'd said it.

"Because I want to." Alex crossed the room to sit again at the table.

"Why would you want to?"

"Gina, I really don't think this concerns us." Grady's voice was firm.

"Maybe you're not concerned, but I am." Her blue eyes flashing, Gina gestured toward the window where Lucia could be seen talking with Carrie and snipping yellow blooms from a bush. "What happened with that Duncan boy almost killed your mother."

"What do you mean?" Alex could feel the blood rushing to her cheeks.

"We knew all about it, Alex. You mother called us in Birmingham, practically hysterical. Grady was just finishing his internship. She upset him to no end, asking what he thought they should do."

"I see." Alex looked at her brother. She hadn't known he knew so much about that summer.

Grady laid a comforting hand on her shoulder. "I was concerned, Alex. Ty had a wild reputation. I told Mom and Dad at the time that it was your decision, but . . ."

"And you were right," Alex said quietly. "It was my decision then, just as it is now. If I want to see him, it's no one else's business."

"But even if all that hadn't happened that summer, he's still the man who's buying the mill. It's like he's taking it away from your mother—like she's losing it all over again. Don't you care?" Gina's voice was belligerent.

"Don't be ridiculous." Alex slid off her chair and headed out of the room. "That mill was lost years before we ever had to let it go. We all know that. And somewhere deep inside I think Mother knows it, too. We can't keep on with this charade that the world is exactly as it was. And I can't live my life for someone else. I have to be happy."

"Just don't expect me to be happy for you while you break your mother's heart." Gina stood quickly and brushed past Alex on her way out. She ran upstairs and they heard a door slam, the sound echoing through the house.

"Do you feel the same way?" Alex asked Grady.

"Of course not." He stood and pulled on his jacket. With his concerned expression, he reminded Alex almost painfully of their father.

"Then what do you think I should do?"

"That's not for me to say. I want you to be happy, and if Ty Duncan can do that, I'm all for him." He brushed an affectionate kiss across her cheek. "But I would like to know why he left twelve years ago. I could hate him for that."

"I know." Alex sighed heavily and leaned against the doorjamb. "But I'm afraid to ask, Grady. I don't want to relive all of that. It happened long ago, and I don't think it really matters now."

"I think you're wrong about that, but I can't tell you what to do." Grady patted her arm and disappeared down the hall, looking tall and confident in his navy sport coat and gray trousers. So much like Father, Alex thought. But Grady's stronger and steadier than Father, she added. Sam

Thorpe had never dealt so well with the ups and downs of life.

"But I'd love to talk to you, Father," Alex whispered to the empty room. "You were the only one who even halfway understood about Ty. You understood dreams." Sadly Alex turned to her kitchen chores, missing her father anew.

The day passed slowly for her. The threat of rain hung heavy in the air, and the atmosphere in the house was equally strained. Carrie was gone with Billy. Grady was catching up on his reading in the study. Her mother napped and Gina stayed in her room. Alex merely waited for the phone to ring.

It didn't.

Around six o'clock she decided not to wait any longer. She dialed his number impatiently and was relieved when Ty answered.

"I've been waiting to hear from you all day. You said you'd call." Despite her best efforts, a note of reproof crept into Alex's voice.

"I've been tied up." For Ty it had been a family day, spent with his sister and her husband and children. Sally had gotten over her anger, but she'd pointedly avoided asking him about his evening with Alex.

"I want to see you," Alex said, unashamed by the desire.

Sally and her family were gone, and his mother was preparing to leave for evening church services, so Ty suggested, "How about a drive?"

"Fine. I'll meet you at the inn in a few minutes."

"No." The word was curt. "I'll pick you up. I'm not going to hide from your family, Alex."

"Ty..." she began in protest, and then stopped. She really had nothing to hide. As she'd told Gina earlier, Alex wasn't going to live her life for anyone but herself. "Okay," she said, relenting.

"See you in about twenty minutes."

Time seemed to creep forward. Alex hovered by the front door, peering through the old etched glass that surrounded the mahogany portal, anxious for the sight of Ty's crimson car. When he pulled in the circular drive she practically flew across the veranda and down the steps.

Ty watched her run toward him with a feeling of happiness so intense he had to look away. To hell with the past, he thought once again; Alex wants to be with me now, and that's all that matters.

Chapter Four

Mr. Clemmer is in a meeting, Mr. Duncan, but he asked that you wait in his office. He shouldn't be long.''

The pretty brunette secretary smiled at Ty as she led him down a hall on the bank's second floor. She ushered him into a large corner office and, after he'd declined a cup of coffee, left him alone.

Ty looked around the elegantly furnished office with interest. Evidently his old school buddy had developed a taste for antiques. An intricately carved eighteenth-century armoire graced one wall, its shelves filled with a collection of carved decoys. Leather-bound books lined the shelves on another wall. Oak filing cabinets stood in a row under one bank of windows, while a massive mahogany desk was centered in front of another.

Easing down in a leather armchair, Ty prepared himself for a wait. If Charlie Clemmer was anything like he used to be, a few minutes could turn into a half hour.

Why did Charlie want to see him? That question had been bothering Ty ever since he'd gotten the phone call from the bank vice president's secretary earlier this morning. If it had been Walt Clemmer calling to request he stop by, he would have understood. Walt was handling the deal for the mill. As far as Ty knew, Walt's nephew Charlie wasn't even involved. Maybe this was personal. But if it was, why hadn't Charlie himself called?

He probably wanted to impress me, Ty thought. Some men—and women—thought having someone make their calls made them seem more important. Ty didn't believe in asking his employees to take care of personal business, and he had nothing but disdain for people who did.

Restlessness propelled Ty out of the chair, and he wandered over to the bookcase. As he absently studied some of the titles, he wondered if something had gone wrong with the deal. Walt had virtually guaranteed it would go through. Ty had called his partner, Chuck Martin, earlier this morning to let him know how things were proceeding. Chuck had urged him to stay in Grayson until the purchase was finalized.

"You need a vacation, Ty. Spend some time with your family and let your mother fix you some decent food. Who knows? You might like it enough to stay."

Ty had laughed at Chuck's suggestion and quickly steered the conversation toward business. He felt strange not working on a Monday morning. No matter where he might travel during the week, Ty usually spent Mondays in his office, plowing through accumulated paperwork and initiating new projects.

He and Chuck had divided the company's responsibilities at the outset. Chuck was the product man, a technical expert who spearheaded all product-development and quality-control operations. Chuck knew sales, but Ty was the real front man. He worked with their advertising agency and oversaw the efforts of a nationwide sales force. This involved dealing directly with regional sales managers to ensure that DunMar Carpets continued to increase their market share.

Lately Chuck had been urging Ty to put more of the traveling in the hands of Linda Bartow, their vice president for sales and marketing. Ty had shocked the male-dominated carpet industry by promoting Linda to her current spot. But she had been and still was the best person he knew for the job. The reason Ty still spent so much time on the road wasn't because he didn't trust Linda. He simply had no reason to stay home.

Ty thought briefly of his luxurious but somehow empty condominium. Chuck and his wife, Marti, often kidded him about wasting his money on the place. He spent more time on planes and in hotel rooms than he did at home.

As usual, Ty felt a sharp prick of envy when he thought of his partner's personal life. Married for fifteen years, with three boys and a beautiful home, Chuck and Marti seemed to have all the solid reality missing from Ty's life.

Engrossed in his thoughts, Ty turned and stared out the window at the hustle and bustle of Main Street on a Monday morning. The scene was pleasantly busy, lacking the harried rush of the big cities where Ty spent most of his time. Maybe Chuck is right, he speculated. Maybe I should stay right here in Grayson and oversee the new plant.

Automatically his thoughts turned to Alex. Last night had been perfect. They'd driven down by the river, parked the car, sat and talked. It hadn't seemed possible they'd have so much to say after the long conversation they'd had Saturday night. But they hadn't run out of talk. And the past hadn't even been mentioned.

The thunderstorms that had threatened all day Sunday had finally broken around nine o'clock. He and Alex had sat on in his car. As the rain beat a symphony of warning on the roof, inside there was a sense of security. For Ty, it was the incomparable feeling of being exactly where he belonged.

And the car was the only place they could be completely alone. With her family on one side and his on the other, a car in a downpour seemed like their only choice. No different from twelve years ago, Ty decided with growing irritation.

Later, when he kissed her good-night, there was again that familiar ache of frustration. With Alex eager and willing, it would have been easy to find a motel, to have forgotten everything else in a few short hours of pleasure.

A younger Ty would have done just that. But now, when he knew just how much there was to lose, he had to back away, bide his time and pray they could make it work this time.

"I know one thing, there must be some kind of good-lookin' dame down on the street for you to be so preoccupied."

Ty started. He'd been so lost in his thoughts that he hadn't heard the door open. He turned to face a grinning Charlie Clemmer. The years hadn't been kind to his old friend; Charlie's hairline had receded a good two inches off his forehead, and his thin blond hair was brushed forward in a feeble attempt to disguise the bald spot. He had always been stocky, and his pudginess had grown into a sizable roll around his middle. He looked at least a decade older than his thirty-two years.

Laughing heartily, Charlie caught Ty's hand in a meaty grasp. "Ty Duncan, you sly old devil. I never thought you'd darken the streets of this town again, much less come back the conquering hero."

Ty accepted the handshake and the teeth-rattling pat on the back good-naturedly. The good-ole-boy rites never changed. "I'd say the hero business is a slight exaggeration—I'm just a businessman. But I have to admit I never thought you'd be sitting in the corner suite of the bank, either, Charlie-boy."

Still chuckling, Charlie took his seat behind the desk. "I guess you could say we both did all right, didn't we, pal?"

Ty crossed back to the armchair. "You said it."

"Well, I guess there was never any doubt that I'd make it." Charlie leaned back in his chair, a pleased smile spreading across his thick features.

"I guess having an uncle who runs the bank never hurt anybody." Ty forced his voice to remain light, not wanting to antagonize the man yet unable to resist the barb.

Charlie's smile faded somewhat, but he continued in a chatty tone. "Ty, I just want you to know how great I think it is that you've done so well and that you want to bring some of that prosperity back to your home town."

"I wish I could say I was operating under purely philanthropic motives, but I happen to think this is a terrific deal."

"Well, those empty buildings aren't making us any money just sittin' there, I can tell you that." Charlie pursed his lips and opened the folder he'd carried into the office with him. "I honestly hope you can find a way to make it work."

"Find a way?" Ty echoed, his eyes narrowing as he studied the seemingly innocent features of the man behind the desk.

"I don't know exactly how to bring this up." Charlie rested his arms on his protruding stomach.

"Oh, I think you know what you want to say." Ty made no effort to keep the sarcasm out of his voice.

"Are you sure DunMar Carpets can expand into a commercial line right now?"

"We're more than able to assume that risk."

"But you failed at the same attempt not three years ago." Charlie slid a piece of paper across the desk toward Ty, who picked it up.

It was a copy of a carpet-industry publication's story from less than three years back announcing the dissolution of DunMar's infant commercial-carpet production division. Ty and Chuck were both quoted as citing lack of marketing research as the reason for the ending of the venture.

Ty looked up and into Charlie's beady, gloating eyes. Tossing the paper carelessly onto the desk, he leaned back, trying to appear confident and relaxed. "We weren't ready three years ago. Now we are. We jumped into the game too early, made some mistakes and lost some money. It won't happen again."

Charlie shook his head sadly. "I certainly hope not. But this failure..." He picked up the article again. "This does make us a little uneasy."

"Uneasy?" Ty's brows knit in puzzlement. "Why do you care? When we give you the check for the purchase price, your involvement ends. It's not as if we're arranging financing through you."

"Now, now, Ty," Charlie chided. "You know that's not the way things are done here. We have a vested interest in making sure the next owner of the mill makes a go of it."

Ty searched his mind unsuccessfully for a reason for the man's attitude. Something was up, and he didn't understand what. He responded to the only explanation he could think of. "So someone else has made an offer? I'm entitled to know that, Charlie. It's only ethical to give me a chance to match their price."

"I would like to say several companies were beating our doors down after that property, but as you say, it wouldn't be ethical to lie. Yours is the only offer."

Ty breathed a silent sigh of relief. "Then I still don't understand the problem."

"Okay, I'll give it to you straight." Charlie leaned forward, his mouth tightening to a thin line, all pretense of friendliness gone. "The businessmen of this town are sort of like a club. Outsiders have to possess certain qualifications before they get in."

"And I'm an outsider, even though I was born and raised here?" Ty's voice rose in anger.

"Well, you never did play by the rules, Ty. Nobody knows that better than me. You cared more about chasin' women and drinkin' than you did about anything else."

Ty almost growled in exasperation. Would the past never let him be? "For God's sake, I was a kid! What does that have to do with now?"

"Maybe a lot. We have to think about the future. When Sam Thorpe ran the mill into bankruptcy, it almost destroyed this town and this bank. We're just digging out from the mess now."

"Then why not sell to me? Then you're free of further financial risk."

"And what about the people who go to work for you? What about the house loans they take out? The money they borrow for new cars? What happens when DunMar Carpets decides they made another mistake? Who pays back the money those people owe us?"

Silence blanketed the room after Charlie finished his speech. The two men glared at each other for several long moments before Ty spoke, struggling to contain his fury. "You're saying that a company with profits in the millions, a solid industry reputation and money in hand is not going to be allowed to buy that property because one of the principals was once a wild, irresponsible kid?"

Charlie shook his head. "I didn't say the deal was off. I just said we've got some questions."

Suddenly the whole ridiculous conversation made sense to Ty. Charlie was playing a game. Ty sat back, eyes narrowing. "I get it, Charlie-boy. You don't have the slightest intention of calling off this deal. You don't even have the power to do that. But you just couldn't resist rubbing my face in the fact that I was born on the wrong side of town and I grew up poor. You never did miss an opportunity to do that, did you, Charlie?"

Ty stood, shoving his balled fists in his pockets to avoid using them on the florid man seated across from him. "You were always lording it over me, even when I was sneakin' across the state line to buy your liquor and trying to beg you a date. You were always reminding me that you were just a little bit better than I was...."

Charlie began arranging the papers on his desk into neat piles, his pudgy hands fluttering nervously. "That's not it at all, Ty. I have a genuine concern—"

Ty interrupted him with a derisive snort. "Genuine concern? That's funny!" He leaned over the desk, his palms flat on the glossy surface, his face just inches from the banker's. "You expected me to beg you for the privilege to buy this mill. And when I left you were going to feel like such a big shot. A funny little scheme, right?"

"No, Ty...I just..."

"I wonder if your uncle would think it was funny if I called this whole thing off. What if I trotted over to the other corner office of this sainted institution and told him his soft, fat little nephew had insulted me? What if I decided my company no longer wanted to locate here in Grayson? Tell me, Charlie-boy, would that be funny?"

"I can see you've misunderstood my intentions," Charlie sputtered brokenly. His face was ashen, and large beads of perspiration glistened on his forehead.

His voice low and threatening, Ty said, "I understand perfectly. But you've forgotten that I always call your bluffs. Just like when you said I wouldn't dare call your uncle and invite him to the little party we were havin' up at his cabin on the lake."

"So you really did call?" Charlie asked incredulously.

"Yep. And he came, didn't he? He walked in the door just in time to watch you smash a chair into the wall and bust out a sliding glass door. I stuck around just to see your expression when he showed up."

Charlie swallowed convulsively and shrank back in the chair. "Okay, I made a mistake. I'm sorry." He managed a weak smile.

"Yeah." Ty straightened and turned on his heel to leave. At the door he added, "You are sorry—one of the sorriest excuses for a man I ever met." Closing the door firmly behind him, he strode through the building and out onto the street.

That conniving little coward, he thought, seething inwardly as he headed for his car. So now I'll let him wonder if I'm going to tell his uncle. That oughta be worth a couple of sleepless nights and plenty of indigestion.

"Damn this town!" Ty muttered as he fumbled with his keys. "Damn it to hell." Just as his key glided into the lock, he looked across the street and saw Alex. She was with a man he didn't recognize.

Fighting a sudden, unreasonable swell of jealousy, Ty studied the couple. Something in the tense set of Alex's shoulders and in the way the man touched her arm told him this wasn't just any acquaintance. The man had meant something to her. Hesitating only a fraction of a second, he dodged the traffic and quickly crossed the street.

Alex looked up and saw Ty coming toward them and groaned inwardly. She didn't need this.

Early this morning she'd called Tom Jacobs's office and arranged to meet him for a cup of coffee. When he arrived, she wasted no time in telling him there'd be no more dates. Tom had been dumbfounded, confiding that her mother had been feeding him encouragement for some time. He pressed Alex for a reason, and she told him the truth. Ty Duncan. Tom had taken the news well enough, but she didn't want him to have to meet Ty right now. That seemed a little cruel.

However, watching Ty stride toward them, she realized she had little choice. She even smiled as he approached. It was impossible not to appreciate the sheer physical presence of the man—the tall, athletic build, the stubborn curl of his dark hair, the determined set of his strong jaw. No wonder she'd never forgotten him. No one else had ever measured up beside his memory.

She smiled nervously as Ty came to a stop beside her. "Good morning, Ty. Ty Duncan, this is Tom Jacobs. Tom, this is Ty."

Tom momentarily showed his surprise, but he recovered his poise quickly and grasped the hand Ty proffered. "I'd say I was pleased to meet you, but—'' He broke off and shook his head. ''This is a little awkward.''

''Is it?'' Ty said coldly.

''Ty—'' Alex began, but Tom stopped her.

''I'd just like to say you're a very lucky man, Duncan. I'd give you a fight, but if I know anything about Alex at all, it's that when she makes up her mind about something, it's set. I'm sure we'll be seeing each other.'' He touched Alex's cheek with his hand. ''Goodbye.''

Alex stared openmouthed after him for a moment. When she looked back to Ty, his glowering expression made her fumble for words. ''I can explain...''

''No need.'' The words were curt. ''He looked like a nice enough fellow.''

''He is. He's a lawyer and doing very well. But I just...'' She faltered under Ty's unflinching gray gaze.

''Maybe you should go after him.''

''What?''

''He seems so suitable, so genteel. I'm sure your mother loves him.''

''I don't see...''

''You know, Alex, it's best to maximize your options. Perhaps you should keep the good Mr. Jacobs around. Who knows? I might leave you again.'' Without a backward glance, Ty crossed the street, climbed in his car and drove away.

Alex stood, numb with shock, and watched him leave. When she realized several people were staring at her, she forced herself to walk toward her own car.

Last night Ty had been warm and loving. Now he acted like an impersonal stranger—cold and distant. How could things have changed so quickly? Seeing her with Tom couldn't have upset him that much. But why had he stalked away? And why had he said he might leave?

Questions thundered through Alex's brain till her head pounded. By the time she got home all she wanted to do was to retreat into her room, alone.

That wasn't to be. Her mother's imperious voice stopped her in the foyer. "Alexa, please come in here a moment."

Lucia was in the front parlor. *Probably sitting by the window, waiting for me to come home so she can grill me about Ty,* Alex thought crossly.

"Alexa!" Lucia's voice brooked no argument, so Alex went into the parlor, squaring her shoulders as if she was about to face a police interrogation.

"Have you had a nice morning?" The question was deceptively innocent, but experience told Alex the real meaning in her mother's words: Had she seen Ty?

"Actually, Mother, I've had a lousy morning. Is there something in particular you wanted?" Alex stood stubbornly in the doorway.

Lucia pressed a hand to her chest, pretending affront. "Goodness. Is there something wrong with wanting to talk with my daughter?"

"You only want to preach at me about Ty, and I really don't feel like listening!"

"Well! I must say, if he puts you in a mood like this perhaps you're better off without him."

"Say whatever you want, Mother. But wait and say it to someone else, won't you?" Alex snapped as she left the room, not waiting for her mother's reply.

She spent the afternoon alone, trying to read and catch up on correspondence. For the first time, Alex regretted her chosen occupation. Teaching school left her with summers free to relax, but now, as her thoughts centered on Ty's mysterious behavior, she wished for another job, something that would occupy her mind to the exclusion of everything else.

Before dinner she joined the rest of the family in the sitting room and offered her mother a quiet apology for her rudeness. Nevertheless, dinner was a silent, strained meal, and Alex was happy to flee back to her room afterward.

Sleep eluded her, so she did something she'd been avoiding for days. From the top shelf of her closet, hidden behind a stack of old sweaters, Alex pulled out a box. Inside was the history of her relationship with Ty. She hadn't looked at it for years.

"Any normal person would have thrown this junk away," she said aloud, sifting through the snapshots and mementos.

Pieced together, the box's contents told the story of the millworker's son and the boss's daughter, of a handsome older boy whose brazen gray eyes had followed the girl through the high-school corridors, a boy who had once claimed a dance with her in the school gym. His wildness had frightened Alex at first as much as it had intrigued her. So he had backed away, leaving her with the image of his insolent grin echoing in her memory for months.

But the tale really began the summer after her graduation, when her father had decided she should work in an office at the mill, and the boy, now a man, had teased and cajoled her until she'd consented to a date. There had followed a summer of moonlit drives and movies, of drinking beer at a disreputable bar and eating hot dogs at a Fourth of July picnic. A summer of promises made and dreams shattered.

The tears gathered in her eyes, and Alex bit down hard on her bottom lip to keep them from falling. She pulled an envelope from the box, and brittle dried rose petals drifted to the floor. A sound—half sob, half laugh—escaped her lips. These were the only flowers Ty had ever given her, picked from one of her mother's prize bushes beside the patio. He'd thought it a nice gesture, and Alex had been delighted and amused. Her mother had been furious.

"Oh, Ty, I want more than memories. I'm sick of memories!" In frustration, Alex flung the contents of the box across the room.

She sat in the midst of the mess for a long time. But she didn't cry. She didn't allow herself that weakness. Enough tears had been shed over Tyler Duncan. Whatever had been bothering him today had been a misunderstanding. They'd resolve it tomorrow. She was not, absolutely not, going to just forget it and lose him again.

Close to midnight the phone rang, echoing shrilly through the silent house. Alex grabbed the receiver before it could ring a second time and wake everyone.

"Hello."

"I'm sorry."

With just those two words from him Alex was ready to forgive Ty anything, but she had to understand why he'd acted as he had. "What happened?"

There was a long silence before he answered, "It was a rotten morning, Alex. I took it out on you."

Fighting the urge to capitulate, Alex closed her eyes and said, "That's not good enough, Ty. You really upset me, and I want to know why." She held her breath, almost fearing his answer.

"I . . ." He stopped, then plunged ahead, recounting the ugly scene with Charlie Clemmer. For Ty, who'd resisted sharing his feelings with anyone for so long, telling her was a blessed relief.

" . . . I don't know, Alex," he finished. "It's just that he succeeded. He made me feel poor and insignificant again. Then I walk outside, and there you are standing with this other man, and it's obvious that he's meant something to you. . . ."

"Not really," Alex interjected.

"Well, maybe not, but that's the way it looked. I felt . . . so . . . inadequate. The way I used to feel. The way I felt when everybody told me I wasn't good enough for you."

Alex's voice was quiet but strong. "I never told you that. I never thought it."

Ty gave a short laugh. "Never? Not for a minute? That's hard to believe, considering the end."

She waited to answer, bringing her trembling voice under control. "Don't accuse me of that, Tyler Duncan. Don't accuse me of not caring. I'm not the one who left."

Tyler's sigh was clearly audible, heavy with misery. He wanted to remind her that she could have followed him, joined him, but there seemed no point to it. "You're right."

Anger made her forge ahead, the words tumbling out. "Don't make decisions about the way I feel about you. By doing that you're as guilty of railroading me as you used to accuse my parents of being. I don't give a damn what Charlie Clemmer or anyone else thinks of you. I don't care what my family or your family says. I want to see you, Ty. I want to take up where we left off. I thought that was what we were doing. But if you don't feel that way, if the last few days have been some sort of nostalgic trip, tell me now. You're not going to hurt me again."

The cold fury of her tone slapped Ty like a stinging spray of water. "I do want to see you, Alex. This isn't a game. I'm sorry for today."

It was impossible to doubt his sincerity, and a slow, soft smile spread across Alex's face as she leaned back against the headboard of her bed. "You'll have to prove it, you know."

"Prove it?"

"Take me on a picnic tomorrow."

His deep chuckle sent ripples of anticipation through her. "Is that all?"

"I'm sure we'll think of something else." Her voice was full of seductive suggestion.

"I'm sure we can. I'll pick you up at noon."

"Great. Goodbye."

Alex cradled the phone receiver against her chest until the dial tone became a loud, insistent buzz. Even then she replaced it reluctantly, unwilling to sever even that imaginary link with Ty.

The next few days were like pages from Alex's book of dreams. She and Ty were together almost constantly. They picnicked by the river, swam at the country club, ate drive-in hamburgers and played a series of fast and furious games of tennis. There was quiet, serious conversation and loud, boisterous frolic. The past was never mentioned.

On Thursday they made the two-hour drive into Chattanooga. At a large shopping mall, Ty trailed along as Alex flitted from store to store. They played a make-believe shopping game, picking out all the furniture and accessories they'd use to decorate a house. It was a silly way to spend the afternoon and both of them knew it, but it was fun. So they laughed and bickered over styles and prices, acting just like an old married couple.

That thought struck Ty as he watched Alex finger delicate drapery material. An anxious clerk was hovering at her elbow, eager to make the sale. As Ty gazed at Alex, caught up in his yearning, she turned and sent him a brilliant smile. "What do you think, honey?"

I think you should have been my wife, Ty wanted to say. I think we should have been married for twelve years, with a mortgage and bills and a comfortable set of problems. I think we should be fighting about our kids and making love in the mornings. I wish we hadn't made so many mistakes.

Those were the things Ty longed to say, but he couldn't, not here, not now. Instead he disarmed the clerk with his rakish smile and said, "I think I'm hungry, and I refuse to make a decision on an empty stomach. We'll come back later."

Grasping her arm firmly, Ty pulled Alex away from the drapery department and drew her down a side aisle. He ducked behind a stack of sale-priced lawn chairs and kissed her soundly.

"What was that for?" she asked, smiling up at him, a little breathless from the swift but passionate caress.

"That was just one kiss to start making up for all the kisses I've missed." His gray eyes were dark with emotion as he drew an unsteady hand through the shining softness of her hair.

"Really? Then here's another."

They kissed like love-struck teenagers until a smiling young store manager cleared his throat and suggested they might prefer shopping elsewhere.

"Thrown out of J.C. Penney!" Alex announced delightedly when they were once again out in the mall. "Imagine what the school board would say."

"Miss MacGruder would have a field day with your reputation."

"You're right. No more kissing in the mall."

Ty leaned down and kissed the tip of her small, straight nose. "Then let's get out of here. By my calculations I would have kissed you at least twenty times a day for the last twelve years, and that means..." He multiplied swiftly in his head. "Over seven thousand kisses per year times twelve comes to more than eighty thousand kisses you owe me."

"Now I see why DunMar Carpets is a success. There's a mathematical genius at the helm." Linking her arm with his, Alex said, "Let's get going."

They ate in a lively, casual restaurant in a renovated older home that rambled in levels and terraces down a hillside. The view of the city at night was superb, the food excellent, the wine mellow and relaxing. And though they laughed and talked over their meal, Alex was very quiet on the long drive home.

Ty knew what she was thinking. She'd expected to stay the night in Chattanooga, away from their past, away from their families. She hadn't asked, but he could see it in her eyes. He knew without a doubt that with one word from him they could be in a motel and that he could have Alex—naked and gloriously passionate under him. But he couldn't. Not yet. Not until he was sure where they were headed.

Friday morning Walt Clemmer called with the good news. The bank had accepted DunMar Carpets' offer for the mill. Ty was elated. As soon as the formalities had been completed, they could begin preparing the buildings for operation. He phoned Chuck to tell him to get the ball rolling with their bank and lawyers.

"Are you going to stay in Grayson?" Chuck asked.

"For now." Ty made his decision that quickly. "There's really no one else who could oversee this, although I do want some people to come out and give me a hand." He named several employees. "I'm going to turn all the advertising decisions over to Linda for the time being, and she can also handle that trip to Dallas."

"No problem. I think she's been chomping at the bit waiting for this to happen."

Nodding in agreement, Ty planned quickly. "I'll be in the office Monday to stay a few days and clear up some details. Go ahead and place the order for the machinery we agreed on. There's a lot of work to do, both here and there."

"I'm glad you're staying, Ty. We'll be fine on this end."

"Just as long as you get down here when it's time for the installations. That's your area."

"Don't worry about it. See you Monday."

As he replaced the receiver, Ty resisted the urge to give a shout of triumph. Everything was working out. His company had the mill. Maybe, soon, Alex would his, too.

"What happened?" Rose Duncan stood in the kitchen doorway, wiping her hands on her apron.

"We've got the mill." Ty caught her to him for a hug, then reached again for the phone. "I have to tell Alex."

Ty saw the sadness in Rose's eyes as she watched him dial the number, but she offered no comment. She'd avoided any confrontations about the many hours he'd been spending with Alex. His sister, too, had maintained her silence, but Ty could feel her disapproval waiting just beneath the surface, waiting for the right moment to break through. He appreciated his mother's attempt to understand and accept.

His call caught Alex in her kitchen, where she'd been chatting with Suzie, who'd dropped by for a visit. Alex listened quietly to his news, made plans for dinner and hung up the phone with a pensive smile curving her lips. She wondered suddenly how her father would feel if he knew the mill had passed into the hands of Harris Duncan's son.

"Earth to Alex. Come in, Alex." Suzie snapped her fingers playfully in front of her friend's face. "You were obviously in another solar system. That must have been Ty on the phone."

"Yes, it was. He's bought the mill."

Suzie studied her intently. "That's good news in a way, isn't it?"

"Of course it is," Alex returned stoutly. "It means jobs and opportunities. Ty is very excited."

"Your mother will be upset."

"She expects it." Alex's mother had said nothing about the time her daughter had been spending with Ty. Nonetheless, her disapproval was clear. Grady and Carrie seemed to approve, but Gina continued with her puzzling hostility. No, news of the sale would come as a shock to none of them. However, Alex knew it would still hurt her mother, and she dreaded telling her.

"Despite the mill business, you seem happy." Suzie touched Alex's hand affectionately. "I'm glad."

"I am happy." The words came as something of a surprise. It had been so long since Alex had viewed her life with anything more than stoic acceptance that admitting happiness felt almost unnatural. But she was happy, and the reason was Ty. "This has been a wonderful week."

Suzie leaned her elbows on the table, her eyes curious but her tone hesitant. "Alex, I never asked you what happened between you and Ty that summer. One minute you were together. Then I left for college, and when you wrote me there was no mention of him. The next thing I knew you were going to school in Florida instead of Nashville as you'd planned, and you never mentioned his name again."

"We broke up." Alex gave a careless shrug that was a triumph of discipline. If she couldn't go into all this with Ty, she certainly couldn't explain it to Suzie.

"You didn't come home for Thanksgiving, and at Christmas you seemed sad and pale. We didn't really see each other until the next spring, planning my wedding. You seemed okay by then, and I figured you had finally gotten over him.''

"I did. But now he's back." Alex carefully avoided her friend's eyes, focusing her attention on the blue-and-white place mat in front of her.

"I heard that Ty just up and left town that summer."

"He did."

"Why?"

"I don't know." Alex got up, went to a cabinet and took out two glasses.

"Don't you care?"

"No." Alex opened the refrigerator. "Do you want iced tea or lemonade?" she asked, effectively closing the subject.

Suzie didn't mention Ty again until she was ready to leave. Seemingly on impulse, she gave Alex a quick hug. "I can tell there are things about Ty you don't want to discuss...."

"Suzie, please, I—"

"No, I'm not trying to pry, truly I'm not." She touched Alex's cheek. "I like seeing you happy. And if you feel he's right for you, don't let him go!" Without waiting for a reply, she was out the door.

Later that day, Alex thought about Suzie's advice as she got ready for her evening with Ty. She wondered how her friend would feel if she knew everything about what had happened that summer. Would Suzie still urge Alex to hang on to Ty? She wondered.

She also wondered about her mother. Lucia had taken the news of the mill's sale with good grace. Then she'd made plans to have a rare dinner out with Grady, Gina and Carrie at the country club. Lucia was embarrassed by her incapacitation, but tonight she was going out, head held high, to show everyone that she didn't care about the mill's sale to Ty Duncan. Alex doubted anyone cared. She thought her mother's pride was misplaced, but she did admire her courage.

Ty hadn't said where he was taking her for dinner, but he'd said to dress casually, so Alex obliged. Her red cropped pants and striped cotton sweater were comfortable and flattering. She was anxious to see him, but as she headed downstairs she couldn't shake a vague feeling of trepidation. There was no reason for it. She and Ty had spent a beautiful week together. Now it looked as if he would be in town for quite a while. This week could be the first of many.

But would it? How long could they go blithely along, not mentioning the past, not examining their painful memories? Alex shied away from the thought. There was something strong and loving growing between her and Ty. They had to avoid the past and allow a future to take root and flourish. Fortified by that thought, she settled on the veranda to wait for him.

He arrived soon after, wearing worn blue jeans and an old football jersey.

"I can't believe you still have that old thing," Alex said, pointing to the faded green jersey with Warriors printed in peeling white letters across the back.

"I went to a lot of trouble to steal this after Coach Roberts threw me off the team for fighting. Do you think I'd ever give it up?" They got in the car, laughing.

"He had to have known you took it. Why didn't he ask your parents for it?" Alex pressed.

"The man was scared of me. Afraid I'd beat him up!" Ty grinned wickedly as he turned the car west toward the lake.

This route was a familiar one to Alex. When she'd been a little girl, her family had still owned a cabin on the lake, a cool oasis on hot summer days. When the family's and the mill's finances had begun sliding downhill, the cabin had been the first thing to go, the proceeds of the sale financing Grady's college and medical-school expenses.

During her teen years the lake had been a gathering place for Alex's friends. They met at one another's family cabins or at the public beaches. The mild climate allowed swimming from May until October, and they took full advantage.

It was at the lake that Alex and Ty had first made love, on the darkened beach under a July moon.

The road twisted and turned through the hills and valleys surrounding Grayson, past fertile farms where green fields and growing crops were touched with amber by the setting sun's rays. With every mile Alex was pulled back in time. She was very quiet as she remembered....

It had been a hot day, one of those simmering mid-July Saturdays when people mop their perspiring faces and squint accusingly at the fiery orb in the sky. Alex was supposed to visit an aunt in Chattanooga with her parents, but she'd begged off, pleading a headache. And when her father's Lincoln disappeared down the drive, she called Ty. Soon they were headed for the lake.

They swam, sunbathed and ate, building a fire in a barbecue pit to roast hot dogs and melt marshmallows. When the sun set and the other picnickers and swimmers packed up and left, Alex and Ty remained on the sandy strip of beach, talking, laughing, savoring their aloneness.

There had been an awareness between them all day, a knowledge that soon their relationship would pass from casual to something much deeper. Alex supposed she'd known that from the beginning, from the first time Ty had kissed her. He'd kissed her in a way unlike any of the other boys she'd dated—thoroughly, with much more than a boy's demands.

She knew the dangers. She knew her parents were disturbed because she was still seeing Ty nearly two months after their first date. Her parents hadn't actually forbidden her to date Ty, but Lucia kept reminding her daughter that college was waiting in the fall. She said there'd be a whole crop of interesting and much more suitable young men from which to choose. Alex didn't listen and didn't care. For right now, her world started and ended with Ty.

Perhaps if the night had been a little less pleasant, the stars a trifle less bewitching, the beach less deserted, perhaps then they wouldn't have made love. But the summer air was sweet; their kisses were intoxicating, and Alex succumbed to the urgency in Ty's touch. For the sensible, obedient girl she'd always been, her capitulation was something wild and unreasoned. Ty was at first surprised, then delighted by her response.

At twenty he wasn't an inexperienced lover, but his tender feelings for Alex lent a new delicacy to his touch, a gentleness that was both instinctive and protective.

One kiss led to another, one bold touch to still another until both of them were naked under the dark carpet of the sky, their bodies warm even in the cool breeze off the lake.

Forever after, Alex had only to close her eyes to remember Ty's hand between her legs and his lips on her breasts. Then there was the sharp pain of his entry and the delicious ballooning of pleasure that buoyed her up and almost to the edge of full satisfaction.

Afterward they lay entwined, their passions spent. But Alex felt no remorse. Ty had taken precautions; there'd be no pregnancy, and all she could think of was making love again. They did, and though the pain lingered, her passion reached a woman's zenith and went beyond.

Ty was sweet and solicitous as he awkwardly helped her dress, and to this day, twelve years later, Alex had no doubt he'd meant the words of love he'd uttered....

"Aren't you going to get out of the car?"

Ty's quiet question jarred Alex out of her reverie, and she realized they'd reached the lake. When she turned to him, her brown eyes reflected the memory of passion and betrayal.

"Hey, what's wrong?" He stroked his hand gently across her cheek, concern in his voice.

"I guess I was thinking of something else," she answered hesitantly.

"Then stop it. We're celebrating, remember?" Getting out of the car, he pulled the front seat forward and took out a wicker picnic hamper. With his hand outstretched, he waited until Alex joined him, and they walked through the trees down the path to the beach.

The spot he'd chosen for their picnic was far from the place where they'd first made love. But just as it had been that long-ago night, the beach was deserted. Twilight was spreading across the water, leaving only about an hour of light before darkness fell. Determinedly Alex shook off her melancholy and joined Ty in unfolding a blanket on the sand and emptying the basket.

He'd brought crisp fried chicken, cold potato salad and flaky homemade biscuits. "Did your mother do this?" Alex asked, surprised.

"Yeah. When I told her I wanted to celebrate with you, she said she understood and spent the rest of the day cooking."

"Do you think she's softening any toward me?" Though Ty hadn't said, she knew his family wasn't thrilled with their renewed relationship. They had never approved, and that, like so many things, couldn't have changed completely.

Ty tossed a scrap of biscuit to a squirrel that had scampered to the edge of the beach. "Maybe. I think she just wants me to be happy."

"And are you?" The question was quiet, but Ty couldn't miss the underlying seriousness.

He draped his arm around her shoulders and kissed the gentle curve of her cheek. "Of course I'm happy. I'm with you."

The words sent warm pleasure tingling through Alex and she relaxed, enjoying the meal, his company and the peaceful surroundings. After they ate they walked on the beach and stood near the boat dock, watching the moon rise lazily over the mountains.

Back at their picnic site, Ty built a small fire and produced a bottle of champagne from the basket. "It's a little warm, but I think it'll do."

"Where'd you get that in Grayson?"

"I smuggled it in from Chattanooga last night." He popped off the top and poured foaming liquid into two plastic cups.

"To the newest DunMar Carpets venture," Alex proposed with a laugh, touching her cup to his.

Ty grinned, drained his cup and quickly poured more champagne. They cuddled on the blanket in front of the fire, kissing and laughing, trading toasts. He kept refilling Alex's cup until her head spun from the potent drink.

"You know I don't handle alcohol too well," she protested. "Are you trying to get me drunk so you can steal my virtue?"

"As I recall, alcohol wasn't necessary," Ty teased.

With his casual words the bubble of happiness inside Alex seemed to burst, and she sat up abruptly. The past was intruding, and it wasn't the pleasant memories of lovemaking she recalled; it was the ugly ending of their summer idyll.

"Alex? What's wrong?" His hand cupped her chin, gently guiding her face around till he could look into her eyes. "What did I say?"

All the yearning in her heart poured out with her words. "I wish I'd only just met you, that there'd never been another time for us. Because no matter where we go or what we do, I keep remembering how it all ended. I know it's stupid. I know I'm not eighteen and I don't have to do what my parents want me to do. But sometimes I look at you and I think this is all some kind of weird flashback."

In the flickering firelight Ty's expression was thoughtful, his silvery eyes shadowed. He took his time replying. His words, when they came, were slow and carefully measured. "I think we need to confront the past," he said. "We need to pull it all out and see if we can't make some sense of it. I have a lot of questions, and I know you do, too. Let's talk about it."

Alex pressed her hand to her trembling lips and gazed with sightless eyes across the darkness of the lake. An overpowering loneliness flashed over her, and there was a curious wrenching deep within her—a memory of sadness and loss and complete, utter aloneness. She didn't think about this anymore. She hadn't for a long, long time. And she had never discussed it. She simply couldn't tell anyone. Not even Ty. The memory was like a yawning black pit, and she was too frightened to ever go near the edge.

"I can't," she whispered at last. The tears started then, streaming down her cheeks, washing her face in sadness.

"Aw, honey." Ty's strong arms went around her shaking body and drew her close. His mind was churning with questions, but he couldn't bring himself to put her through the hell of answering them now. It all seemed suddenly so hopeless. Here they were, responsible adults, but the people and events that had separated them years before still had the power to keep them apart.

"You don't have to tell me now." He drew back and held her tear-streaked face with gentle hands. "But, Alex, someday we have to talk this through. That's the only way it'll finally be behind us. But I don't think you can talk about this until you're sure of how you feel about me now...."

"But, Ty, I know—"

"No, you don't," he insisted. "A lot has happened. Fast. I'm a little confused by it all myself. I mean...the decisions were all made for us years ago, and maybe what we're feeling now is just unfinished business."

"No, it's not," Alex said stubbornly. "I know this is for real...for now." She touched urgent, demanding lips to his.

"No." Ty pushed her away with firm but gentle hands. "I don't think you're sure. I don't think you completely trust me. And I want you to. Because then, and only then, will you be able to tell me what happened after I left—and you'll be ready to hear my explanations.''

He lifted her downcast face to his. ''I'm going to leave for Atlanta tomorrow. I won't be back until next week sometime. I want you to think about us. And soon, very soon, I want some answers.'' Ty stood and began packing up the remains of the picnic and dousing their fire.

Alex watched him with sad, thoughtful eyes. She felt as if a fantasy had just ended. She'd deluded herself into believing they could just go on from here. But now Ty had made it clear they had no future unless they examined the past. The thought terrified her.

Chapter Five

The house where Alex lived with her family was just one of many large, comfortable homes on its street. These houses had been built by the men who had brought industry to the small southern town at the turn of the century. All were lovely homes. However, it had always seemed to Alex's admittedly prejudiced eyes that her home stood a little apart.

Since being built nearly a hundred years earlier by Alexander Nelson, the house had witnessed its share of family dramas—births, deaths, marriages, tears of joy and pain. It had been modernized, expanded and redecorated.

But Alex liked knowing the house was essentially the same as it always had been. When she walked down the curving stairway in the central foyer she imagined her great-grandmother walking the same stairs, touching the same satiny wood of the banister rail. She could almost see her ancestors gathered in the cool recesses of the front and back verandas, away from the hot Alabama sun. She could understand why her beauty-loving, idealistic father had been enchanted by his first sight of the house. Like him, Alex took pleasure in the house's gentle symmetry—the tall fluted columns lining the front and back, the even distribution of windows and doors and the balancing first-story wings.

Even during the worst of times, when there was trouble over Ty or when the mill was failing and her father lay dying, Alex had taken comfort from the tranquility of the big white house. To her it had always possessed a familiar serenity in the face of a storm. She'd missed that feeling when she'd moved away.

So why was that different now?

As she waited for Ty to return from Atlanta, Alex felt imprisoned by her home's graceful walls, as if the memories they sheltered were blocking the future.

She blamed it on the weather. On Friday night, after Ty had dropped Alex off, the rain had started. On Monday it still fell, a gray curtain broken intermittently by periods of overcast gloom. Lethargic and unreasonably sad, Alex stayed indoors and brooded over Ty.

"Are you okay?"

The hesitant question came from Carrie, who stood in the doorway to the library, a frown marring her pretty face.

Alex managed a smile. "It's just such a dreary day. I wish it would stop raining." She settled more comfortably against the hunter-green cushions of the window seat, smoothing her khaki shorts down over her thighs.

Carrie perched on the edge of the square oak desk. "I just wondered. You seem upset, and you and Mom barely even speak to each other."

The last thing Alex wanted was to upset the young girl, so she tried to downplay the feud with Gina. "We just had a disagreement."

"Over him?"

Alex knew she meant Ty, and she nodded her head.

"Is he gone again?"

"He went to Atlanta for a few days to get some things straightened out at his office. He'll be back later this week."

Alex fixed her concentration on the water dripping from the overhang of the roof. She didn't dare think he wouldn't come back.

"Then why are you so sad?"

"I'm not sad. I'm just . . ." Alex stopped, not knowing how to explain her feelings. Was she frightened? If so, of what? Why couldn't she think about what had happened twelve years ago without quaking inside? Ty wanted a relationship with her now. There was no reason *not* to be open about the past. But Alex couldn't rid herself of the nagging feeling that talking about the past would only open a fresh crop of problems.

"You're what?" Carrie prompted, leaning forward.

Alex sighed. "What's going on between Ty and me is too complicated to explain, honey. . . ."

"If it's that complicated, why bother?" Gina interjected from the doorway.

Carrie and Alex turned to look at her, and Gina stepped into the room, a cold gleam in her blue eyes. "Ty doesn't seem to be making you very happy, Alex."

"Gina . . ." Alex began warningly. She didn't want to argue in front of her niece, but she also wouldn't let Gina push her around. "I really don't want to discuss Ty with you."

"Because you know I'm right."

"Gina!"

"Ty Duncan is no good. He deserted you once and he'll do it again. I notice he hasn't married anyone else in all these years. Commitment evidently isn't his strongest point." She laughed shortly. "Or did you think he'd been pining away for you since he left?"

"Mother!" Carrie said, visibly upset by her mother's cutting remarks.

Gina gave her daughter a distracted look, as if she'd forgotten the girl was in the room. "Run along, honey. I want to talk with your aunt."

"No, I—"

"I said, go!" Gina snapped.

"It's okay, Carrie," Alex interrupted quietly. "Go on. Your mother and I need to have a talk." She waited until her niece was gone before continuing, "I don't understand why all of this is so important to you, Gina."

"Because your mother is important to me. I happen to love her very much."

"And I don't?"

Rubbing at her temples, Gina came and sat in the green plaid chair that faced the window. She leaned forward. "I know you love your mother, Alex. I didn't really mean to suggest otherwise. But I think right now you're blind to everything but your own feelings. You're being tempted by someone you once thought you loved, and—"

"I did love Ty," Alex cut in firmly.

Gina pursed her lips into a thin line and continued. "Okay, you loved him. But he's wrong for you. Always has been, always will be. And it's killing your mother, watching him make you miserable all over again."

Alex studied the other woman's lovely face closely. Could concern for Lucia alone bring on this display? Somehow Alex doubted concern was the whole story. Gina had acted strangely about Ty from the beginning, and there seemed to be no plausible explanation.

"Gina, this is between Ty and me. I can make my own decisions, and if they hurt Mother, then I'm sorry. I told you before; I have to live my own life."

Now Gina rose from the chair and walked to the desk, her slender fingers drumming nervously on the polished surface. Her voice shook slightly as she asked, "Did Ty tell you why he left?"

"I've asked him not to."

For just a moment Gina's shoulders sagged, and when she turned around she was smiling. She looks relieved, Alex thought in surprise. Why?

"Do you think he'll do what you want and not tell you?"

"He's not going to push the information on me, Gina. I don't want to even think about that summer, and I've told him so. We both made a lot of mistakes—mistakes I want to forget. But I still care for him. I'm just going to wait and see how things develop.'' Alex frowned and swung her legs to the floor. ''Why is everyone so hung up on the past? It's over and done with. We were kids. There's no way to change it now.''

''You're right.'' Gina sat down beside her. ''I think you're absolutely right to forget what happened.''

''You do?'' Alex was puzzled. A few minutes ago Gina had been saying Ty hadn't changed, that he was the wrong man for her. Now what was she up to?

Gina laid her hand over Alex's. ''Have a fling with him, Alex. Get it out of your system once and for all. Like you said, you were kids then. What do kids know about love? I think after a while you'll see what your mother means about him and it'll all be over for good.''

Shaking off the other woman's hand, Alex stood and said angrily, ''I don't want a fling, Gina. This is more than just sex.''

''I know you think that, Alex. Your memories are full of young romance. But Ty's not your kind at all. He's too raw. Too basic. He'll never make you happy.''

Backing away, Alex shook her head. ''You're wrong. This is more than memories, more than physical attraction. Maybe he can't make me happy, but that's up to me to find out. If I don't, I'll just go on wondering for the rest of my life. No one is going to make this decision for me.''

''We're just trying to keep you from being hurt again!'' Gina protested.

''I think that's a chance I have to take for myself. And I really don't want to discuss it with you again.'' Alex turned and left the room without giving Gina a chance to reply.

She avoided any further confrontations with her sister-in-law over the next few days. But she did think about the conversation. It was unusual for Gina, normally so aloof, to take such an interest in Alex's affairs. For some reason it

was terribly important to Gina that Alex and Ty not be together. And Alex couldn't begin to understand why.

The conversation did accomplish one thing; it shook Alex
out of her depression. While she waited for Ty to return
from Atlanta she spent time with Carrie and with Lucia.
Any mention of Ty was studiously avoided, and Alex was
glad. Her family's feelings about him only clouded the issue. And she had enough to worry about. What was she
going to say the next time he demanded answers about the
past?

Ty spent Wednesday night working late at his office. In
the past three days he and Chuck had finalized all the plans
for the new plant. The deed would be transferred later in the
week, the machinery would be delivered within the month,
and start-up was planned for sometime in early fall. When
Ty got back to Grayson he'd start hiring a crew and begin
renovations and repairs to the buildings.

It was nearly eleven when he signed the last letter on his
desk and looked over the instructions he was leaving for
Linda Bartow. The sales-and-marketing VP was looking
forward to Ty's absence as a chance to spread her wings a
little. They'd spent most of the last two days together, going
over details she needed to know for trips to Dallas, San
Francisco and Los Angeles.

If Ty hadn't made a strict rule for himself about dating
employees, Linda would have tempted him. She was thirty-
five, three years his senior, a veteran of a male-dominated
industry who had somehow managed to retain her feminin-
ity. The tall, slender blonde had earned Ty's respect with her
abilities, and he admired her life-style. She'd raised a
daughter without the help of the child's father, and because she traveled so much she lived with her parents. She
was an intriguing combination of ambition and old-
fashioned principles. Perhaps, if Ty hadn't been haunted by
the memory of Alex, Linda could have become someone
special. As it was they were good friends, and she'd com-

mented on the difference she perceived in him the moment he'd returned from Grayson.

"How was the home town?" she asked.

"Still the same," came the terse, almost angry response.

"I take it that's not good?"

Ty looked up at his friend, a slow smile animating his face. "I guess I shouldn't take my troubles out on you, huh?"

"That depends." Linda leaned back in her chair and returned his smile. "If I ask what's the matter, then you can tell me. Otherwise keep your problems to yourself, boss."

"Are you asking?"

"Yes."

"Then maybe you're exactly the person I need to talk to. Let me buy you lunch."

They took a two-hour break, and Ty did something that surprised Linda as much as himself. He told her all about Alex, about their young, impossible love and its painful end, about the last week and Alex's reluctance to explore the past.

Linda let out a slow sigh when he finished. "I guess now you want the advice, right?"

"That was the idea," Ty answered, suddenly uncomfortable with the personal revelations he'd just shared with his colleague. "But I know I'm putting you on the spot, and—"

"No, you're not. I'm your friend, so I'm going to tell you what I think." Linda touched his arm softly. "I think you should take whatever she's got to give—and I suspect that's quite a bit—and not worry about what went on twelve years ago."

"Could you?" Ty challenged.

"We're not talking about me." Linda leaned forward, her amber eyes steady on his. "You still love her, Tyler Duncan. You'd be a fool to let it slip away again."

Her advice encouraged Ty, and he went about his work with new enthusiasm, eager now to get back to Grayson.

Maybe he and Alex *could* work it out. He worked overtime, delegating more and more of his work. Somehow all that mattered was getting back to Alex.

Finishing up Wednesday night, he decided to call his mother and let her know he'd be home in time for dinner the following evening. Her somewhat sleepy voice answered on the fourth ring.

"I'm sorry I woke you, Mama."

"I had just closed my eyes for a minute, son. When are you coming home?"

"Tomorrow."

"For how long?"

"Indefinitely."

As he'd expected, she was pleased. "I'm so glad."

"I am, too." He asked about his sister and her family, and was almost ready to hang up when his mother said, almost casually, "I saw Alex tonight."

Struggling to sound just as nonchalant, he replied, "Oh, really? Where?"

"She was going into the movie theater with her niece. I was just passing by. She looked very nice."

"She usually does."

There was a long, weighted pause before Rose spoke again. "Do you still care for her?"

Ty's voice deepened with emotion. "I love her, Mama. I always did."

"And you think she loves you?"

"Maybe not now. But she will. I'm going to do everything I can to make her love me again."

Rose sighed. "I used to pray you'd meet someone else and forget her. But I guess I always knew that wasn't the way it would be. I can't tell you not to see her. You're a grown man, and you've always done just what you wanted anyway. But I do want to say one thing..." She faltered.

"Mama?"

Her words came out in a rush. "Forget what happened before. Start over. That's the only way you'll find happiness."

"That's what everyone says, but it's so hard not knowing why she didn't join me. I'll always wonder about our—"

Rose cut him off. "There are some things you might be better off not knowing. I'll have dinner ready for you tomorrow night, son. I'm happy you're coming home again."

They said goodbye, and Ty replaced the receiver, puzzled by his mother's words. For a woman who had always insisted on complete honesty from those she loved, Rose's advice was strange. He didn't know if he could follow it. Other people found it easy to tell him to forget. But it wasn't their past or their pain.

Suddenly weary of unanswered questions, Ty switched off the lights and moved through the darkened offices, eager for tomorrow to come. Tomorrow he would see Alex.

After nearly a week of rain, Thursday brought hot summer sunshine. The petunias and zinnias in Grayson's town square were in full bloom, their colors brilliant in the light, their scent perfuming the air. Summer sounds drifted through the town—the drone of lawn mowers, the high-pitched laughter of children, rock music spilling from open car windows.

As Alex turned down the street where Ty's mother lived, she realized July was only two days away. The summer was slipping away. At its end would she merely go back to the classroom? Or would there be a difference? Would Ty still be here?

She drew to a stop in front of the house, wondering if she was doing the right thing. Ty's mother had called earlier and invited her to dinner. She'd said Ty would be home this evening.

The invitation had first shocked and then pleased Alex in quick succession. Perhaps this was a beginning. If Ty's family accepted her, maybe it was a start for the two of them. With that thought to sustain her, she cut the engine and stepped out of her car.

It was impossible not to remember the last time she'd been here. She'd come looking for Ty when he hadn't met her as they'd planned. She'd found him gone, his father hostile, his mother in tears. They'd blamed her for their son's departure. Alex had left in a panic so suffocating, its power had almost choked her.

Now Rose Duncan met her at the door, her smile somewhat hesitant but still welcoming. "Can you believe this heat? They say it's going to rain and it's clear. They say it's going to be clear and it rains. Who can predict?"

"Certainly not the television weathermen," Alex agreed, laughing softly. "Thank you again for inviting me."

"Oh, goodness, it's nothing. Ty asked me to, and I was happy to do it."

"Ty asked you to?"

"Yes, he called last night."

Alex followed Rose through the living room to the kitchen, her heart nearly bursting with happiness. Ty wanted her here. Surely that told her something about their chances for a future.

"Have a seat," Rose said, gesturing to the small dinette table set before corner windows. Alex obeyed and looked around with interest. The room was clean, neat and homey. Green plants lined the windowsills beneath starched white café curtains. Cookbooks crowded the yellow countertop, and a delicious spicy aroma filled the air.

"That smells heavenly," Alex said, taking a tall, frosted glass of lemonade from Rose. "You're a wonderful cook. I always wonder how you make the meals at school so delicious when you have to prepare so much."

"Oh, it's nothing." Rose shook her head dismissively and began breaking lettuce into a glass bowl.

"Oh, but you're wrong! It's a real talent. I taught in Florida for a few years, and the food there was horrible. You do a great job."

"Well, it's tough on the budget we work with, I can tell you that." Rose seemed to relax under Alex's praise. "But then I don't have to tell you about school budgets. Are you anxious for a new year to begin?"

"I was just thinking about that. Before we know it the summer will be gone. It's hard to believe."

"Oh, time flies, Alex. You'll appreciate that more and more as you get older. Why, it seems like just yesterday I used to stand at this window and watch Ty and Sally play while I got dinner ready. Now Sally's got kids of her own." Her expression pensive, Rose reached for a plump tomato.

"Were they good kids?" Alex couldn't resist asking. She always found it difficult to imagine Ty as a boy.

"Sally was a dream. But Ty? Well, you can imagine." His mother laughed softly. "I remember the time he let a snake loose in the house. I went to the neighbors' and refused to come home until he and his daddy found it." Alex joined in the laughter as Rose recounted the story of the search.

And so it went. For almost half an hour they talked freely about everyday matters, about the school and the town, foods they both liked, places they'd like to visit. The older woman finished the dinner preparations, poured herself some lemonade and joined Alex at the table. They were laughing together when Ty came in the door.

Of course, he'd known Alex was here. Her car was parked in plain sight on the street. However, he hadn't expected this pleasantly homey scene—his mother and the woman he loved chatting at the kitchen table.

"Ty!" Rose got up and hugged him tightly.

"Hello, Mama." He returned her embrace, his eyes on Alex. She seemed to be looking everywhere but at him.

"I invited Alex to dinner, just as you asked." Rose drew back and, safe from Alex's sight, winked.

Ty was amazed—his mother, acting sly? This was a new twist. But, considering her usual attitude toward Alex, the change was welcome.

Alex sat nervously at the table, watching mother and son. Why had Ty wanted her here when he came home?

"I'm glad you're here," he said now, crossing the room to touch her shoulder gently, causing the awkwardness between them to vanish. He turned back to his mother. "I'm going to get out of this suit and get comfortable. Have I got time for a shower before dinner, Mama?"

"If you hurry."

Alex busied herself helping Rose get the dinner on the table, and when Ty joined them less than fifteen minutes later they were ready to eat. The meal was delicious—tangy barbecued chicken, crisp salad, flaky rolls and potatoes baked to perfection. When Rose produced a lemon meringue pie, Alex and Ty both groaned in protest.

"Mama, you're trying to kill us."

"Oh, hush up and dig in. I've seen you eat half of one of these."

Dinner finished, all three of them helped straighten the kitchen. The quiet domesticity thrilled Alex. When they had been younger, any visit she or Ty had paid to each other's homes had been like a foray into an enemy camp. Now Rose was doing her best to make things easy. Her efforts touched Alex.

"You two head out on the porch and sit for a while. I'll dry the rest of these pans." Rose shushed their protests and herded them out the door.

As they passed through the living room, Alex paused in front of a bookcase and picked up a framed photograph. Two good-looking children smiled at her from the picture. "Are these Sally's kids?"

"Yeah. Cody's eight and Laura's six. They're a handful." Ty's voice held more than a trace of affection.

"That old?" Alex murmured. "Sally must have gotten married right out of high school." Alex replaced the picture and followed Ty through the room.

"She did. She and Keith have had a tough time. He lost his job when the mill closed, but I think they're back on track now." Ty held the front door open for Alex to precede him outside.

Once the door shut behind them and they were enveloped by the fading twilight, he drew her into his arms, his lips capturing hers in a tender salute. "I've missed you."

"Oh, Ty." His name was no more than a sigh as Alex's arms wound around his neck, drawing him closer. "I've missed you, too. I was so afraid...."

"That I was gone again?" he whispered.

"No, I knew you'd be back, but I didn't know how you'd feel. When you left you seemed so angry with me. I thought I'd ruined it. Then your mother invited me to dinner, and she said it was your idea that I come...."

"I have a confession to make about that—I didn't tell her to ask you. That was her idea."

Alex drew back and stared up at him. "Why?"

"I don't know. Maybe it's her way of saying she approves of us at last."

"That would be nice. With her, Grady and Carrie on our side, maybe everyone else will just give up."

"Is your mother giving you a hard time?"

"That's the funny part. Mother hasn't said much lately, but Gina seems intent on pulling us apart."

"Gina?" Ty rubbed his chin thoughtfully.

"I know. She's never cared what I did before this. We've never been close. Now she just acts so strange, so nervous and—"

A car horn shattered the still evening air, drawing Alex and Ty apart abruptly. He peered through the darkness toward the street. "It looks like Sally and Keith. I guess this really is family night." He tugged the cord that turned on the porch light, clasped Alex's hand and drew her with him down the steps and across the lawn.

Ty made unnecessary introductions, and they all stood looking at each other in awkward silence. Though Keith and the children seemed friendly enough, Sally was openly hostile.

"Let's go in," Ty suggested at last.

"We don't want to intrude," Sally protested.

"Don't be silly. Mom's got a lemon meringue pie."

"It's delicious," Alex added after a moment's hesitation.

Cody turned to his mother eagerly. "Aww, come on, Mom, I'm hungry."

Sally gave in to her son's pleading. "All right. But only one piece." They all trooped inside.

Rose and Ty did what they could to ease the tension-filled atmosphere, but there was no disguising the animosity Sally had for Alex. No matter what Alex said, Ty's sister made a point of disagreeing. Her husband looked uncomfortable, her mother was apologetic, and storm clouds were gathering in Ty's gray eyes. Even the lively chatter of the children wasn't enough to distract Sally. She made it clear she didn't think Alex belonged at her brother's side.

Finally Alex had had enough. She rose to leave, smiling in apology at Rose. "Dinner was wonderful. Thank you again for inviting me. It was nice to see all of you." Her glance lingered on Sally, and she said purposefully, "I *will* see you all again soon." There was no missing the frown Sally sent her way. Alex smiled a little as Ty accompanied her out to the porch.

"I'm sorry..." he began.

"It's okay. Not everyone can be won over in a night." She touched his arm and lowered her voice. "But I think we need to talk. Can you get away later?"

"Of course. But where?"

"You remember Suzie's parents' lake house."

"I think so. Second road on the left off Lake Road?"

"That's it. I've got the key. Meet me there."

Ty would have had to be blind to miss the meaning in her words or the intensity in her golden-brown eyes. There was eagerness in the sweet curve of her mouth. If he went to her tonight, he knew they'd do much more than talk. "Are you sure?" he murmured.

"Surer than I've ever been about anything," she whispered. Without another word she disappeared into the darkness. Ty stood watching until her car's engine sprang to life and she drove away.

"Ty?"

He turned at the sound of his sister's voice, allowing his anger to spill over. "What's the matter with you, Sally? Did you have to treat her like that?"

Sally shrugged and came across the porch to stand beside him at the railing. "I can't understand why you'd be fool enough to care."

Ty stepped closer, his voice low and threatening. "Just what is it to you, anyway?"

"Have you forgotten that summer?"

"Of course not! But what do you know about it, anyway?"

"I know it all, Ty. I may have only been sixteen, but I heard you and Mom and Dad screaming at each other about her. I heard the talk. I was here when she came looking for you."

"Looking for me? Alex came here?" Ty caught Sally's arm in a painful grip. "When was that?"

"Sally!" Rose's firm voice pulled the brother and sister apart as effectively as force would have as she stepped from the house, shutting the door behind her. "Sally, you only think you know what you're talking about. You've said and done enough for one night."

Sally turned on her mother, her voice low with fury. "How could you invite her to dinner, Mother? After the things she said about us, the things she said about Ty—how could you?"

"What things?" Ty interrupted.

"That doesn't matter!"

"Yes, it does," Sally insisted. "Tell him, Mother."

"No!" Rose snapped. "That was a long time ago, and it's best forgotten. Alex was only eighteen. She was hurt and angry. I'd forgotten about it, and I suggest you do, too. Both of you."

Ty stared at his mother with a puzzled frown. "What did Alex say? Why was she here? Dad said he met her at a restaurant. What happened?"

"What happened is that your sister is confused."

"No, I'm not!"

"Be quiet, Sally!" Rose turned back to her son. "I told you last night, Ty. Forget the past. Put it behind you. You say everyone, including Alex, has told you to forget it. You say you love her. Prove it. Take things from here. You won't help anything by dredging up old hurts."

Ty ran a hand over his face and sighed in frustration. "It's not as simple as that, Mama. There's a big gap in our past. How do we get past that?"

"You didn't have any choice about the way things turned out, son...."

"I know that. I know I had to leave. But I'm still ashamed. I should have fought. I should have faced it with her. Dammit, you and Dad should have helped me stay!" His voice rose again in anger. "We should have been stronger!" He turned and walked down the steps.

"They didn't have a choice, Ty!" Sally called after him. "It wasn't their fault! Alex had some choices to make, too, you know!"

Perhaps it was the pounding of his heart or the angry roaring in his ears, but Sally's voice seemed to come to Ty from a great distance as he stalked to his car. He burned with fury. Everywhere he turned there were more questions. He didn't understand why he couldn't find any of the answers.

He pulled out onto the road in a screech of tires and headed for the lake. He knew Alex didn't want to tell him what had happened any more than his family did. But she was going to. Tonight was the turning point. He was going to find out.

At the lake house Alex waited, nerves singing, for Ty. She'd asked Suzie for the key earlier today, after Ty's mother had invited her to dinner. She'd hoped to convince Ty to come up here so they could be alone. Everywhere they went their families were waiting to give them advice, waiting for them to hurt each other again. At least here there was no real history to encroach upon the present.

The house was unpretentious—one large, high-ceilinged room, a small bath, a kitchen and a wide screened-in porch that wrapped around three sides. There was a large bed tucked into the corner and two long, comfortable couches in front of the stone fireplace. When Suzie's family used the cabin they often slept on the porch in cots and sleeping bags.

The air was cooler here at the lake than in town, and Alex could smell rain in the air as she opened windows to clear the mustiness. There was an eerie feeling to being up here alone. If she stepped out on the porch she'd be able to see the darkened water of the lake and the glow from the lights at the pier and the boy's camp on the other shore. But here in the house she felt completely isolated. She started to turn on a few more lights when she heard the crunch of gravel beneath tires. Ty had gotten away more quickly than she'd expected.

Whatever he had planned to say to her, whatever demands had formed in his mind on the drive up to the lake vanished when Ty saw Alex standing in the doorway. The lights from inside formed a gentle halo around her body. She looked soft, welcoming and utterly feminine.

It seemed only natural to pull her into his arms and taste the tempting fullness of her mouth. It seemed only right that she should draw him across the room toward the big mahogany bed, that she should press her body against his in that ancient, urgent message of need.

Her lips were a drug, a sweet, intoxicating addiction. They burned on his, igniting his passion, fueling his desire. If Ty had *wanted* the younger Alex, he *hungered* for her now. The ache inside him grew, pushing aside all his questions.

He parted her lips with his questing tongue, and she accepted the intimate exploration eagerly, responding with a passion Ty couldn't mistake. When finally the kiss ended, he touched her face in wonder. How was it possible to need someone this much? How could twelve-year-old desires rage this hot and this insistent?

"Make me forget you ever went away," Alex murmured, touching her lips to his chin, nipping him lightly with her teeth.

Drawing his hand through her shining cap of hair, Ty cupped her neck gently and pulled her away. He stared down into the golden-brown depths of her eyes and smiled. "This feels right."

"Because it is. It always was." Her lips curved in sweet, sexy invitation, and Ty's mouth touched hers again. His last bit of hesitation died, forgotten in the splendor of having Alex in his arms again.

He teased her with his lips while his hands tugged the white cotton blouse free of her slacks. His fingers skimmed the heated skin of her back, and Alex sighed with pleasure. He drew away and began to undo the blouse's buttons, and she trembled. But her eyes never left his, and the emotions that shone from them warmed him to the core of his being.

For Alex, the memory of that night would always be touched with gold. She knew it was a trick of the light, of course. Only two lamps burned, their dim light giving everything a dreamlike quality. Their golden glow turned Ty's lean, hard body to fluid beauty and lent a magic to their movements.

Every touch was a promise of more. Each kiss seemed to seal their love. The words were never spoken, but they lay between them anyway. When Ty laid Alex on the bed, there was reverence in his touch. This was much more than a physical act; it came from the heart.

If possible, Ty was stronger than Alex remembered. His shoulders were broader, his arms and legs more powerful. But his hands were gentle as they roamed over her body, bringing her to a fever pitch of desire.

Alex was also different from Ty's memory of her. Her breasts were fuller, her hips more softly rounded. And she was bold in her loving. Youth and uncertainty were gone. She answered Ty's touch with a woman's demands.

Ty found the changes exciting, and he whispered his pleasure just before he slid into her welcoming depths.

All that remained was the swift climb to heaven on earth. It came so quickly, so completely, that both of them were left trembling. But when Ty twisted away, pulling Alex on top of his body, there was a smile on his lips. He pushed her up to straddle his lean hips while he caressed her full breasts, and their rosy peaks hardened and bloomed in his hands.

In the room's golden light, Ty's gray eyes were slits of silver. They saw too much. Alex, suddenly shy, slid to his side and curled against his strong body. Now that it was done and they were lovers again, she wondered at her audacity.

But she was happy. "Ty, why did we ever let it slip away?"

He laughed. "Ask me an easy one, like why the world is round or why people die. I don't know what happened to us." He flung a strong leg across hers and shifted until he was once more on top of her. Before his lips descended to hers again, he murmured, "And right now I don't care about anything but loving you."

And so they loved. Throughout the night, when the rain came again, sweeping across the lake and spilling onto the porch, they shared the pleasure of each other's bodies. Together they explored their passions as thoroughly as a brief span of hours will allow.

In the darkest part of the night, just before dawn cut the sky over the mountains with pink, Ty slept. Alex lay beside him, wide awake, measuring her happiness by each quiet breath he drew.

Before the morning could come completely to life, she woke him, and he smiled at her sleepily, moving her gently back into the safe circle of his arms. If she'd had her way, they'd have stayed like that forever....

Sadness darkened Alex's eyes as she slipped out of bed and began drawing on her clothes. She had to go home. Her family might be worried. It was time to leave this cocoon of happiness and see if their love could survive the real world of family pressures and outside interference. It was a test they'd failed once before, and Alex feared the outcome this time.

If he'd waited a little longer to ask the question, Alex might have been ready. As it was, her mind was clouded with weariness and memories of passion, and he took her by surprise. He was still lying in bed watching her dress when he asked, "Tell me now, Alex. What happened to our baby?"

She stared at him as if in shock, holding her sandal in one hand while the other groped vainly for some means of support. While the answer to his question formed in her brain, the words wouldn't come.

So instead she ran.

Snatching up her purse, she fled from the cabin, away from his question, away from memories and the accusing look in his gray eyes. My God, she fumed as she started her car, what gives him the right to ask?

In the cabin, Ty watched the summer sun spread across the lake and cursed himself for his clumsiness.

Chapter Six

It was all so unlike her. Alexa Thorpe had always been such an obedient child. Such a sweet girl. So correct in her behavior. A perfect daughter, friends of her parents had always called her.

They'd been right. She'd never caused her parents one moment's worry. Until her eighteenth summer. Until Tyler Duncan awakened her body to passion, her mind to possibilities, and she threw caution to the wind.

That hasn't changed, Alex decided, pulling her car to a stop in front of her home. Ty always managed to make her behave in wildly uncharacteristic ways. Like last night, when her body turned into fire under his touch. And this morning, when she'd run away.

Who would believe she was the same calm, reasonable Miss Thorpe who taught the sons and daughters of Grayson the beauty of poetry and prose? No one. Only Ty could make her crazy. Only he knew the secret self she kept so well hidden.

With a weary sigh, Alex looked at the house. It was barely six o'clock. Hopefully she hadn't caused any worry, and with any luck she'd be inside before anyone knew it.

Luck wasn't on her side.

"Alexa? Is that you? We've been worried sick!" Lucia Thorpe propelled her wheelchair down the foyer, a frown tightening the delicate skin of her forehead.

"I needed some time alone, Mother. Suzie loaned me the keys to her parents' lake house." Alex comforted herself with the thought that that much was true. "I'm sorry. I should have called."

"Do you really expect me to believe you were up there alone?" Lucia came to a stop in front of Alex. "I'm not that much of a fool."

Gripping the smooth wood of the stairway's newel post for support, Alex said quietly, "All right, Mother. I was with Ty. I don't like lying to you, but I wanted to spare your feelings."

"Did you?" Lucia's blue eyes blazed with anger. "Did you really spare any thought at all about my feelings? I don't believe that's any truer now than it was twelve years ago."

Alex took a deep steadying breath. "Mother, I don't want to go over this with you...."

"Well, you are!" The older woman leaned forward in her seat, hands clenched in her lap. "What is his appeal, Alexa? I'll never understand."

"I wouldn't expect you to."

"Oh, I admit Tyler has the sort of crude appeal some women like." Lucia shook her head in disapproval. "But I never thought *my* daughter would be one of *those* women."

Fury at her mother's insulting tone snapped Alex's thin hold on self-control. "Just what are you calling me, Mother? Trash? Isn't that what you called me when Ty and I came to you and Dad, scared out of our minds, to tell you I was pregnant? If I was trash then, I guess I'm trash now. Because I just spent the night with him, and I'm not ashamed. In fact I'm glad. Glad, glad, glad!"

"Alex, stop!" It was Grady who prevented her from continuing, who halted the flow of angry, hateful words. He rushed down the stairs, his dark hair rumpled from sleep, gathering his robe about him. "I don't think either of you want to discuss this right now. You're too upset."

"You're right," Alex said, struggling to keep her voice steady as she looked back at her mother. "I don't want to hurt you, Mother, but I don't think you should question me like I'm a teenager. I'm a grown woman—"

"And you should have called us," Grady interrupted shortly. "We're your family; you live in this house, and when you didn't come home it frightened us. We didn't even know where you were."

"Oh, let her be." Lucia seemed to shrink into her wheelchair. Her eyes were dull now, empty of anger, and she looked very old, very vulnerable. "I didn't want to argue with you this morning, truly I didn't. But when you didn't come home..." Her voice trailed away, and she twisted the rings on her fingers before continuing in a stronger voice. "I knew where you were. I knew you were with him. And I worried. I just can't believe Tyler Duncan will ever do anything but hurt you. He did before. How can you want—"

"I wish everyone would stop trying to figure out what I want." Alex shut her eyes to block out her mother's pleading expression. "You didn't understand me twelve years ago. You don't understand me now."

"But once I did," Lucia whispered, and Alex opened her eyes to stare into the other woman's. "Once you were my sweet, lovely daughter. And I knew you. I knew what you wanted, where you went and with whom. But I haven't known much about you ever since that summer. Since he changed you."

"But he didn't change me. I changed myself. I had to," Alex said firmly, dropping to her knees beside her mother's chair. "I couldn't stay the same little girl forever."

"I thought we'd die when you went away."

"He didn't cause that. I left because I couldn't stand seeing the disappointment in your faces anymore."

"I tried," Lucia said, wiping at the moisture that overflowed from her eyes. "That's why I wanted you to come back here to live with us. I wanted to be close to you again. But things were never the same...."

"Oh, Mother." Alex sighed and laid her head against her mother's arm. "You don't act like you want to be close. You try to force me into the little mold you've created. In your image. But I'm not like you. I never was."

"Your father said the same thing—that I couldn't keep trying to change you." With trembling fingers, Lucia smoothed Alex's dark hair back from her forehead. "I'll try harder to understand you, Alexa. You can even go back to Florida if that's what you want. I won't try to stop you. But please, I beg of you—don't get involved with Ty again. There's too much history, too much pain."

Alex frowned at the near panic in her mother's voice. It was the same panic she'd sensed in Gina. What was it that frightened them about her relationship with Ty? It just didn't make sense.

She rose slowly to her feet. "Mother, tell me why you can't forget the past. After all, Ty's a successful man. So many of the things you objected to about him don't apply any longer. Why can't you just let this alone?"

Lucia stared at her daughter for a long moment, her mouth thinning into an angry line. "I know you think I'm just an interfering snob."

"I didn't say that, Mother."

"But you think it." Lucia pressed the reverse lever of her wheelchair. "Well, maybe I am a snob. But I won't stop interfering when I think one of my children is making a mistake. And falling for Tyler Duncan's smooth lies again is a mistake, Alexa. I know it."

The chair turned, and Lucia disappeared through a doorway farther down the hall. Alex watched her go and knew, with an overpowering sadness, that she and her mother were no closer to understanding each other.

"Please don't do this again." Grady's disapproving voice cut into Alex's thoughts.

"Do what? Spend the night with Ty?" Alex ran a weary hand through her hair. After running out on him this morning she might not have another chance, but she didn't feel like bowing to any of her family's wishes. "I can't promise that."

"I'm not trying to tell you what to do about Ty," Grady retorted. "I'm asking you to have a little respect for other people's feelings. We were worried about you."

"I'm sorry," Alex replied with genuine remorse.

"I want you to think about Carrie," he continued.

"Carrie?"

"She's all caught up in this big romantic notion about you and Ty, Alex. What you do influences her. You live here."

Alex stared at him, incredulous. "Oh, come on, Grady. Carrie's too smart to make the kind of mistakes I did—"

He interrupted her with a gentle touch to her cheek. "Yeah, I always thought you were pretty smart for your age, too. Sometimes our minds stop working when our hearts are involved."

Her shoulders drooped with sadness. "I guess you're right, Grady. I'll be more considerate." Alex started up the stairs.

"And be careful," Grady added. "I don't want to see your heart broken again."

Without acknowledging her brother's last comment, Alex continued upstairs to her room. The door shut behind her and she sagged against it. Dear God, why did everything that happened remind her of that summer twelve years ago? The scene her family had just enacted had been sickeningly familiar. Only before it had been her father, not her brother, who had charged downstairs. And Ty had been beside her as she'd faced her mother's ugly accusations.

Alex crept across her room and huddled on the window seat, reliving another time, another morning....

It had been September when she and Ty had faced the truth. It had been the week right after Labor Day, when the sun had all the ferocity of summer but the evening shadows carried the velvet look of autumn. It was the time of year when the song of insects along the country roads begins to falter as they acknowledge the passing of their season. It was then Alex and Ty knew she was pregnant.

Neither of them could believe it was happening. They'd been careful. So careful. But when the time for her period had come and gone a second time, they had known their problem was more than a percentage of failure listed on the side of a box. A doctor in Chattanooga had confirmed that reality.

A shopping trip for college clothes had been Alex's excuse for going into the city, and she'd forced herself to buy a few things in anticipation of her mother's questions. But all the time she'd been screaming inside. There was no one in whom to confide. Suzie had already left for college, and even if she hadn't, Alex doubted her friend would have been much help. So she spent the day alone—never had she felt so alone.

Ty had picked her up at seven that night. Her parents had been more cordial to him than usual. Alex would be in college in another two weeks, and they made no secret of the fact that they expected the distance would *not* make her grow fonder of Ty.

Alex began to cry as soon as she got into his car. Until today she'd held on to the faint hope that she wasn't really pregnant. Now that hope was gone, and she was more frightened than ever. But even in her fear she loved Ty. She clung to the certainty that he would have a plan.

He didn't. If possible, he was more frightened than she. The streetwise, always resourceful Ty Duncan didn't know what to do. It hadn't been supposed to happen like this.

They had made plans. She'd go to college. He'd save his money, move closer to her school, get a job and begin his own education. The desire to be worthy of Alex in every way had become a burning passion with Ty. Eventually, they'd figured, there'd be marriage, a home, children. Those things would come in the future. They hadn't planned on this complication.

They drove to the lake, of course. It had been their haven all summer. Where else could they confront this catastrophe?

He stopped the car in the parking lot overlooking the public beach. "You don't have to have the baby," he suggested hesitantly.

"Not have the baby?" Alex echoed.

"There are clinics in Atlanta. Good clinics. The doctor could probably give us the names. There wouldn't be anything to be scared of."

Turning her red, swollen eyes to his, Alex said softly, "Is that what you want?"

He touched her cheek. "Only if you do. Do you?"

For Alex, the idea was tempting. It would all be over quickly. She'd go on to school. Her parents would never know. The baby would be gone before it seemed too much of a person, and she and Ty could go on with their plans.

But would they? The question stayed with her. After they went through this, would it ever be the same? Or would it hang between them like a festering wound?

Even at eighteen, Alex knew what the past could do to people. She'd watched the memories of wealth and unchallenged success eat away at her parents' marriage as the mill became less and less profitable. The past could be a bitter acid.

What if this were the only baby she and Ty could ever have? Instinctively Alex's arms folded in a protective gesture across her stomach. If that was true, sometime in the future they might hate themselves for destroying it. With that thought, the baby she carried became a real, living person to Alex. It wasn't a moral issue, but simply a decision based on love. The love of Ty and the child he had given her.

"No. I don't want an abortion," she said at last with conviction.

Ty expelled a long breath. "Then we'll get married."

She studied him solemnly in the gathering twilight, searching his features for some sign of pleasure or love. All she saw was fear. "If that's not what you want—say so."

"Do you think I'd let you do this alone?" he demanded angrily.

"Well, you don't look exactly thrilled about marrying me!" Alex leaned her head against the half-open window, and the tears began to fall again.

"Dammit, Alex. This just isn't exactly the way I planned it; it's not the happiest moment of our lives."

"But I thought you loved me."

"I did. I do," he corrected quickly, reaching for her. "I'll always love you, Cinderella. And I won't leave you. We'll get married, and everything will be fine."

Hesitantly, awkwardly, the young man kissed her tears away, soothing her with reassuring words—words she wanted to hear. But there were still decisions to be made, decisions they argued about nearly all night.

Alex wanted to be married right away, without telling anyone. Presented with a marriage certificate, her parents would have to accept the union. Otherwise, she feared what they might try.

Ty, on the other hand, felt both their parents should know. It was strange to Alex that Ty, the rebel, was the one who wanted to do everything by the book. But he did, and his arguments were persuasive. By dawn they were in agreement. They'd go first to her parents and then to his before they left to be married.

Lucia Thorpe was waiting for them. When Alex opened the front door, her mother was halfway down the stairs, angrier than her daughter had ever seen her.

The words she used to describe Alex's behavior had been born out of fear and fury, but that didn't lessen their hurt. Lucia hurled accusations at Alex and Ty, not allowing them to respond until Sam Thorpe came down the stairs and quietly demanded an explanation.

"I'm pregnant," Alex said simply, watching her father's reaction through tear-filled eyes.

"Oh, my God!" Lucia cried.

"We're going to get married, but Ty thought we should tell you first. We're going to see his parents next."

Sam Thorpe was a tall man, well over six feet, but he seemed to shrink a little at his daughter's words. He put an arm around his wife and said, "I'm glad you had sense enough to come to us first, Tyler. Let's go in the sitting room and talk this over." Ty and Alex had no choice but to follow.

Her parents preached caution. There were other options, they insisted. Alex and Ty reassured them that marriage was what they wanted, with or without anyone's approval.

Sam and Lucia were stubborn in their disapproval. And, almost surprisingly, so were Ty's parents. Neither couple thought marriage was the best choice for their child.

Finally, after three days of constant battle, Alex and Ty made plans to meet the following afternoon just outside town. There she convinced him they had to go through with their plans, no matter what their parents did or said. He held her tightly, whispering, "I love you," before she drove away.

But the next day came, and he didn't show up.

After two hours of waiting, Alex, frantic with worry, went to his parents' house and found him gone. They couldn't or wouldn't tell her where.

First there was shock. Why would Ty leave her? As Alex stood staring at his parents, she groped for an explanation. It didn't seem possible that Ty, who had promised to always love her, would be capable of running away, of leaving her pregnant and alone. What about all their plans?

Plans. The word echoed in Alex's mind. Ty had always been so full of boastful plans and schemes. He was so determined to become somebody in the eyes of everyone in this town who had ever looked down on him. And though she'd never given voice to the thought, Alex had sometimes feared their relationship was just a means to an end for Ty. Perhaps he thought having Alex Thorpe on his arm would guarantee him acceptance. She was the good little rich girl with the spotless reputation; she was Ty's ticket to the right side of town.

But now? Now everything had changed. Without her parents' blessing, Alex and her baby were liabilities instead of assets to Ty. She was tarnished in his eyes, her usefulness gone. Now she'd just hold him back, keep him prisoner in the life of hard work and broken dreams he so wanted to escape.

These bitter thoughts swirled within Alex and boiled over in a black fit of anger. How dare Ty toss her aside like some broken doll?

"I should have known he couldn't be counted on," she told his parents, raising her chin proudly.

"What do you mean?" Harris's eyes narrowed in challenge.

Alex forced herself to laugh. "Well, isn't it obvious? Ty was more concerned with what I could do for him than in facing his responsibilities."

"And what could you do for my son?" Harris Duncan demanded.

"I made him feel like somebody," Alex countered.

"He didn't need you for that."

"He thought so." Alex fought to keep her voice steady. "But now that our marriage doesn't have my parents' approval, now that Ty can't coast along on my family's standing—" she paused, swallowing hard "—now he's run out on me and his child."

Ty's mother put her hand on Alex's arm. "You don't understand—" she began.

Harris silenced her with a harsh "Shut up!"

The room seemed to spin as Alex stared at Ty's parents. This couldn't be happening. How had she so totally misjudged Ty and his feelings for her? He certainly wasn't the person she'd thought he was. For Alex, wealth and social class had nothing to do with the really important things like honor and loyalty. Those were the qualities she'd thought Ty had in abundance. Was she wrong? Either way, she'd obviously been wrong; now she needed to save face.

"It's just as well Ty's gone," she said in what she hoped was a cold, unfeeling voice.

"Why is that?" his father asked.

"Because it's better that I found out now what kind of person he really is." With every bit of pride she had left, Alex said, "My parents are right. He isn't good enough for me."

"Why, you..." The man had started out of his chair, gray eyes blazing, but his wife had held him back, her expression a mixture of pity and despair. But she couldn't stop his words. "That's exactly what he decided about you, missy. He doesn't want to be saddled with a wife and kid when he's just getting started."

"Just as I figured," Alex returned, wanting only to hurt those people closest to Ty. "He really is worthless, just as my mother said."

Ty's father shouted a long stream of ugly curses at her, but in her pain, Alex didn't even flinch. It was Rose who almost broke through her bitter shell. "What about the baby?"

The baby. The reason for all this fuss had been shoved out of Alex's mind. Somehow Ty's betrayal had seemed more to do with her than with some nameless, faceless infant. Now the panic returned. What was she going to do? Alex steeled herself against the agony. She couldn't give in to the smothering hopelessness. Not while she was here. Not while she faced people who could tell Ty she cared.

So, pretending it didn't matter, she said, "I can't wait to get rid of this baby. I don't want anything to remind me of Ty Duncan. You can tell him that if he ever asks."

With curses ringing in her ears, Alex turned and fled. It wasn't until she was miles away that the tears began. She cried herself to the point of exhaustion, then, gathering her wits about her, she'd returned to face her own parents.

It was her father's disappointment that had never faded from Alex's mind. All the rest, even the bitter scene with Ty's parents, had become a little dim, a little less traumatic. But her gentle, caring father's face remained in her memory vividly. He'd tried to understand that she still loved Ty. He'd tried to comfort her when he was gone.

However, Alex hadn't let anyone get through to her. She very carefully sealed herself away into a place where only she and the baby existed. And when the day arrived when she would have been leaving for college, she took her tuition funds and left for Florida without telling anyone.

It was weeks before she called her parents. Alex would never forget, when she'd seen him again, how tired her father had looked, how beaten and old. She'd felt so guilty, so responsible for his anguish.

"I'll never stop paying for that summer," Alex lamented now, looking around her room with heavy, listless eyes.

So many people had been hurt—herself, her parents, his family. Yes, even Ty. Once, years ago, she'd thought he wouldn't care what had happened to her and their baby. That thought had helped her hate him. But the feeling had passed. She'd known Ty too well to really believe he didn't care. She knew there had to be another reason why he'd left.

There were people who, given what he'd done, would never even have spoken to him again. But when he'd come up to her at the restaurant that day, it had never occurred to Alex to cut him, to hurt him. Why? Why had she fallen under his spell a second time? Why was she putting herself in a position where she had to answer to him for what had happened?

"I don't know," she murmured to herself. "I just don't know." Suddenly Alex couldn't think about it any more. Her body was exhausted; her mind was too dazed by weariness and heartbreak to continue searching for answers. She left the window seat and crawled under the warm comfort of her bed's silk spread, falling asleep as soon as she closed her eyes.

Ty was just as weary, just as mentally drained. After Alex had fled, he'd dressed, straightened the cabin and driven away, cursing the fact that he'd ruined the magic of the night. He should have known not to be so abrupt. He never should have fired that question at her.

But he'd felt so good. So complete. For the first time since he'd run out on Alex, he'd felt like a man instead of a coward.

For nearly twelve years, Ty had lived with the shame. At first it had burned at him like a physical torture. He'd known that Alex would feel abandoned when he didn't meet her as planned. That was why he'd left the note with his father with instructions to make sure she got it soon. He'd known she'd understand once she saw the note. He'd known she'd join him when she could in Atlanta.

She didn't.

The weeks came and went, and even though he went every weekend to the meeting place he told her of in the note, Alex didn't come. He called his father, who assured him the note had been delivered.

Ty even tried calling Alex. He hung up every time her mother or father answered. And whenever the maid answered he was told Alex wasn't home and that there was no way of knowing when she'd return. After nearly two months, Ty accepted the truth—Alex had listened to her parents and had given up on him.

In facing that cold fact, Ty's young love had turned to pure hatred, hatred for Alex's entire family and their wealthy, easy way of life. Everything soft and mellow Alex had found in Ty disappeared. He was once again the cocky loner.

Only the ambition remained. He'd never lost that. It had been Alex who had encouraged him, Alex who had believed in his dreams. She had taken his boastful claims and given him the confidence he needed to make them come true. Ty had worked hard, pouring his energy into becoming a success. Instead of fighting the system, he became part of it and won.

Somewhere along the line, he'd lost his bitterness. At some point he'd ceased to hate Alex for not having followed him. Perhaps it was maturity. Perhaps it was the realization of how hard it would have been for them to make a go of a marriage. No, Ty hadn't hated her for years. How could he hate her when he'd never really stopped loving her, when every woman he met and every relationship he started failed in comparison to her and what they'd had?

His sister was probably right when she accused him of coming back to Grayson solely to find Alex again. Of course, he hadn't known she'd be here. He'd only hoped to find her and their child.

That wasn't entirely true, Ty mused. A part of him had always known the child wouldn't be with Alex. Despite her attempts to prove otherwise, Ty couldn't picture Alex holding out against her parents for too long. They would have insisted she either have an abortion or give the baby up. He knew the baby was gone from him forever. Gone from Alex, too. How he knew, he couldn't say, but he'd been sure of that before he'd ever spoken to Alex that first day back in Grayson.

So why couldn't he let it be? Why had he pushed today? He didn't know why he'd been so stupid. Ty pulled to a stop in his mother's driveway and pounded the steering wheel in frustration.

Rose Duncan was sitting on the front porch, breaking green beans into a bowl. Her eyes were full of questions, but she didn't ask her son anything other than whether he'd had breakfast.

Ty touched her cheek softly in gratitude. He was tempted to ask her about Sally's reference to things Alex had said. That memory seemed to be at the root of his sister's hatred for the woman he loved.

But he didn't ask. There was time for that later. He'd just learned firsthand that nothing was to be gained by pushing people. So instead Ty showered, made some phone calls and spent the afternoon at the mill talking with a contractor about the renovations.

Sally was with their mother in the kitchen when he returned. It was a quiet, apologetic Sally who promised her rudeness toward Alex would not be repeated.

"Okay, sis," Ty said. "I accept your apology, but I want to know what you were talking about last night. What kind of terrible things did Alex say to Mom and Dad?"

His sister moistened her lips, and Ty didn't miss the warning look that passed from mother to daughter. Something was wrong here.

Rose filled the awkward silence. "Your sister overheard part of a conversation and has been carrying around the wrong idea about Alex ever since. I straightened Sally out last night."

"What conversation?" Ty pressed.

Sally continued staring at her hands, and their mother seemed to be choosing her words very carefully. "Alex came here after you didn't meet her like you said you would."

"You never told me that," Ty said in a low voice.

"It didn't seem important."

"Dad said he met her at a restaurant to give her my note."

Rose twisted her hands in her gingham checked apron and avoided Ty's eyes. "Alex was upset, and before we could calm her down she said some pretty hard things and left. It wasn't the time to give her the note. I understood why she said those things, Ty, and I never gave any real thought to them. But Sally was in her bedroom, she didn't understand the situation, and she heard what Alex said. Your sister was too young to know why people say things they don't mean, Ty. I guess those words have stuck with her for years."

"I'm sorry, Ty," Sally said again. "There were a lot of things about you and Alex I didn't understand until last night. I'm going to apologize to her, too."

Ty studied them both with narrowed eyes. He didn't believe this was all there was to this situation, but he'd bide his time about finding out. He gave Sally his easy smile and hugged her tightly. Whatever she'd done, he knew it was out of love for him.

Sally stayed for dinner. Afterward she and Ty went for a walk through the neighborhood.

The places they passed had the look of their childhood, and the brother and sister fell into conversation about old times. It was Sally who mentioned Alex.

"Mom says you and Alex are pretty serious again."

"I'm serious. I'm not exactly sure how Alex feels." Ty picked up a stone from beside the road, weighing it in his hand as he eyed the grapes hanging from a vine in Mr. Simpson's backyard. He'd knocked many a bunch to the ground when he was a kid, just for the thrill of making them fall. God, the summers had been so simple then. It took age and complications to make you appreciate that simplicity.

"Did she have the baby?" Sally's quiet voice broke into his thoughts.

Ignoring her question, Ty threw the rock. It fell just shy of the grape arbor. Among other things, I've lost my throwing arm, Ty thought.

"Ty, tell me." Sally grasped his arm and pulled him around to face her.

"I don't know. She hasn't told me," he answered at last.

"Oh."

He sensed that Sally knew more than she'd told him. "What does that mean? Do you know something?"

Sally leaned against the Simpsons' fence, her eyes thoughtful. "There were lots of rumors at school the year you two left town. Mom and Dad had threatened to kill me if I said one word, so I kept my mouth shut. But people had plenty of questions. You left in a hurry, without even saying goodbye to your friends. And Alex didn't go to college in Nashville like she was supposed to. She ended up in Florida.''

"That's right, she's told me that much."

"But some people said she didn't start school that fall because she went away to have a baby."

"Who said it, Sally?"

"Just some girls."

Ty snorted in disgust. "That doesn't prove anything. It was just gossip. Didn't you see her in town at Thanksgiving or Christmas?"

"No, I didn't. But that doesn't prove anything, either. She and I never traveled in the same circles."

"But it still looks like someone would have said something."

"By that time there was a new scandal to talk about."

"But didn't you wonder? Didn't Mom and Dad say anything?"

Sally touched his shoulder. "I know you don't understand why we weren't interested, but it was a horrible time at home after you left. Mom and Dad fought all the time, and I didn't see how bringing up the baby would help anything. I kept my mouth shut."

"Why did they fight?" Ty was puzzled. His parents had always gotten along well, and they'd been in such total agreement that he and Alex shouldn't marry.

"I never knew exactly what the arguments were about, Ty, but I got the feeling Mom didn't think Dad had handled something in the right way. I guess it was the strain of it all, and they worried a lot about you."

That seemed a plausible explanation, so Ty didn't pursue the subject further. "Whatever happened to the baby is in the past now. We were two stupid kids. If Alex did give the baby up, I know our child's been in a good home."

"But don't you wonder?" Sally asked, thoughtful. "Don't you have any curiosity about whether it was a boy or a girl? I can't imagine giving Cody or Laura up!" She shivered as if the thought disturbed her.

"Of course I wonder, but there's not much I can do about it now." Ty turned back toward their mother's house to retrace the route they'd just taken. "But it was Alex who was the important one, the one I didn't want to lose. The baby was just something that happened."

The truth of the words hit Ty like a blow. Alex *was* the important one, and last night he'd almost gotten her back. Oh, it hadn't been just the sex. It had been the closeness, the feeling of harmony they'd always shared. Last night he had belonged to someone again. He'd never felt that close to anyone but Alex. Why had he spoiled the feeling by asking about something that couldn't be changed?

I've got to talk to her, Ty thought; I have to tell her I don't care about the baby. Unconsciously his pace quickened until he broke into a jog as he approached the house.

"Hey, what's the hurry?" Sally complained.

"I've got to see Alex," he explained over his shoulder. Sally rewarded him with a knowing, sweet smile.

Alex's day had been a nightmare. She'd been asleep no more than two hours when Clarissa had called her to the phone. It was Suzie. She was at the hospital, and the doctor thought she was miscarrying.

"Jason and Dad are both in Birmingham on business. It'll be hours before we can track them down and they can get back. Mom has Melanie at home. I could use a friend, Alex." Suzie's voice broke on her name.

"I'll be right there."

So, hollow-eyed and exhausted, Alex sat with Suzie most of the day, waiting. They talked about shared memories, about amusing things Suzie's daughter had done, about plans for the rest of the summer. They talked about everything but the child Suzie was losing. Around two, after the doctor examined her again, he said the medication wasn't helping. Suzie was definitely going to lose the baby.

With memories of her own pregnancy so near the surface, Alex felt her friend's disappointment keenly. It was so unfair. Suzie and Jason had been trying to have a second child for seven years.

"Oh, Suzie, I know, I know how it hurts," Alex said, trying to comfort her friend.

"But Alex, you can't know. Having a child inside you— even for just a little while—it becomes part of you. Having to let it go is like losing a little part of yourself." Tears streamed down Suzie's white, drawn face. "I know you're trying to help, but you can't possibly know what that's like."

"But I do," Alex said quietly.

Suzie stared at her, realization dawning. "Alex, are you saying—?"

"I was pregnant."

"With Ty's baby," Suzie finished for her. "I knew it. I knew something happened at the end of that summer. But what? Did you have the baby?"

"Shhhh," Alex said. "You don't need to be thinking about me. Just rest. I'll tell you the whole story some other time. I haven't even told Ty."

"He didn't know?"

Tears choked Alex's throat, making it hard to talk. "He knew, but he left."

"My God, Alex." Suzie's eyes filled with fresh tears. "Why didn't you tell me? How could he have done that to you?"

Alex sighed. "He was just young, Suzie. We were both just too young, too confused."

"But does *he* know what happened to the baby? Have you told him?"

Alex cried now, unable to hold back. "I can't, Suzie. I'm just so afraid that's the only reason he came back into my life—to find out about the baby. Isn't that crazy?"

"No, no, it's not." Suzie paused as a flicker of pain moved across her face. "But you have to tell him, Alex. Even if he did leave you, I still think he has a right to know what happened. It was his baby, too."

Before Alex could reply, Suzie cried out in genuine pain, gritting her teeth and saying, "I think you'd better get the nurse."

At Alex's summons the medical team rushed in, and she waited outside in the hall. Jason arrived and found her there. "She's losing the baby," Alex said tersely. She had to look away from the raw emotion on his face.

"Oh, God," he said, burying his face in his hands. "I thought we'd have our baby this time." He straightened. "Is Suzie okay?"

"I think she will be." Alex touched his arm awkwardly. She and Jason had never been really close, but she felt the need to comfort him now. "I'm really sorry."

"You're a good friend, Alex. Thank you for being here."

The doctor came out of the room and gestured for Jason. Alex waited only long enough to make sure Suzie was okay and there was nothing further she could do. Then she drove home.

Though it had been another hot June day, she felt cold—frozen to the core of her being. Poor Suzie. And poor Jason. He'd been just as destroyed as his wife. How would Ty have felt? Alex mused. How must he feel now, not knowing what had happened to their child? She realized with sudden clarity how unfair she'd been to him by not telling him exactly what had happened. She had to rectify that mistake. Soon.

At home, her family had already finished dinner. Alex felt too weary to eat. She just wasn't up to facing her mother's accusations or Gina's hostility. She paused only briefly in the sitting room to report the news about Suzie.

It was the strain that caused her voice to break. It was the thin emotional edge she'd been walking for days that brought the rush of tears. All the anxiety of the past few weeks took their toll, and Alex collapsed into a chair, sobbing.

Grady was beside her quickly, soothing her. For a moment, before Alex regained control of her senses, she thought it was her father who held her. She relaxed, drawing comfort from the deep voice that had never failed to ease her fears, from the strong arms that had always made every problem disappear. But the confusion soon cleared, and she opened her eyes to look into her brother's and to see that the others were clustered about, their concern obvious.

"I'm sorry," she mumbled. "I don't know what happened."

"It's okay," Grady said soothingly. "Drink this." He handed her a glass of water. "I want you to go straight to bed. You're exhausted."

"You're right." Alex drank the water thankfully and felt her body begin to uncoil from the tense spring she'd wound herself into. She began to feel embarrassed. "I guess I was so upset about Suzie. I don't know why else I—"

"I know why," Lucia interrupted briskly. "Ty Duncan. He's got you so tied up in knots you don't know whether you're coming or going. He's a troublemaker. Always has been, always will be...."

"Oh, Mother, shut up!" Alex cried with more strength than she felt. "Please just be quiet. I'm sick and tired of hearing the same old speech about him and me and why we're not right for each other. For God's sake, anyone would think you'd be happy to see your daughter involved with someone as rich as Ty is. Money has always meant so much to you."

"Alex—" Gina began.

"Keep out of this. I don't know why you think it concerns you," Alex told her sister-in-law bluntly, sitting up and eyeing her mother. "What is it you're so afraid of, Mother? That I'd be happy with Ty?"

"You wouldn't have been happy if I had let you marry him then, and you won't be happy with him now," Lucia predicted grimly. "That's what I'm afraid of."

"But I loved him. I love him now."

Dimly Alex heard the doorbell ring, and the babble of voices that greeted her pronouncement. But none of it really registered. The only thing that clicked in her brain was the statement she'd just uttered. She loved Ty.

Until this moment, she'd been afraid to admit the feelings were still there. As long as she didn't put a definitive label on what she felt, he couldn't hurt her again. By admitting her love, however, she made the stakes much higher. It made having his love again that much more important.

So lost in thought was she that at first Alex didn't think Ty was real when he followed Carrie into the room. She was afraid he was the product of weariness and her imagination. However, no mirage could possess those quicksilver eyes or the deep, smooth voice that said, "Alex, we have to talk."

Chapter Seven

Everyone in the room was silent as Alex rose unsteadily to her feet, her gaze never faltering from Ty's. There was quiet determination in his eyes and in the firm set of his jaw. He wanted answers, and who could blame him? It's time to put all the ghosts from our past to rest, Alex thought.

Her mother, however, had other ideas.

"Alex isn't feeling well, and I think it would be best if you left, Tyler." Lucia wasn't making a request; she was issuing a command.

Ty turned to her, his eyes narrowing. "I'll go only if Alex asks me to."

"No," Alex said. "Stay."

"Alexa, I just don't think you're up to—" Lucia began.

It was Grady who silenced her in his calm, reasonable voice. "Mother, this doesn't concern you."

"No, it doesn't," Alex concurred, not even bothering to look in her mother's direction. She stepped forward, placing her icy hand in Ty's warm grasp. "Come out on the back veranda. We can talk there."

Faintly Alex heard her mother make one last, feeble protest, but she ignored it, leading Ty through the central foyer and out the double doors at the end.

The big back porch, twin to the one at the front, had been the scene of many family dramas. Here, Sam Thorpe had wed Lucia Nelson. Here, Grady and Gina had placed Carrie in her grandfather's arms for the first time. Here, a younger Alex and Ty had kissed and made promises.

The comfortable wicker furniture made it a pleasant place to relax. But it was the ivy-covered trellis at the end that made the porch a private corner of the world, perfect for sharing secrets.

Ty followed Alex to the glider where they sat for a few awkward, silent moments. Finally he said, "I was an idiot this morning."

"No," Alex protested. "I shouldn't have run away."

"I don't blame you." Ty got to his feet and began to pace back and forth, his hands jammed deep in the pockets of his faded jeans. "I realized today that I shouldn't have asked you about the baby...."

"But why not? You have every right to know. It was your baby, too."

He stopped and stared at the pale oval of her face. "Do I? I thought I gave up any rights to anything the day I left you here alone."

Alex sighed and looked beyond him, out across the well-landscaped contours of the backyard and pool. "If anyone had asked me whether you had any rights twelve years ago, or even five years ago, I probably would have said no. But the bitterness faded, Ty. I stopped hating you for leaving."

"I'm grateful," he said simply. "God knows, I deserve to be hated." He paused and took a step forward. "Alex, it really doesn't matter to me what happened to our child. You were young and alone. Whatever choices you made were the right ones. I'm sure of that. I should have left the whole matter in the past where it belongs—"

"No," she interrupted. "We can't do that. Not after the last few weeks." She looked up, directly into his eyes. "After being with you again, I realize I have to tell you. I guess it's so hard because I never told anyone."

"Never told?" Ty questioned softly. He couldn't imagine how she had lived with this knowledge for all these years without sharing it. "What about your parents?"

"They didn't ask."

Ty sat down beside her again, covering her hand with his own. "I don't understand."

She leaned back and set the glider in motion with the push of her foot against the tiled floor. "I think I went a little crazy after you left. In fact, I don't remember much about the first couple of days. Every time I looked at Mother she was crying. And Father...well, he was just so disappointed."

"I bet he was," Ty interrupted in a sarcastic snarl.

Alex shook her head. "Oh, it wasn't you who disappointed him, Ty. It was me. He was upset because of the whole situation. It was too much like real life—this problem of his pregnant unwed daughter." She sighed. "Father didn't deal very well with real-life crises. You know that yourself."

"I don't think you're giving him enough credit," Ty told her, not bothering to disguise the bitterness in his voice. He could think of one time in particular when Alex's father had dealt him a resounding slap of reality.

"You just never understood Father, Ty. All you saw was that he was a failing businessman." Alex brushed the subject aside with a wave of her hand and continued, not giving Ty a chance to correct her. "Anyway, I convinced myself that your going was really a blessing. I figured my parents had been right. If you'd run out now, what would happen when the baby was born? After I made that decision there was nothing anyone, even you, could have done to make me change my mind. I wanted only what was best for the baby.''

Just as I thought, Ty told himself, she gave in to the pressure from her parents. No wonder she hadn't answered his note and joined him in Atlanta. "So what did you do?" he asked tightly.

Stopping the motion of the glider, Alex got up, crossed the porch and leaned against one of the round white columns. Her back was to Ty as she answered. "I went to Florida, and I lost the baby."

"Lost it?" Ty murmured, surprised. He'd expected any explanation but this.

Alex turned back to him, her face shadowed in the gathering twilight. "I guess you could say it was pretty normal. There was some pain and a lot of blood. I was scared out of my mind." Her voice broke on the last word, and Ty quickly came to her side, longing to embrace her but unsure of how that gesture would be welcomed.

"I'm sorry," he said at last. To his ears, the words sounded lame. But what else could he offer her now? When she'd needed him, he'd been gone.

"I'm sorry, too," she whispered.

Then she told him the entire story.

Alex had been alone in a cheap hotel room when the pain had begun. Terrified, she'd found the number of a nearby clinic listed in the phone book. There an impersonal voice had listened to a list of her symptoms, told her she was probably miscarrying and advised her to come in. Before she could get there, Alex had known her baby was gone. The last bond with Ty had been broken.

At the small clinic, a nurse's aide had told her to consider herself lucky. "There's a whole crowd of girls in the waiting room who'd like to swap places with you," she'd said, jerking her head toward the front of the building, where a dozen or so women waited to undergo abortions.

However, Alex hadn't felt so lucky. Although her healthy young body had mended quickly, her spirit had taken much longer.

Some days she just sat in the darkened hotel room, not sleeping, not eating, barely moving. Other days she walked on the beach, trudging for miles in the sand. She went to restaurants and ordered meals she only nibbled at. She went to movies she left in the middle.

It was nearly a month before she called her parents. They flew down immediately. Alex met them at the Tampa airport and announced the moment she saw them, "There's no baby."

Alex shook her head, remembering. "Neither of them asked me another question—not what happened or how I felt or anything. They just started acting as if the baby had never existed." She shrugged. "I guess it was their way of dealing with it all. So I never told anyone. I refused to come home until Christmas, and then only for two days. I got a job on the campus of Florida State and started school in January. End of story." She took a deep breath and looked up at Ty. "Until now."

Ty knew there was a lot of pain hidden in the forthright explanation. He could imagine how alone she'd felt. For all her bravado, Alex had led a fairly sheltered life until that summer. Losing the baby while she was hundreds of miles from home, alone, had to have been traumatic. Yet one thing puzzled him. "Tell me, why did you care so much, considering that I was gone?"

"It was my baby, too!" Alex retorted fiercely.

"You were going to keep it?"

"Of course I was. I didn't know exactly how, but I was determined." She passed a weary hand over her face. "It's so strange. When you're eighteen, everything is either completely possible or absolutely impossible. There's no middle ground. I just knew there'd be a way for me to keep the baby."

"I'm sure your parents were glad Tyler Duncan's off-spring didn't become their problem. I just can't imagine that they never even asked you what happened."

"I didn't come to terms with that for years. There was always this little part of me that felt so guilty."

"You felt guilty?"

"For having gotten pregnant in the first place," she explained. Her eyes narrowed as she gazed at a spot somewhere above Ty's shoulder. "Every time I saw my father I felt so ashamed, like I'd let him down."

Ty snorted in disgust. "My God, did he tell you that?"

"Of course not," Alex said. "You don't understand. It wasn't his problem. It was mine. I only thought he felt that way. He told me years later, the week before he died, that he never asked me about it because he knew how badly I was hurt by the whole thing."

"And you believed him?"

"Yes. My father never lied to me." Alex returned to the glider and sat down, her shoulders drooping wearily. "I sort of got the feeling Father was sorry he and Mother had tried to keep us apart."

"What did he say?" Ty asked.

Alex's lips curved into a tender smile. "Nothing, really. It was just a feeling I had. He and I walked here in the backyard. He mentioned that summer I'd had with you, and I sort of felt like he forgave me."

"There was nothing to forgive!"

She gave him a distracted look. "But there was, Ty. I ran away. I worried him sick. But he acted as if he understood why it had all happened. It eased my mind. The next day he slipped into a coma, and he died the next week. We never talked again."

Damn the bastard! Ty fumed inwardly. He died without telling her the truth. Now how can I tell her? He glanced at Alex's face, soft with memories and love for her father. How could he tell her now that Sam Thorpe was the reason he had left town? How could he tell her how ruthless her gentle, dreamy father had really been?

The question he dreaded came then. Alex said, "Now you know what happened to me, Ty. What about you? Why did you leave?"

Running a hand through his hair, Ty turned, just as she had done, to face the lawn. Darkness had fallen, and he could hear the steady hum of insects and smell the scent of roses in the still summer air. The moments seemed to stretch into hours as he deliberated over what to say.

Every instinct he possessed urged him to tell her the truth. It had been Sam Thorpe who had sent a message to Ty the night before he and Alex had planned to leave. In the note he'd had delivered to Ty at Nick's, Sam had said he was beginning to see things their way; he wanted to talk to Ty alone. Ty had been convinced Mrs. Thorpe knew nothing of the plan to meet. That was the reason for the secrecy, Ty had decided. Sam was breaking a lifelong habit of bowing to his wife's every wish. He'd agreed to meet the man at midnight at the mill.

Sam Thorpe hadn't been waiting. But the men who'd caught Ty in the dark beside the mill had delivered his message loud and clear: leave town, leave Alex alone, or both Ty and his father would lose their jobs at the mill.

The men had left Ty with a bleeding nose, a split lip and a couple of bruised ribs. They'd also left him without hope. Ty had known Sam Thorpe wouldn't hesitate to carry out his threat. If Ty and Alex left the next day, his father would lose the only job he'd held for thirty years. And no one would know the real reason.

It would be easy to fabricate an excuse for firing Harris Duncan. He was in his mid-fifties; his health wasn't the best. He sometimes made mistakes; he cursed his supervisors when they chastised him; he wasn't the easiest man in the mill to work with.

How could a man like that start over? Rose's small salary from the school cafeteria wouldn't support them. And how could Ty help out? If he and Alex married, they certainly couldn't come back here. Where would Ty find a job making enough money to help his parents and sister as well as support a wife and child?

In the blackest part of that September night, Ty realized he didn't have a choice. He had to leave.

He went home, awakening his parents to tell them the situation. Rose was outraged. Harris was coldly furious. However, he, too, realized Ty had no choice but to go.

To his father's credit, Ty remembered there had been no words of recrimination, no I-told-you-so speeches. He'd given his father a note for Alex, pleading with him to get it to her at the first opportunity. Harris resisted at first, but then gave in, taking the envelope and stuffing it in the pocket of his worn pants.

Father and son had been unable to share any real emotion. Harris had merely pressed five well-creased twenty dollar bills into Ty's hand. After bandaging her son's injuries, Rose had packed his clothes and kissed him goodbye. Ty had peeked into Sally's room, silently memorizing the gentle curves of her sleeping face before he'd left in the faint light of dawn.

The only other person Ty saw before leaving was Nick. He'd stopped at the beer joint and caught the old man just as he was ushering the night's last customers out the door.

Perhaps Nick had seen the trouble brewing in Ty's stormy gray eyes. Perhaps he had known even more about what had transpired that night than Ty. The secrets of a small town are rarely hidden from a man like Nick. In any case, he made Ty wait while he called an old friend. And so Ty had left Grayson with the promise of a job in a carpet mill. From that his entire adult life had been shaped. He wondered now where he would have ended up without Nick's help.

"Ty?" Alex asked, bringing him sharply back to the present. He turned and looked at her, silhouetted in the glow of lights from the windows that lined the porch. What was he going to tell her?

By her own admission, she'd only made peace with her father shortly before his death. Could he shatter the image Alex had of Sam Thorpe? And if he did, wouldn't it always come between them?

They had both been wrestling with the mysteries of their past ever since he'd come back into her life. Now Ty had his answers. Alex had told him of her ordeal. Did he have the right to add more pain?

The answer, of course, was no. So he lied.

"I just couldn't face the responsibility," Ty said quietly. "I was scared, and I ran. I don't have any excuses. In a way, I guess I was like you. I convinced myself you and our baby would be better off without me. I also realized somewhere down the line, after struggling to make ends meet for one person, just how hard it would have been for us." Ty cleared his throat and looked away. There seemed no reason to ask Alex why she hadn't answered his note. The fact that he'd left had surely seemed like the final abandonment to her. She'd probably believed he didn't really intend to meet her in Atlanta. His voice was husky as he finished, "But I've never stopped being ashamed of myself, Alex. I never stopped being sorry."

To Ty they seemed like strangers, standing there on that darkened veranda, going over the events that had altered their lives so drastically. He wished suddenly for a script, a plan, anything that would tell him where to go from here. As always, he realized there were no rules or easy answers. He merely waited for Alex to speak.

"What do we do now?" she asked.

"That's up to you."

"No, it isn't," she retorted, a trace of anger in her voice. "I've made it clear from the first that I wanted to try again. You've hesitated. You wanted to know what happened to the baby. Now you know; is that all you wanted?"

"Of course not. I told you earlier. You didn't even have to tell me."

"Then I want to know, dammit. Do I have a chance with you?" She stood and walked toward him.

Ty was amazed. Alex was asking *him* for a chance? It should have been the other way around. Taking her hands, he pulled her gently into the circle of his arms, pressing his cheek against her soft hair. "I'm willing if you are," he murmured.

Only then did Alex relax, and when she did the weariness settled in. She'd been going for nearly forty-eight hours with almost no sleep. Sensing her exhaustion, Ty said, "We don't have to solve all our problems tonight."

"But, Ty..." she protested.

"I'll call you tomorrow," Ty said firmly. "You need some rest. We've both got a lot to think about." After brushing a kiss across her mouth, he turned and left, disappearing into the darkness around the porch.

Alex almost called him back. Couldn't he see she needed him to stay, to talk about their plans? Were the words "I'm willing" enough to sustain her until the next time she saw him?

She went back into the house and straight to her room, thankfully encountering no one. She felt curiously let down, and didn't know why. Had she thought Ty would give her a passionate declaration of love and a proposal of marriage? She was well enough acquainted with the man he had become to know he wasn't that impetuous. Neither was she. So what now?

Wearily Alex sank down on her bed and looked around the familiar room. Someone, probably Clarissa, had placed a tray with a sandwich and a glass of tea on her dresser. Suddenly realizing she was starving, Alex ate the food gratefully, took a quick shower and got in bed. Perhaps the situation would look different once she'd gotten some rest.

And it did. In fact, the whole world looked brighter, cleaner, fresher than it had in ages. Alex was humming a little tune when she headed downstairs late the next morning. Clarissa was placing a vase of yellow roses on a table in the foyer, and she looked up, smiling, as Alex breezed by her.

"I'm starving," Alex said. "What's for lunch?"

After two roast-beef sandwiches and a handful of home-made chocolate-chip cookies, she went in search of her mother.

Alex found her in the library, sitting by the window and gazing out at her treasured rosebushes. Lucia glanced at her daughter. "You seem to be feeling better."

"I feel wonderful," Alex said, sitting down in the window seat.

Lucia hesitated and then said, "You and Tyler talked for quite a while last night."

"Yes, we got some things settled." Alex leaned forward, hands braced on her knees. "I love him, Mother. You're going to have to accept that."

"Despite the way he left you, you still love him?" Lucia queried tersely.

"He told me all about that last night."

"He did?" There was surprise and a trace of something akin to panic in the older woman's voice. Was she that upset at seeing her daughter involved with Ty again?

"I understand it all," Alex continued, watching her mother closely. "Ty was young and scared. He decided he had to leave. I can forgive him that."

The tension in her mother's expression eased. "You're saying he left because he couldn't accept the responsibility of being a husband and father?"

"That's right. And I can understand."

"You have your father's heart, Alexa, too forgiving." Lucia's gaze caught and held her daughter's. "What does this mean?"

"It means I'm going to be seeing a lot of Ty. I don't know exactly where this is going to take us, but I'm willing to take my chances. I expect you to treat him civilly." Alex paused and drew a deep breath. "If you don't, I'll move out."

"I don't want that," Lucia said quickly.

"Good." Alex stood and touched her mother's cheek lightly. "If you'll give him a chance this time, I think you'll be surprised at how much you like him."

Lucia sniffed. "We'll see."

"Yes, we will." With a happy laugh, Alex left the room and went to call Suzie.

As Alex had expected, her friend was home from the hospital, resting comfortably in her own room. Her mother was looking after Melanie, Suzie's rambunctious seven-year-old. Suzie was feeling much better and invited Alex to come over.

Telling the whole story about her and Ty felt good to Alex. Suzie listened to it all without comment until the end. "Why didn't you tell me, Alex?"

"I wanted to," Alex said. "But I didn't think you'd understand. You never really approved of Ty. I was so afraid you'd say 'I told you so.' And then later, that next spring, you were all caught up in planning your wedding. You were so happy. I just didn't want to upset you."

Suzie nodded her head. "I probably wouldn't have been much help. But I know one thing. I would have told you to find Ty."

"What?" Alex asked, amazed. "I thought you didn't like Ty."

"Well, he wasn't like any of the other boys we'd dated. He scared me. But then, you wouldn't have been happy with any of the country-club set, Alex. There was something about you and Ty that seemed so completely right. You were a perfect balance. You calmed him down; he brought out the fun in you."

Alex considered her friend's words for a few moments. Maybe all of that had been true twelve years ago, but what about now? Were she and Ty good for each other now?

As if anticipating the question, Suzie said, "Don't let him go again. You're not eighteen anymore. You don't have to wait around for him to call you. Find him and give it your best shot." With her bright blue eyes sparkling and the gamine smile that spread across her face, Suzie looked like a mischievous imp as she urged, "Time's a-wastin', Alexa Thorpe. I expect to be playing with you and Ty's babies within the next two years."

"Good heavens, Suzie, aren't you rushing things?"

"Well, maybe somebody has to—now quit sitting around in my house and go find him."

Although finding Ty had been Alex's next intention, Suzie's advice was nonetheless appreciated. A quick call to his mother revealed that Ty was down at the mill. Alex left, her heart pounding in anticipation of seeing him again.

It was hot inside the factory's deserted offices, but Ty didn't notice. He'd forced a window open and rigged up a table with two sawhorses, and had spent the day poring over plans for the renovations. The contractor he'd met with yesterday had joined him, and they'd reached some solid agreements.

The other man had left hours before. Ty, however, worked on, jotting down ideas and questions, looking over the cost projections. He could have done the same at his mother's house and been much more comfortable, but he preferred to stay here. Whether it was a conscious decision or not, Ty was putting his mark on the place now. By working here he was enforcing the reality that this was no longer Nelson Textiles but rather DunMar Carpets.

A new sign would go up within the next week, and he'd already hired someone to tame the tangle of weeds that covered parts of the surrounding land. The offices themselves would need very little work—just paint, carpet and new furnishings. As with the plant in Georgia, he wanted the public areas to have a bright, open feel. The right surroundings made for happier employees.

The office he'd chosen as his own had been Sam Thorpe's, of course. It was large and square, a utilitarian sort of room, in keeping with the manufacturing atmosphere. Ty didn't plan to alter that ambience, but he did intend to strip the room of every color and every texture that would remind him of Alex's father.

Laying down his pencil, Ty stretched. There wasn't even a chair for him to use, so he propped himself on the wide windowsill, one leg drawn up, the other swinging to touch the floor. Contented, he looked out over the property. Everything, for once, was going his way.

He'd go home soon and call Alex. Last night he'd decided on his next move. He intended to court Miss Alexa Thorpe in a way that would absolutely astound her. He knew she wouldn't expect it. He knew they could deepen their relationship without all the fuss and bother of dating and wooing. But he wanted that. He wanted it for Alex.

It seemed to Ty that they had missed so much. That summer had been too intense, as if they'd known that September would end it all. This time he wanted it slow. He wanted their togetherness to grow and last.

Considering they'd already become lovers again, some people would have wondered at Ty's romantic notions. Indeed, he hoped the next few months would offer many other such sweet, intoxicating nights. He was counting on them. But he hoped for much more.

The crux of the matter was that Ty wanted Alex to love him again. He wasn't entirely sure she didn't already, but she hadn't said the words, and until she did he was going to romance her in a grand style. They'd had enough of tragedy and compromise. Now was the time to live and love.

"Is the lord and master contemplating his holdings?"

Ty turned to see Alex in the doorway, a smile playing at the corners of her mouth. The happiness he felt at merely the sight of her shook him with its intensity. "Actually, I was thinking of you," he said finally.

She stepped inside the room, advancing toward the window where he sat. "What about me?"

"About how beautiful you are."

"Ummmm . . . tell me more."

"About how much I've missed you all day."

"I've missed you, too."

"And about how much I'd like to kiss you."

Alex stopped just inches from where he sat. "Then what are you waiting for?" She stepped into his outstretched arms.

Not for the first time in the last few weeks, Alex wondered how she'd survived all these years without Ty's kisses. A simple touch of his lips had always brought an avalanche of feelings. And when he kissed her as he did now, hungrily, with a trace of desperation, the only thing she knew was desire, overpowering, all-consuming want.

The flick of his tongue against her lips opened them like a flower turning to the sun. She needed the heat, the warmth, the energy that only Ty could give her. His touch, his nearness, was a simple necessity now, a basic requirement for living.

They kissed like people long starved for love until Ty tore his lips from hers with a soft groan. He leaned his forehead against hers and drew in a long, uneven breath. "Any more of that and we won't get out of this office for a long, long time."

"Promises, promises," Alex teased, her golden-brown eyes bright with laughter.

"What would your father say about using his office in such a shameful manner?"

Alex turned and gazed about the room. "He'd probably be shocked. But I'm sure he'd basically understand. He was a romantic, after all. He worshipped my mother."

"Lady, worshipping implies a rather distant relationship. I was thinking about getting very close to you." He caught her arm and turned her into his embrace, capturing her between his strong, muscular thighs.

Alex giggled. "How close?"

"As deep inside you as I can," Ty growled against her throat.

"Ty!" she protested weakly. In fact, the idea sounded all too appealing, and she closed her eyes as his lips explored the rounded column of her throat. "Ummm, that feels good."

"You're so easy to please," he murmured as his hand snaked up under the loose hem of her pink knit blouse.

"I'll try to be harder."

"Uh-uh, being harder is my job." Ty's fingers reached the front closure of her lacy bra, unsnapping it with practiced ease.

"You do that very well," Alex observed in a shaky voice while his hand cupped her breast. "And that, too," she managed to whisper when his fingers began to tease the nipple into an ever-tightening bud.

"It gets better." With a quick movement he drew her blouse up, pulling her forward until his mouth circled the pink tip of her other breast. His tongue dallied with agonizing laziness with the puckering orb while Alex moaned low in her throat. She touched his hair lightly with one hand, pressing her body closer between his thighs.

His arousal was evident in the tight, worn jeans, and Alex's own desires walked the tightrope between pain and pleasure. She wanted him now, while the smell of dust and perspiration clung to his body. She wanted him in here, in this deserted, echoing building. She wanted him in every erotic, pleasing way they could envision. She gave herself over to sensation, caught in the netherworld of passion.

It was with shock that she realized Ty had stopped caressing her body, that he was actually fastening her bra and rearranging her clothes. "What's the matter?"

"I haven't had lunch, or dinner, and my mother always told me to save dessert till last." He grinned at her, his quicksilver eyes daring her to protest.

"You're cruel, Tyler Duncan." Alex moved out of his arms, trying to gather her scattered emotions into some semblance of order. "I'll pay you back."

"I'm counting on that." He caught hold of her hand. "Now let's go get a hamburger and talk." After swatting her impudently on the rear, he hauled her out of the office.

Everyone in Grayson had the same idea on this late-June afternoon. The drive-in was packed, its outdoor slots filled with cars while teenagers milled about outside and families scrambled for seats inside. Many of the kids called greetings to Alex as she and Ty threaded their way through the crowd. They stared openly at the tall man in tight jeans and T-shirt who walked beside her.

"Now every girl under the age of eighteen will be talking about Miss Thorpe's new boyfriend, the hunk," Alex whispered as they hurried to claim the lone empty booth inside.

"Great. Let's really give them something to talk about." Ty pulled her close, claiming her lips in a brief, hard kiss. When he stepped back, he looked over Alex's head and straight into Charlie Clemmer's eyes.

The plump banker was seated in a neighboring booth, staring at Alex and Ty with a grim look on his face. His dark-haired, surprisingly attractive companion, whom Ty guessed to be his wife, swiveled around to see what had Charlie so captivated.

Plastering a big, false smile on his face, Ty waved. "How are you, Charlie. Is this your wife?"

The other man swallowed deeply but managed to answer, "Yes, this is Mary Evelyn. And these are my boys, Todd and Nathan."

Ty nodded pleasantly as introductions were made and conversation was exchanged. Mary Evelyn knew Alex. "Having a nice summer?" she asked pleasantly.

Alex linked her arm through Ty's and smiled. "Very pleasant."

The grin Charlie's wife gave them was knowing. "Since Charlie and Ty are such old friends, maybe we should all get together sometime for dinner. We'd love to have you over."

"That sounds great," Ty answered, watching Charlie squirm. He hoped Mary Evelyn did issue that invitation. He'd go. He'd drink Charlie's whiskey, sit at his table and enjoy every minute.

"Call me and we'll make plans," Alex added before taking her seat at the booth. Ty gave Charlie another tight little smile and joined her.

"You really enjoyed that, didn't you?" Alex whispered impishly.

"Yeah, I really did."

Her laugh was soft. "I did, too."

Both of them smiled and waved again as Charlie and his wife left with their two children. "How did Charlie find her?" Ty asked.

"They met at college. She's so nice, I've never understood what she was doing with him."

"Maybe it's his money," Ty suggested.

"Well, that can be a powerful motivation."

"Are you after my money?"

Alex winked at him. "That depends. How much money do you have?"

"Enough for dinner," he replied, pulling the plastic menu out of its holder in the salt-and-pepper stand. "What'll you have?"

A simple hamburger had never tasted quite as appetizing as the one Ty shared with Alex. She fed him French fries and finished the last swallow of his shake while they watched the Saturday-night scenes of their home town.

The teenagers circled the drive-in in old cars, their daddies' station wagons or their own slick new compacts. There were couples and groups of boys and girls, all playing their roles in an elaborate production of the mating game. The clothes were different, the faces had changed, but it could have been a Saturday night from their own teenage years.

A thin, awkwardly tall boy strode into the restaurant, and from the cassette deck balanced on his shoulder blared the steady rock-and-roll beat of a twelve-year-old song. Alex and Ty grinned at each other as the tune triggered shared summer memories.

"Remember the night we went wading in the courthouse fountain?" he asked.

"And the police pulled up just after you got out but I was still in the water? Yeah, I remember." Alex shook her head, wondering at her own foolishness.

"They just laughed."

"I just knew they were going to call my father."

"If I hadn't hidden, I'm sure they would have. I'd been in trouble enough when I was younger. They knew me."

Alex leaned forward. "That brings something else up: Did you really paint the high-school principal's Cadillac orange?"

Ty laughed heartily. "Uh-uh, you're not going to trap me on that one. I was sworn to secrecy."

The reminiscing continued as they left the restaurant and drove aimlessly around town. Alex told him about Suzie's miscarriage. Ty discussed some of his plans for the mill. It was a pleasant, easygoing evening. Last night had cleared away most of the lingering awkwardness, and there was a new spontaneity between them.

Around nine-thirty they found themselves headed toward the lake. "Do you still have the key to Suzie's parents' cabin?" Ty asked quite casually.

"Yes." Alex could feel the excitement catching hold in her chest.

"Do you want to go up there?" he pressed, his tone suddenly very serious.

"I left a note at home for them not to worry if I didn't get in until tomorrow morning," she whispered, returning his look with a steady, sure one of her own.

They had come to an intersection, one of those tiny little crossings of country roads that dotted the rural area around Grayson. There was a gas station on one corner, a bait-and-tackle store on the other. Ty drew the car to a stop in the deserted parking lot of the store and turned halfway in his seat, grasping her hands in his.

"I know we haven't talked about where we're going from this point, and where we want to go."

"No," she agreed quietly. "We haven't."

"I don't want to rush it." Ty looked down at their joined hands and his fingers tightened around hers. "Is it okay with you if we sort of play this thing by ear, if we see where it leads us?"

"If that's what you want." Alex blinked rapidly against the moisture collecting in her eyes. No, this wasn't a declaration of undying love, but hadn't they said those words too quickly last time? Hadn't they moved too fast too soon? Ty was right to take each day as it came. That way they could build something solid.

"We're a little like that road over there," he said, releasing one of her hands as he pointed toward the two-lane highway running to the left of the store. "I'm pretty sure it'll take us to the lake, same as the road we usually take, but I've never gone that way, have you?"

"No," she replied, instantly comprehending his analogy. Taking a different, perhaps slower route might still get them to the place they wanted to go. She squeezed his hand. "Let's see where it takes us."

The kiss he pressed on her mouth held a subtle charm, its intent more to seal a promise than to arouse. But desire sparked between them anyway. When he released her, his silvery gaze still held her in his spell, but his hands reached to put the car in gear. "I certainly hope Suzie's parents didn't decide to use the cabin tonight." He grinned and guided the car out onto the road. "I don't know if this car has enough room for what I've got in mind."

Alex returned his smile and told him to hurry.

Chapter Eight

July in northern Alabama is a study in color. Red-white-and-blue flags wave in patriotic celebration against the cloudless sky. In the hot sun roses deepen to crimson, zinnias to orange, petunias to pink and purple. Farms spill their bounty into roadside stands—green beans, yellow squash and red tomatoes.

These were the colors of every summer of Alex's life, but she'd never appreciated their beauty until this particular July, when Ty was hers. Their other summer was forgotten, or perhaps overshadowed, by the present. And though they neither made a real commitment nor spoke the words of love, there was deep contentment in their togetherness. Happiness brightened everything Alex saw or did.

That happiness became her. Alex had never been a truly striking beauty. With her gold-kissed brown eyes, dark hair and rather ordinary features, she was pretty in the way of conservative, well-behaved southern girls. There had always been an air of seriousness about her, a reserved facade that kept her from smiling or laughing too much. But when she smiled, as she did often that summer with Ty, the effect was heart-stopping.

Ty cultivated those smiles. He'd tease her until she grinned at him with slow, brilliant ease. He'd sneak up behind her just to see the surprise in her eyes and the wide, welcoming smile on her full pink mouth. His favorite smile was the gentle, satisfied curve of her lips after they'd made love. And because he'd lived so long without them, every smile Alex gave him was a gift he treasured.

Right now, in the heat of a late Saturday afternoon near the end of July, it was a challenging smile Alex sent him from the other end of the tennis court. They were playing doubles, Ty and Carrie versus Alex and Billy. Game, set and match rested on this point.

"Move out of the way. This is coming through," Ty called, tossing the ball high and sending it across the net with his powerful serve.

Alex sidestepped quickly, catching the ball with her backhand just as it bounced upward. The return was well placed. Carrie stumbled after it, and Ty found himself hopelessly out of position. The fuzzy yellow ball flashed by him, just out of reach of his outstretched racket. He sank to the court in defeat.

"We won!" Billy yelled. It had been a grudge match. Carrie and Ty had demolished the other two last weekend, and since the boy was the star of his high-school team, winning had become a point of honor.

"How did you do that?" Ty called to Alex as he got to his feet. "You haven't returned a serve that well all summer." He grimaced as he straightened his leg.

"I guess you're slipping, Duncan. Maybe you're just getting old!" she taunted gaily.

"Old? Did you say old?" Ty tossed his racket to the side and sprinted around the net.

Alex shrieked and dodged him. They scampered around the court like youngsters until he caught her at last by the fence. Pressing her against the chain-link barrier, his hand gently forced her chin up until their lips were less than an inch apart.

"Do I have to prove that I'm not old?" he murmured.

"Please do," she answered, her fingers grasping the front of his white polo shirt.

"Let's take the kids home and go somewhere where I can fully demonstrate my continued youthfulness and zeal," Ty said softly, his gray eyes bright with meaning.

"We have to go home and get ready for Suzie's party right now or we're going to be late." Alex pushed him away playfully. There was mischief in her voice as she added, "But later..." Her laughter was smothered when he brought her against his chest again, his lips briefly hard and insistent on hers.

He loved her like this, her eyes bright with laughter, creamy skin flushed by the sun and physical exertion. He wondered if she couldn't see the love in his eyes when he looked at her, or taste it on his mouth when they kissed.

Ty and Alex pulled apart, and Billy grinned at them, giving Carrie's ponytail a quick tug as she handed him his racket.

"You two!" Carrie said, shaking her head in mock disapproval.

"But we're having so much fun," Ty answered blithely, throwing an arm casually over the girl's shoulders.

"If I had as much fun as you guys do, Mom and Dad would ground me."

"And they'd be within their rights," Ty replied. "However, when you're as old as I am and as close to death as your aunt has accused me of being, you have to take a few chances."

Alex laughed as she fell in step with Billy and followed Ty and Carrie to the car. The easy camaraderie between Ty and her niece pleased her. And Ty was right; they were having fun.

The last few weeks had been full of activity—swimming, tennis, cookouts, movies and dinners. Alex and Ty had rarely been separated. He was supervising the work at the mill, and he'd gone to Atlanta twice, but for the most part they'd played.

He'd even spent some time at Alex's home with the rest of the family. Carrie, of course, adored him. Grady seemed to like him, and Clarissa was approving. Even Gina had relaxed some of her puzzling icy reserve. Only Lucia remained distant. Her blue eyes were skeptical whenever Alex spoke of Ty, or whenever he was present. As she'd promised, she was never rude, but she remained aloof. Alex sometimes thought it would take nothing short of a miracle to make her mother accept Ty.

She was grateful they had a place to escape her mother's disapproval. Ty had bought a cabin at the lake, a small A-frame with one fully furnished room downstairs and an empty sleeping loft above. It was on the north shore of the lake in a quiet little cove, away from the older lake homes.

A path led down a wooded slope to a smaller pier. Alex and Ty had already spent many hours there, lying in the sun, talking, making love. The only other house in the cove was unoccupied, so their privacy was assured.

I'd rather be at the cabin now, Alex thought hours after the tennis match as she lazed on a lawn chair in Suzie's backyard. Her friends were hosting their annual summer barbecue, and the patio and lawn were filled with the cream of Grayson's younger society set. Alex studied the people spread before her.

The well-dressed women clustered in colorful groups, sipping their drinks and discussing their babies, homes, husbands and jobs. The men congregated near the keg of beer and the bar, talking business, trading jokes and comparing golf scores.

At the center of it all was Ty.

It amused Alex to see her friends and acquaintances, many of whom had snubbed Ty in school, fawning over him now like a newly discovered rich relation. Once it had become common knowledge that she and he were an "item," the invitations had fluttered in for parties and get-togethers in homes or at the country club. In the past three weeks they'd gone to five or six of these affairs. The faces varied little from party to party, and Ty was always the focus of attention.

Alex couldn't decide who hovered over him more, the men or the women. Some of the females, known predators, zeroed in on him early, making their gestures of willingness. These Ty rebuffed with his devilish grin and the casual yet meaningful way he drew Alex to his side.

The men were much more subtle. They circled about with apparent disinterest and then swooped in with deadly aim, armed with business proposals, investments and community projects. Ty deflected their attacks with slickly choreographed moves and vaguely worded answers that left them wondering if he'd said yes or no.

Tonight it was the men who were most persistent. Several of them had pinned Ty by the corner of the patio, and an earnest discussion of tax shelters was under way. Alex noted Charlie Clemmer, portly in yellow slacks and an unflattering striped knit shirt, hovering at the group's edge.

The man seemed to have banished all memory of his attempt to harass Ty. He now enjoyed regaling people with tales of their youthful exploits. Alex had to give Charlie credit; he knew which way the wind blew, and right now Ty was smelling like a rose. The thought made her smile.

"Something funny?" Suzie asked, dropping down in the chair beside Alex's.

"I was just thinking how the green of money casts people in a rosy glow." Alex nodded to Ty and his group of admirers.

"I see what you mean." Suzie giggled. "However, I don't think it's money that makes Ty so attractive to June Cartwright." She gestured toward a raven-haired beauty in a pair of tight shorts who was threading her way through the crowd toward Ty.

"Don't kid yourself, Suzie. If he didn't have a dime she might pause to admire the scenery, but she'd never try to collect any souvenirs."

Both women laughed, but Alex stood when she saw the brunette extricate Ty from the group of men. "I think I need to make my claim a little clearer. See you later."

Alex joined Ty and June, slipping a possessive arm around his lean waist. Ty smiled down at her, and his own arm encircled her shoulders before he dropped a light kiss on her cheek. June withdrew gracefully.

"Thanks," Ty whispered as they strolled toward the long buffet table. "The woman's a menace."

"The pleasure was all mine. She was licking her chops over getting you alone." Alex began to fill a plate with spicy barbecued ribs, buttered corn on the cob, flaky biscuits and creamy coleslaw. As usual, Suzie and Jason had outdone themselves with the spread of food.

"They do this every year?" Ty asked after they'd found a seat at one of the picnic tables placed throughout the yard.

"For about five or six years now," Alex answered. "They also have a big open house at Christmastime. Suzie doesn't like to entertain all the time, so she pays back everyone they owe with two big gatherings."

"It's a great house for a party," Ty said, eyeing the roomy lines of the mellowed-brick home. "And for a family." His eyes rested on Jason, who was filling a plate for his daughter. Melanie had insisted on joining the party instead of spending the night with her grandparents. Her indulgent parents had given in as usual.

Alex followed Ty's gaze and then turned back to him, catching the flicker of yearning in his eyes. He loved children, loved catering to the whims of his niece and nephew and loved spending time with his business partner's three boys.

With a brief stab of sadness, Alex thought of the child they had lost. But she didn't dwell on it. She preferred looking ahead. Perhaps there'd be children for them one day—rowdy boys with their father's thick ebony hair, gentle girls with his quicksilver eyes. Or perhaps the girls would be rowdy and the boys gentle. Alex didn't care. What mattered was that the possibility of having children with Ty existed. Just two months ago, there'd been no hope of that for her.

Lost in thought, Alex let her expression soften, and her brown eyes were dreamy as she gazed out across the crowded lawn.

"Hey," Ty said, waving his hand in front of her face. "Where'd you go? I lost you there for a minute."

She came out of her dreamworld with an effort. "I was just thinking."

"I hope it was of me."

Under the table her hand slipped into his. "Of course." The look they exchanged was full of intimate, shared memories.

The sound of a throat being cleared caused them to look up. Jason and Melanie were standing beside the table. "Is it okay if we join you, or is this table strictly off limits?" the earnest young attorney asked.

"You can sit down this time," Alex teased, patting the chair beside hers. "But don't interrupt this kind of thing again, okay?"

"Gotcha."

The party continued, and there was no further chance for private conversation. However, later that night at the cabin, as Ty made slow, sweet love to her, Alex remembered her thoughts of a child, her dreams of a family. She wanted to share those hopes with Ty, but she held back, uncertainty keeping her silent. They never talked about anything further in the future than the next week. How could she speak of children?

While Ty slept, Alex lay awake, praying for patience. Surely someday, if she waited, all her dreams would come true.

Ty's family had been pleased when he'd bought the lakeside retreat. To them this purchase, more than the mill, meant he was once again putting down roots in Grayson. They were anxious to have him here permanently. He hadn't made any promises.

Truth was, Ty didn't know how he would adjust to the town. It was the slow pace that bothered him. He had become used to quick decisions, unexpected travel and rapid change. Here time seemed to run half a beat slower than elsewhere. No one hurried. Even the work on the mill was proceeding a little slower than he and Chuck had planned.

But on his quick trips back to the main office Ty worked frantically, clearing up details in short order, anxious to be back in Grayson. He knew the reason, just as Chuck and Linda did. His co-workers cheerfully put in overtime in order to send him back to Alabama—back to Alex.

He turned now and watched as she slid open the glass door and stepped out on the cabin's large deck. In the bright Sunday-morning sunshine, she looked tanned, rested and happy. Ty grinned and drew her close beside him at the porch railing.

"I thought you were going to get the charcoal started," she said. "Your family will be up here in half an hour or so. You promised Cody and Laura burgers."

"You shouldn't have kept me in bed so late this morning."

"Did you really mind?" Alex teased.

"No," he murmured, pressing a kiss to her forehead before picking up a bag of charcoal to begin preparing the grill. When he finished arranging the chunks of charcoal, he turned to find Alex still standing by the railing, smiling at him. "What's wrong?"

"Nothing. Everything's perfect," she answered simply, and went back inside.

These Sunday afternoons with Ty's family were becoming a habit Alex enjoyed. The children were well behaved, open and easy to love. Sally's husband Keith was still a little quiet around her, but he was beginning to come out of his shell. Alex and Rose were becoming good friends. Even Sally seemed to be accepting the woman in her brother's life.

Alex bustled into the small kitchen at one end of the cabin's main room and finished mixing the ingredients for homemade chocolate ice cream. Today was a special occasion, Cody's ninth birthday. On the counter was a heavily decorated cake, complete with thick bakery frosting and a miniature baseball diamond in honor of his favorite sport. She checked the supply of ice in the freezer, then went outside to prepare the picnic table with a colorful tablecloth, plates and napkins. She wanted the day to be a special one.

It was.

Everyone overdid it on hamburgers, potato salad and baked beans, so they wisely left the cake and ice cream for later. The two children were anxious to go swimming, and Cody filled in the mandatory half-hour wait by opening the brightly wrapped gifts piled to overflowing on and around a small table. He was thrilled with everything, but it was the home computer from Ty that astounded the young boy.

"Ty!" Sally objected. "This is too much."

"No, it isn't," Ty replied. "This is something he really wanted, and it will help him in school."

"It will, Mom, honest it will," Cody chimed in, his gray eyes full of wonder at the gift.

"Oh, all right, but you're spoiling them." Sally frowned slightly at her brother.

As if in confirmation, Laura interrupted, saying, "I'll be seven in November. You won't forget that I want a dollhouse, will you, Uncle Ty?"

"See what I mean?" Sally said in triumph.

Everyone laughed while the pretty little girl with her father's blue eyes and her mother's soft brown hair climbed into Ty's lap. He tweaked her nose affectionately. Over her mother's protests, he assured her, "I won't forget. You'll get the biggest dollhouse I can find."

The birthday gifts were stored away in the house, and the entire group went down to the lake. Rose read in a lounge chair in the shade of a tree while the rest of them lay in the sun or roughhoused in the water. Ty was thinking of buying a boat, and he and Keith were arguing good-naturedly about the merits of various makes when Alex and Sally went back to the house to dish up the ice cream and cake.

After the heat of the afternoon sun, the air-conditioned cabin was cool. Alex shivered a little in her damp bathing suit. "I'm going to put on a T-shirt. Do you want one, Sally?" She crossed the room and pulled a couple of Ty's shirts from the top drawer of a chest.

Sally slipped into the loose garment gratefully. "You spend a lot of time up here with Ty, don't you?"

Alex weighed the casual, almost offhand question carefully before she answered. Was the other woman merely making conversation, or was she disapproving of the fact that Alex and Ty were sleeping together? Neither of them had tried to hide their relationship from their families in the last few weeks. Carrie had asked a lot of questions, and Alex had tried to answer them honestly. She and Ty were adults, she'd told her niece. They cared deeply for one another and wanted to be together. Did Sally somehow think it was improper?

As if sensing Alex's unease, Sally continued, "I don't think there's anything wrong about it. In fact, I don't think I've ever seen Ty as happy as he is now."

Breathing a quick sigh of relief, Alex moved over to the kitchen, unwrapping the towels from around the ice-cream freezer and getting bowls and plates out of a cabinet. "I hope you do approve, Sally. You mean a lot to Ty. I want you to like me."

The taller woman laughed and began dipping ice cream into bowls. "I never thought I would, but I do like you, Alex. You're not at all the way I always thought you were."

"And how was that?"

"Stuck-up, snobby."

Alex began placing candles on the cake. "I guess I understand how you got that impression. In high school I was a little snooty. But I changed. Ty changed me. And then..." She paused and looked up into Sally's eyes, gray eyes so much like Ty's. "Then, when I got pregnant, I really discovered that we're all just people. Bad things can happen to anyone—rich, poor or in-between." She watched Sally closely for her reaction.

"Ty told me everything that happened," Sally murmured, and put a sympathetic hand on Alex's shoulder. "I'm sorry."

"Thank you," Alex whispered before turning to look through a drawer for matches.

"At least now you two have a second chance." Sally set the bowls of ice cream on a tray.

"Yes, we do." Alex sighed, a trifle sadly.

"What's wrong?"

"It's nothing." Picking up the cake, Alex started out of the room, wishing she hadn't let her guard slip with Ty's sister.

"No, what is it?" Sally pressed.

Taking a deep breath, Alex plunged ahead, "It's just that sometimes I wonder where Ty and I are going."

"You haven't talked about it?"

"No. We're sort of playing it by ear. But I get impatient. I wonder..." Alex tried to wave the subject aside by heading toward the door.

Sally was frowning as she followed her outside. She hesitated briefly, but then spoke in a rush. "Don't give up on him, Alex. Ty loves you."

Surprised, Alex turned to stare at her.

"Oh, he may not have said it, but I know him, Alex. He loves you, the same as he always did. I think you're the reason he came back here. You're the reason he's staying. The mill is just an extra added attraction. Just give him some more time. You two went through a lot, you know." Sally patted Alex's arm awkwardly and walked to the edge of the deck, calling to the rest that ice cream and cake were served.

Alex set the food out on the table automatically and joined in the laughter as Cody made his wish and blew out his candles, but she couldn't get her mind off Sally's words. Every time she looked at Ty she wondered about his feelings for her.

Once Ty had called what they felt for each other "unfinished business." In the back of her mind Alex had partially accepted that. Oh, she knew her own feelings had almost nothing to do with the past. If she'd never known Ty before, she thought she'd still be in love with him now. However, was the same true for him?

She wasn't naive. Alex knew there had to have been many women in Ty's life since he'd gone away. He had changed from a handsome boy to a devastatingly attractive man. He was rich, intelligent, sophisticated. If the two of them hadn't shared a bittersweet romance, would Ty have ever even looked at her?

Alex knew he cared for her. She knew he desired her. But how much of that was tied up in memories? Was she really the sort of woman with whom he could build a future?

Without selling herself short, Alex knew she wasn't beautiful. She was an attractive, thirty-year-old high-school teacher in a small southern town. With a world full of bright, willing younger women, she wondered if Ty would even spare her a second glance if they didn't have a history.

But Sally said he loved her. Alex sat across the table from the brother and sister, watching them laugh and joke. They were very much alike, and despite the years Ty had stayed away, they were close. He'd confessed to Alex that Sally's ability to sense his thoughts had always been a little unnerving. Surely if anyone knew how Ty really felt, it would be Sally.

The thought cheered Alex, and she shrugged off her doubts. The only choice she had was to follow Sally's advice and wait for Ty to tell her his feelings. She put aside her worries and enjoyed the rest of the day with his family.

For the next few days, Ty and Alex continued as before, spending most of every day and night together. On Tuesday they took Cody and Laura fishing, coming home exhausted with only two puny fish and a wealth of mosquito bites for their efforts.

On Wednesday it rained. While Ty spent the day at the mill, Alex stayed at the cabin. The air had turned unseasonably cool at the lake, and she'd lit a warming blaze in the fireplace. A casserole bubbled in the oven, filling the cabin with a rich, spicy aroma. The room's only light came from the fire, and Alex, seated in front of the hearth, her head pillowed on a large cushion, felt her eyelids growing heavy.

Ty stood on the cabin's threshold, drinking in the quiet peace of the scene. All these years, when he'd come home to an empty apartment, he'd wondered what was missing. Even when a willing young woman had joined him there, he'd always felt alone. Now, here in a tiny, crude house lacking many of the creature comforts he'd grown used to, he finally had all he'd ever wanted.

With scarcely a moment's hesitation he lay down beside Alex in front of the fire, waking her gently with a kiss. She struggled out of the fog of sleep, and his kiss deepened, invading the far reaches of her mouth with his seeking tongue.

"Ummmmm," she murmured. "What a nice way to wake up."

"I can think of nicer ways," Ty whispered, his hands impatiently tugging her full cotton skirt up over her thighs.

"Yes, much nicer," Alex agreed, shifting her body so that he could pull her lacy panties down her legs and toss them aside. His mouth claimed hers again while his hand stroked the soft skin of her inner thighs, his fingers moving ever upward until they encountered the moist, welcoming juncture between her legs. She moaned, a low, throaty sound of pure pleasure.

"Do you like that?" he said against her mouth. Alex's only answer was the nod of her head. "So do I." He grasped one of her hands and held it against the front of his jeans, closing his eyes as she cupped the full, straining bulge.

Alex kissed him again, her mouth wet and open, while her hand unsnapped his jeans and drew the zipper downward. With what seemed like agonizing slowness to Ty, her fingers finally closed around him. Now he was the one who moaned.

"Do you like that?" Alex murmured.

His answer was the lazy motion of his hand between her legs and the hot taste of his lips on hers.

Alex quivered under his touch and felt his reaction in the hardening against her palm. So she followed her instincts, tugging his jeans farther down his legs and rolling him back onto the floor, following him, her hips spreading over his, her hand guiding him inside her. He braced himself with his hands, sitting up so that their bodies were joined from shoulder to hip. Alex locked her legs around him and, looking deep into his eyes, began to move.

Ty met each thrust of her hips with a parry of his own, taking pleasure in watching the ebb and flow of sensations on her face. So deep inside her was he that it seemed they surrounded each other, flowing in and out of each other's souls like a tide—ceaseless in its coming and going, measureless in its power to give satisfaction.

For it was satisfaction Alex sought, satisfaction she searched for with total abandon. She drew off her soft sweater, and Ty's fingers nimbly unhooked her pink lace-edged bra, covering her ripe, puckering nipples with his hands, dipping his head to capture them with his mouth. Throwing back her head, Alex accepted his attentions with eagerness, her hands holding him against her breast. She rocked even harder against his body, till the tide of their passion turned into a waterfall, a tumbling spill of erotic delight. With a tiny cry she relaxed and fell back with him against the cushion on the floor.

Later, warmed by the fire and their fevered lovemaking, they lay content in each other's arms until the smell of the burning casserole began to permeate the room.

The impetuousness of this joining was nothing new. Their need for each other was always just beneath the surface. Caught up in the magic of another summer, they made love whenever and wherever they could—in the car on isolated country roads, behind locked doors at the mill while workmen pounded nails and repaired leaks, in the library at Alex's home while her family slept.

As her lover, Ty was all Alex remembered, all she had ever hoped to find again. However, they were joined by more than sex. They had become friends. They laughed. They talked. They shared viewpoints and ideas. And sometimes there was no need for words. There was joy in silently watching the sun set over the mountains beyond the lake, in feeling the coolness of a summer morning or hearing the high, sparkling laughter of a child.

Ty was especially pleased when Alex expressed interest in his company, and he took pride in telling her all she wanted to know. In turn she told him more about teaching, about her frustrations with parents who didn't care and children who didn't try.

As July turned to August, Alex and Ty drew closer. The shadows of the past disappeared as today's needs and today's common interests sent them forward toward a shared tomorrow. Sally had said Ty loved Alex. He was with her day and night, attentive, kind, loving. For now, that was all Alex needed.

As always, it was her mother who shattered the peace.

The first full week of August took Ty away to Atlanta for a few days. After only forty-eight hours Alex missed him as if he'd been gone for a week. She spent the morning in the kitchen, her lesson plans from last year spread across the round table by the bay window. In three weeks school would begin. In only two she would be meeting with the other teachers, preparing for another year.

The sound of her mother's wheelchair caught Alex's attention, and she greeted Lucia with a smile. "Are you ready for lunch? Clarissa went shopping about an hour ago, but she left some chicken salad. Gina and Carrie are gone, so I guess it's just you and me."

"I'm not really hungry." The older woman drew to a stop beside the table. "Getting ready for in-service training?"

"I decided to get some work done while I could. Ty is in Atlanta."

"He goes there quite a bit."

"The main part of his company is there."

"Oh." The word was weighted with meaning, and Alex frowned, wondering what her mother was thinking.

"Is there something wrong with that?" she asked, trying to appear unconcerned as she picked up her pen and flipped through a stack of papers.

"If it doesn't concern you, then I guess I shouldn't say anything." Lucia plucked the morning newspaper from the table and opened it, appearing to scan the front page.

Alex ground her teeth together, wanting to ignore her mother's comments yet unable to do so. "Should I be concerned about Ty going to Atlanta, Mother?"

Her mother peered over the top of the paper and turned a page, giving a little sigh. "Oh, Alexa, I just wish you weren't so trusting of other people. You're just like your father."

"I have every reason to trust Ty," Alex replied stoutly.

Lucia's short laugh was her only answer. She shrugged her shoulders and went back to skimming through the paper.

Pen poised in hand, Alex sat watching her mother, wishing she could let the subject drop. Her mother had always known the exact buttons to push to get to her, and Alex had never built up the necessary defenses to dilute the effect. Now, as always, she pursued the matter.

"What are you getting at, Mother?"

Laying the paper down resignedly, Lucia gave her daughter a pitying glance. "Don't you ever wonder if there's someone in Atlanta whom he sees?"

"No."

"I don't know how you can be so naive, dear. I mean, Tyler is attractive in a crude sort of way, and he does have money."

"If there was someone in Atlanta, it's over now," Alex said with determination.

"You're probably right. Tyler was never stupid, and he knows a good thing."

"What does that mean?" Alex's voice was tight with growing anger.

"He's come back the conquering hero. He owns the place where his family worked for three generations. He's got the right sort of woman." Lucia folded the paper and laid it on the table, pointing to a picture. "And he's got the entire town eating out of his hand. He enjoys being the big fish in the little pond."

Alex studied the newspaper photograph. It showed Ty posing with members of the chamber of commerce at the ceremony officially welcoming his company as a part of the business community. He looked handsome, self-assured and very pleased with himself.

Looking back at her mother, Alex said, "What does this matter? His company is going to be an important part of Grayson's future."

"And having you on his arm at all these little parties you've been going to, that hasn't helped his welcome?" Raising her eyebrows meaningfully, Lucia shook her head.

Alex rose to her feet and began stacking her papers, agitation making her movements jerky. "All right, Mother, you've succeeded in making me feel worthless, just as you always do."

"I'm only trying to help you see him as he really is," Lucia retorted.

"And how is that?"

"A nothing, a nobody who made a little money."

"Mother, Ty is far from a nobody. He's a sensitive, intelligent man. He's come a very long way in a very short time. Not many people make it to his level of success so young. Your problem is that you're stuck in the prejudices and assumptions of a time that is gone forever." Alex picked up her stack of papers and walked to the doorway. "This is not 1940, Mother. And you're not a debutante belle, cavorting with only the 'best' people."

Lucia rolled around to face her, blue eyes blazing angrily. "I know those days are gone. And more's the pity. At least then a smart woman knew to get a wedding ring before she crawled into a man's bed."

"Mother!"

"Has he said anything about marriage?"

"Mother, I—"

Lucia's voice rose. "I said, has he asked you to marry him, Alexa?"

Alex snapped, "No! I haven't expected it. We're getting to know each other again...."

"When will you know each other well enough to think about marriage? When you're pregnant again?"

Alex gasped. "I'm not going to stand here and let you turn what I have with Ty into something cheap and ugly, Mother. I love him." Her voice was vehement and thick with emotion.

Lucia looked down and straightened her already perfectly creased skirt. "So you keep saying. But does he love you?"

With a little cry, Alex whirled around and ran through the hall, slamming the stack of papers she carried onto a foyer table and snatching up her purse. She didn't care that she was leaving her mother, who was never left alone, without anyone in attendance. All she knew was that she had to get away from Lucia's hurtful words, words that struck at the heart of all of Alex's fears and doubts.

She knew in her heart Ty wasn't the sly opportunist her mother thought him. He'd said they'd follow the road and see where it took them. But where were they going? Would they simply drift through another summer?

With nowhere else to go, Alex drove to Ty's cabin and spent the afternoon huddled on the couch, utterly miserable, beset by doubts. She called home once to make sure Clarissa was home to see to Lucia's needs, and left a message not to expect her home anytime soon.

It was in the darkened, silent cabin that Ty found her later that night. He switched on a lamp and sent her a surprised look. Her red, swollen eyes gave evidence of recent tears. "What's wrong?" he asked, crossing the room to sit beside her.

"I missed you," she answered in a small voice. She trembled as his arms closed about her.

"What happened?"

"Mother." The one word explained it all to Ty. Lucia wasn't about to give up. She didn't want her daughter involved with him, and she would stop at nothing to make sure they were torn apart.

"What did she say?"

Alex laughed shortly, the sound catching in her throat like a sob. "Oh, she had lots of nice things to tell me about women who crawl into bed with social-climbing nouveau-riche playboys who run off to Atlanta to other women."

"Damn her." The words were torn from Ty. He'd have liked nothing more than to choke the interfering old woman.

"That's the way she sees it, Ty. I keep hoping she'll just want me to be happy." Alex's eyes filled with tears as she looked up at him. "Why is it we never get past trying to win our parents' approval?"

"I don't know, honey." He caught her close again and pressed a gentle kiss against her temple, breathing in her natural sweet fragrance. "You don't believe all those things she said, do you?"

"Of course not!"

"Then why let it bother you?"

"I don't know."

"Then forget it."

"I wish it were that easy." Alex sighed and then sat up. "Let's go away for a while. Take me to Atlanta or somewhere. This town is suffocating us."

"Okay," Ty agreed quickly, eager to please her. "I need to go back to the office Monday, anyway. You can come with me. I want everyone to meet you."

"I'd like that."

"Then we'll go over to South Carolina. The company has a condo at Myrtle Beach."

The beach. Alex closed her eyes, thinking gratefully of the ocean, the sun and the sand. "That sounds like the answer to a poor schoolteacher's prayers."

"Good. We'll leave Sunday morning."

Tenderly he kissed the soft curve of her cheek and rocked her in his arms.

Chapter Nine

I'm going to call Marti and Chuck and see if they'll have dinner with us," Ty told Alex as he led the way inside his Atlanta condominium. He set down the suitcases he was carrying and glanced at his watch. "We're a little later than I expected, so I'd better call them now. Make yourself at home."

Alex nodded, closed the door and followed Ty through a narrow black-and-white tiled foyer into a spacious living room. While he dialed his friends' number, she looked around with interest. Disappointingly, the room told her little about Ty she didn't already know.

It was an elegant yet masculine room. The plush carpet underneath was silvery gray, the walls white, the furniture a sleek mixture of black leather, chrome and glass. In the abstract paintings, pillows and accessories, the somber theme was brightened with snatches of teal blue and plum. White mini-blinds shuttered a wall of glass behind the black lacquered pedestal desk where Ty sat talking on the phone.

Nowhere were there photographs or mementos. The room looked as perfect and as impersonal as a designer showcase.

To the left, Alex spied a dining area where a smoked-glass table was flanked by six gray tweed-upholstered chairs. A bar separated the room from a kitchen filled with gleaming aluminum appliances. It was a beautiful group of rooms, but it didn't feel like a home. Alex wondered if Ty spent any time here at all. And if not, where did he spend his time? Her mother's suspicions, well planted, threatened to grow.

She turned as Ty hung up the phone and began opening the blinds that covered the windows. "Chuck and Marti want us to come over for dinner. You're really going to like them."

"I'm sure I will," Alex replied, feeling a bubble of nervousness rise in her chest. She wanted Ty's friends to like her. To keep her mind off the coming meeting, she gestured to the room. "Your condo is gorgeous. You told me it was nothing fancy."

"It's okay," Ty said carelessly as he tugged the last set of blinds open. "I don't spend a lot of time here."

"Because you travel so much?" Alex joined him at the window and stood looking at a flower-lined brick terrace. She hoped that was the reason for the home's impersonal feeling.

"With no one to come home to, this place isn't very welcoming." He looped an arm across her shoulders. "It's nice to see you here. You'll warm the place up."

Alex returned his smile, pleased with the compliment. "Then show me around. I want to unpack and get ready to meet your friends."

Ty led her back to the entry foyer and down a short hall. To the right was a small, book-lined den. A worn easy chair in front of the television set told Alex that Ty spent at least some time here. Another door on the left revealed a guest bedroom and bath decorated in a striking mixture of peach and gray.

The door at the end of the hall revealed the master bedroom suite. "Oh," Alex murmured, stepping inside. "This is beautiful."

The carpet was again gray, but here there was more color. The walls were a textured paper of creamy pearl. The bedspread was rich plum, and the paintings on the walls glowed with purples, violets and blues. Another wall of glass separated the room from a small, plant-filled terrace. The brick walls were high enough to ensure total privacy, but allowed sunlight to spill into the room.

"This is my favorite part," Ty told her with a mischievous grin as he pulled open a mirrored door and led the way into an expansive bath.

A huge plum-colored tub was set in the floor to their right. Beyond it, sliding glass doors opened onto the private bedroom terrace. To the left, two steps down, were a walk-in closet and a vanity with double sinks. The shower and toilet were through a door at the end of the room. Everywhere the colors were black, white and plum.

Alex looked at Ty with eyes that were round with pleasure. "This is the perfect seduction pit, you know."

"Of course. I bought the unit before it was finished, and the interior designer modeled the whole layout to suit the needs of a bachelor." He grinned wickedly.

"Did she ever come back to try it out?" Alex asked, touching the sleek marble finish of the vanity top.

"Who?"

"The interior designer. Did she ever come back as your guest?"

Ty laughed, shaking his head. "She's the mother of one of my employees. Married forty years, with five kids and fifteen grandchildren. Her only vice is designing seductive bathrooms."

"I wonder where she gets her ideas."

"Staying married that long requires a romantic soul, don't you think?" Ty asked.

"I suppose." Alex stared about her in wonder until the sound of running water caught her attention. Reflected in the mirror over the sink, Ty was standing beside the tub, shedding his navy polo shirt. "What are you doing?"

"I'm going to put this tub to the use my decorator intended." He quickly divested himself of his clothes and advanced toward Alex with a predatory gleam in his eyes.

"Ty, I haven't even unpacked, and I . . ." she began feebly.

"So what?" Ignoring her protests, Ty helped her out of her clothes. He spent several moments kissing her, and the tub was completely filled by the time Alex was undressed.

She stepped into the tub, closing her eyes as the warm, soothing water closed over her body. Ty flipped a switch, and the water began to bubble and churn as he joined her. Sighing, Alex leaned against the side, letting the motion of the water lull her into total relaxation.

"All we need is bubble bath," she murmured. Through partially closed eyes she watched with amusement as Ty poured some crystals into the water, and soon they were surrounded by fragrant white foam.

"You've seen too many James Bond movies," she teased. "Now you're going to expect some sort of erotic bathroom adventure."

"Exactly," he concurred, pulling her away from the side and into his embrace. He trailed his hand through her dampened dark hair and, cupping her neck, brought his lips up to meet his.

The oil from the bath crystals made their skin slippery, and Ty rubbed his body enticingly against Alex's. He could feel the tightening of her nipples as her breasts flattened against his chest. His body stirring in response, he guided her backward to rest against the side. Her smooth legs wound around his hips, drawing him closer against her even as her lips made promises of coming delights.

"You don't know how many times I've fantasized about this," Ty whispered, his hands slipping lower to close on the rounded shape of her buttocks.

"About having me in your sinful tub?"

"No, about having you in my life." Grasping her hips firmly, he slipped inside her.

Alex's eyes flew open, and she stared up into his turbulent gray ones. "You fantasized about me?"

Ty pushed himself a little deeper. "Always."

"Why?" she said breathlessly, her wide brown eyes just inches from his.

"Because no one else ever came close," he murmured, beginning to move inside her with strong, measured strokes.

"Close...to...what?" Alex managed to gasp out the words, her body trembling from the arousal sweeping upward from her loins.

The rhythm of his body stopped, and he brought her hand up to his chest and held it over his heart. "Close to this."

Alex stared up at him for a long moment before she whispered, "I know. Believe me, I know what you mean."

They shared a lingering intimate glance before Alex's legs tightened around Ty's body and he surged into her.

Her hands gripped the edge of the tub, and she laid her head back against the side, her hair trailing out on the tiled floor. She shut her eyes, delighting in each thrust of Ty's body. Her senses swam and then melted together until she couldn't decide which was more sensual—the feel of him pulsing inside her or the fragrance of the jasmine-scented water, the taste of his mouth or the deep timbre of his voice as he murmured tender endearments against her throat.

Ty was enchanted by the sight of Alex. The pink tips of her breasts rose enticingly out of the white bubbles, and a rosy flush of excitement stained her cheeks. A shimmer of bath oil gleamed on the tanned skin of her shoulders. She drew a shuddering breath, and her lips parted. He watched, fascinated, as she moistened her mouth with her tongue. She was every dream he'd ever had, every desire he'd ever expressed.

The hands that held her soft, yielding bottom now slid upward, his thumbs skimming across her breasts. Shivering slightly, she opened her eyes and looked at him, a look that was soft with yearning, clouded with passion. With a languid motion she let go of the sides of the tub and allowed her arms to wind around his neck, drawing him closer still as his arms encircled her body. His movements inside her, slow until now, increased in tempo, and her golden-brown eyes widened, then closed as he pushed her up, up and over into a final burst of pleasure. He followed quickly.

Ty held her there in the bubbling water against the side of the tub, his breath coming in gasps. "I meant what I said," he said low against her ear when at last he could speak. "There's never been anyone else I cared for."

Her answer was a smile that dazzled and arms that clasped him even closer.

There was more Ty wanted to say. He wanted to pour out his heart to Alex, to tell her how very much he loved her, how that loving had never ceased. But as always he felt the need to go slowly, to take their relationship one careful step at a time.

So he made himself content to merely hold her, to stroke her body tenderly, to feel her response to his closeness. Holding his feelings in check was the hardest task Ty felt he'd ever undertaken.

The serious mood was dispelled in a quick shower where they washed the traces of bath oil from their bodies and hair—then it was a rush to get ready for dinner in time. But Alex was almost grateful for the haste; it gave her less time to dwell on the meaning behind Ty's words or to get nervous about the coming meeting.

She'd chosen her evening's outfit with care, hoping to impress Ty's friends. The simple white dropped-waist dress set off her tan, and her dangling gold earrings and bangle bracelets added an elegant note. Ty assured her she looked just fine as they drove to the Martin's home in a nearby Atlanta suburb.

They drew to a stop in front of a rambling colonial house. Bicycles and toys littered the walk, and the front door stood ajar, as if someone had forgotten to close it. The scene was welcoming.

Inside, the same welcome reigned. Marti and Chuck Martin were in their late thirties. He was tall and thin, studious-looking in his round glasses. She was a petite redhead with a friendly smattering of freckles across her upturned nose.

Regarding Alex with frankly curious green eyes, Marti said, "Go ahead and laugh now over the name."

"What?" Alex replied, puzzled.

"Marti Martin," the redhead supplied. "My mother told me I was asking for punishment if I married this guy, so I like to get the laughter out of the way up front when I meet someone new."

"I'd never laugh," Alex returned, smiling.

"Good. I'm kind of attached to the name after fifteen years." Marti slipped an arm affectionately around her husband's waist. "Why don't you guys go outside and start cooking that barbecued chicken while Alex and I get acquainted?" She shooed Ty and Chuck outside, but the men were quickly replaced by the Martins' three boys.

"Danny's thirteen, Mitchell is ten and Buster's four," Marti said, introducing the trio of carrot-topped youngsters.

"Are you Unca Ty's girfwiend?" Buster demanded, fixing Alex with an unwavering gaze.

"Yes, I am."

He studied her solemnly for several moments before breaking into a gamin smile. "Okay," he said, and all three boys scampered away.

"Well, you've passed the test. Buster absolutely rules this house. He was our last attempt at having a girl, and ever since he arrived the other boys have sort of accepted his opinion on everything." Laughter bubbled naturally out of Marti, and she shook her head.

"Why do you call him Buster?" Alex ventured, following her to the kitchen.

"Can you imagine calling him Randolph Charles Henry Martin the Third?"

Now Alex giggled. "I guess Buster does fit a little better."

"Right. Never has a household been so dominated by a four-year-old." Marti turned the corner into the kitchen. The room was obviously the center of family activity. A jigsaw puzzle was laid out on the dinette table, opened bags of cookies and chips littered the counters and a pile of towels and toys lay near the French doors. Through them Alex glimpsed a pool and patio where Ty and Chuck hovered over a grill.

"How about some wine?" Marti asked.

"White, please." Alex perched on a stool near the room's central work island and accepted the glass of Chablis Marti proffered.

"So you're the one."

"Pardon?"

"The one who's been keeping Ty in his home town."

Alex sipped at her drink, swallowed and said casually, "Business is keeping him occupied, too."

"But you're the attraction."

Smiling, Alex replied, "I hope so."

"I do, too." At Alex's quizzical look, Marti continued, "Over the past eight years I've tried to set Ty up with every eligible female who crossed my path. It never clicked. Then, early this summer, Linda Bartow told me Ty was seeing an old girlfriend again—"

"Doesn't she work for Ty and Chuck?"

"Yes, and she and Ty are friends."

"I'm looking forward to meeting her."

"Good. I invited Linda and her daughter for dinner tonight, also."

"So you're all friends."

Marti's glance was shrewd. "Honey, when a woman who looks like Linda Bartow goes to work for your husband, you make it a point to become her friend."

"Oh," Alex replied lamely, and glanced about the room, trying to remember everything Ty had told her about Linda. Maybe she was the reason his condo looked barely lived-in. Maybe Ty spent more time at Linda's than at home.

As if sensing her unease, Marti reassured her. "You've got nothing to worry about from Linda. There's nothing between her and Ty but friendship. Maybe once there was a chance for something else, but Ty never gave it a second thought." She opened the door to the microwave and began placing potatoes inside. "Something tells me you're the one Ty has been carrying the torch for all these years."

"Has he carried a torch?" Alex asked, pleased by the other woman's frankness.

Marti stared at her openmouthed. "In case you haven't noticed, Alex, the man is a certified hunk. Women have been chasing him for years, even before he and Chuck started the company and started making real money."

"Yes, but that doesn't mean I'm—"

Marti interrupted. "It means something. Back when Chuck and Ty were on the road selling for the same company, Chuck would come home with all kinds of stories about women throwing themselves at Ty. He wasn't a monk, I'll grant you that, but he never got serious about anyone. Why, this summer is the first real vacation I've known him to take for years."

"Why?" Alex felt compelled to ask.

"He buried himself in the company."

"It's paid off."

"Yes, but I'm glad to see he finally realized there's more to life than making and selling carpets. You're good for him, Alex. I've seen the changes in him the few times he's been back in town this summer. I see it now."

Marti opened a cabinet and withdrew a stack of plates. "Now come on, let's drop this serious stuff. Help me set the dining-room table and tell me about yourself. Ty says you teach high-school English. Maybe you can tell me how to get a thirteen-year-old to forget about horror movies and read the classics."

The two women talked and worked companionably for the next half hour, and Alex opened up to the pert redhead. Marti was forthright and honest and plainly delighted to see Ty involved with Alex.

"Where is everybody?" a female voice called from the front of the house.

"That's Linda," Marti told Alex. Then she called, "We're in the kitchen. Come on out."

A few moments later one of the most stunning women Alex had ever seen walked through the door. Model slim, Linda Bartow had the bright blond hair one associates with California beaches. Her skin was flawless, her features perfect, her unusual amber eyes shining with friendliness. She wore her simple blue jersey sheath with understated elegance. It was difficult to believe the thin teenage girl trailing behind her could possibly be her daughter.

"You're Alex," Linda said in her pleasant southern drawl. "Ty has told me so much about you. This is my daughter, Sarah."

"Hello." Alex included both of them in her cheerful greeting, and relaxed. Gorgeous Linda might be, but she seemed genuine and friendly.

Ty ambled into the kitchen at that moment. "I see you've met," he said, crossing the room to stand beside Alex.

"Yes, but since Sarah and I are running late as usual, we've only just said hello," Linda told him.

"You're always late, Linda." Marti chuckled. "I figured out long ago you wanted to avoid any part of the cooking."

Linda's laugh was low and husky, like her voice. "You know I hate cooking, Marti, but I always help do the dishes."

"Chicken's done!" Chuck interrupted from the doorway. He carried a heaping platter of barbecued chicken.

"See, I'm right on time," Linda said, and everyone laughed.

Dinner was fun. The conversation was quick and witty. The four children were well behaved. Her nervousness and suspicions completely forgotten, Alex talked about college English requirements with Linda and Sarah and argued good-naturedly with Chuck about a book they'd both read.

Ty made his affection for her obvious throughout the evening, holding her hand when the adults went to the living room for coffee, kissing her from time to time. The looks the other three sent their way were approving, and Alex was grateful for the unconditional acceptance. From everything Ty had told her, she knew these people were important to him. She wanted to be counted as one of them.

As Linda and Sarah were leaving, Linda took Alex's hand and gave it a little squeeze. "Welcome to the group. I'll see you in the morning at the mill. Ty says you're going to come in to work with him."

"Yes, I'll see you tomorrow." Alex squeezed her hand back. "And thanks, Linda."

The blonde gave her a wink and glanced at Ty. "I'm glad to see this bachelor so happily shackled."

On the drive to his condo, Ty thought how well Alex had fit in with his friends. Not that he needed their approval, but he was happy anyway. "Nice evening, wasn't it?" he said at last.

"It was great."

"Why so quiet?"

Alex sighed. "I was wondering how you managed to work so closely with Linda and not fall in love with her. She's stunning."

"She's okay."

"Okay? Ty, she's perfect."

"Maybe she is, but neither Linda nor anyone else has ever compared with you."

Alex was silent as Ty brought the car to a stop in front of his home. Before he could open the door, she put a detaining hand on his arm. "Thank you for making me so happy," she said simply, a slight catch in her voice.

Leaning forward, Ty kissed her lightly on the forehead. "I assure you, ma'am, the pleasure is all mine."

Later that night they made love beneath the cool satin sheets of Ty's water bed, and Alex curled tightly against his side. Ty lay awake until he felt her relax into slumber. Then, holding her loosely, he stared out at the darkened terrace, wondering how he'd ever come to deserve a second chance.

The next few days were a dizzying circle of new faces and places for Alex. Monday she accompanied Ty to the mill, and there she discovered a new dimension to his personality.

From the moment they walked through the door, Ty was the complete executive. He took Alex on a quick tour of the facility with its noisy tufting machines and hard-at-work employees. She was introduced to key people, men and women who had been with DunMar Carpets from the beginning. Everyone looked busy and the work seemed difficult, but Alex sensed an air of well-being, as if it were a pleasant place to work.

There was respect on the faces of these people as they talked with Ty, and he seemed to genuinely care about them. He asked workers about children and spouses, calling the family members by name, bringing a smile to many faces with his thoughtfulness.

"How do you remember everything about so many people?" Alex asked him when they finally retreated to his office on the second floor.

"I learned it in sales. To sell a man or woman something you have to establish a rapport with them. To do that you've got to remember something more than how much money they spent with you last quarter."

"I guess that makes sense."

"Sure it does. The same applies to management. You just can't expect the best from people if you don't act interested in them." Ty gestured at the piles of papers littering his desk. "Do you mind reading or something while I work through this mess?"

"Of course not." Alex drew a paperback book from her bag, but she read very little. She turned the pages, but it was Ty who captured her attention. He made what seemed to be a hundred phone calls, haggling with suppliers, soothing a major dealer in Detroit and chastising one of his district sales managers. Pretending to read, Alex sat quietly in the corner, impressed by Ty's efficient manner.

Linda stopped by late in the morning. Her friendliness of the evening before was still evident, but as she discussed several problems with Ty she was all business. "I want you to meet the new buyer from Big Star Carpets in Houston."

"I can't fly out before the first of next week," Ty told her, sending Alex a smile.

"He's coming here—tonight," Linda said briskly.

"Dinner?" Ty asked.

"He expects to be wined and dined. If this order comes through, it'll be the largest single buy they've ever placed with us. He wants to meet the top dog."

"But you're the top dog." Ty gave her an impudent grin.

"I know that and you know that, but this guy wants to go a little higher."

Ty sent Alex a helpless look. "Do you mind?"

"Not at all," Alex agreed. "I'd sort of like to see the top dog in action myself."

Ty stood and pulled on his jacket. "Well, come on, ladies, I'll take you both to lunch and we'll map out our strategy for the evening. The guy won't know what hit him when I show up with two beauties."

At lunch Linda explained to Alex what a chance Ty and Chuck had taken by promoting her to vice president for sales and marketing.

"It was bad enough when they made me district sales manager," the blonde explained. "When I became VP they actually got calls of protest."

"Why?" Alex said.

Linda gave a short, mirthless laugh. "It's a chauvinistic business, and other companies didn't want any precedent set."

"But you didn't listen, did you?" Alex asked Ty.

"Not for a moment. Linda's the best for the job." Pushing his seat away from the table, Ty excused himself. "I'm really sorry, but I just remembered a call I have to make."

Alex followed his progress through the restaurant before turning back to Linda. "Are things always this frantic?"

"Pretty much. But Ty loves it this way. In fact, if he has any flaws as a boss, it's that he sometimes can't understand when his employees don't love the company the way he does. He hasn't always accepted that many of us have families and commitments other than our work."

Alex found Linda's candor a testimony to the friendship and trust the woman had in Ty as her boss. Many people wouldn't dare criticize an employer—even slightly. "*You* seem awfully dedicated, Linda. Do you put anything ahead of your work?"

She nodded. "My daughter and my parents always come first. Once, when my mother became ill, I left an important meeting in Chicago to come home. At first Ty was furious, but Chuck took my side and we worked it out." Linda glanced at Alex, her eyes candid. "Maybe now, since Ty has someone he cares for, he'll be more understanding."

"Maybe," Alex agreed, hoping the other woman was right. Later, as she waited for Ty to finish up a "few" more items of business that took all afternoon, she wondered if anything would come before his company.

It was obvious he was a tough businessman. How else could he and Chuck have come so far so fast? Unbidden, Lucia's taunts about Ty using Alex to further his position in the Grayson business community came to mind. Alex tried to put aside her unease, telling herself Ty wasn't that hard or ruthless. However, as the day wore on, she began to see that Ty brooked no argument on matters he thought important to the business.

He was always courteous and polite, but he was always firm. While Alex listened, he ran down a foul-up in shipping that had cost the company a large order. She couldn't help but feel a pang of sympathy for the person who had caused the error and received Ty's dressing-down. He also talked with the personnel director who would be supervising the taking of applications for workers in the new Grayson plant. Ty had specific ideas about the type of employee he wanted and the procedures to be used in testing and hiring.

At dinner with the buyer from Houston, Alex saw still another side to Ty's business nature. He was charming and deferential, even as he refused to give the Houston firm an additional two-percent discount. Alex listened, amazed, as the buyer agreed to all of Ty's terms and even upped his order substantially.

"The top dog turned that guy into a pussycat," she said in the car going home.

"He just wanted to see how far he could push us," Ty replied easily.

"You were pretty tough."

"I thought I was nice."

"Slick as glass nails being hammered into his heart."

"Oh, come on, that's just business."

Alex sighed. "Does anything come between you and success?"

Catching the serious note in her voice, Ty glanced at her in concern. "What do you mean?"

"Nothing," she mumbled.

"No, what is it?"

Pausing only a second, Alex said, "After watching you today, I just wondered if anything was as important to you as this company."

Ty concentrated on navigating through the heavy traffic for a moment. "DunMar Carpets means a lot to me, but not enough to hurt anyone I care about—not you, my family or my friends. What made you ask that?"

"Watching you operate today," Alex explained tersely. "You seemed so different than when we're together, so...so cold."

"That's ridiculous. I just do my job."

"Well, I say my father missed out when he didn't put you into sales at Nelson Textiles."

"Your father missed out on a lot of things," Ty tossed out, his voice laced with bitterness.

"What does that mean?" Alex demanded.

"It means he wasn't much of a businessman."

"You mean he wasn't ruthless."

Ty's laugh was low and ugly. "Just not ruthless enough in the right places."

"And what does that mean?" Alex pressed.

But Ty had said enough. His lips were set in a grim line as he pulled the car to a stop outside his condominium. "Alex,

I don't want to talk about your father, okay? My memories of him just aren't the best. Let's drop it before we fight.''

"But—" Alex began.

"I'm not going to discuss him," Ty said, getting out of the car and punctuating his feelings with the slam of his door.

Following him inside, Alex decided to let the subject drop. However, it puzzled her that Ty never wanted to discuss her father. Sam Thorpe certainly hadn't been overjoyed by the prospect of having Ty as his son-in-law, but he hadn't been openly hostile, either. His arguments had centered on the fact that they were both young and lacked college educations. Her father had tried his best to curb Lucia's acidic attacks on Ty's family and background. He'd tried to understand their feelings. Alex had told Ty all of this. So why was he so bitter toward the man?

They went to bed without exchanging another word. After several minutes, Ty turned over on his side. "Alex?"

"Yes."

He lay completely still, considering his words carefully. Ty had decided at the outset never to tell Alex it was her father who had forced him to abandon her twelve years ago. She'd put the man so high on a pedestal that it was doubtful she'd accept that he was capable of such cruelty.

"What is it, Ty?" she pressed.

"I don't want to fight about your father. We just see him in different ways."

"Obviously."

"Let's forget it, okay?"

She sighed. "Fine." Ty's arms closed around her body, drawing her close to his side.

"And stop worrying about how important the company is to me. It's no competition for you."

Her heart thudded so hard against her chest Alex feared Ty would hear it. He kept telling her these sweet things—almost, but not quite, saying he loved her. Why didn't he come out with it? And, for that matter, why didn't she come right out and ask him? The words formed on her lips just as she heard his breathing change to the deep, even rhythm of sleep.

The next day Alex went shopping with Marti, splurging on beachwear and several naughty nighttime concoctions of ribbon and lace. She balked at spending so much money on such impracticalities, but Marti urged her on, saying, "Won't it be worth the price just to see Ty's face when he sees you in them?" Cheeks flaming, Alex agreed.

That night, Ty watched her pack for the beach, his eyebrows raising as she drew a scarlet-and-black lace teddy out of a shopping bag. "What's this?" he demanded, pulling the delicate garment out of her fingers.

"That's supposed to be a surprise," Alex protested, grabbing for the teddy.

"Let's check it out." He held the miniscule concoction of fabric and lace in front of her, studied it for a moment, then looked up at Alex, the familiar gleam of desire in his gray eyes. "This is going to be interesting."

"I knew you'd like it."

"Yeah, but you don't need ribbons and lace to drive me wild."

Ty tossed the teddy in Alex's suitcase and tumbled her unceremoniously across the bed, his hand tugging her lilac gown up over her thighs. Her laughter caught on a sharp little intake of breath as his lips brushed across her sensitive inner thighs. Then she gasped as his mouth pressed, hot and fierce, between her legs. His daring, intimate touch flooded her body with erotic sensation until she couldn't stifle the cries of pleasure that rose to her lips.

Much later, they fell asleep on top of the covers, suitcases still waiting to be filled.

After a short flight on the company plane the next day, they were in Myrtle Beach. Ty had reserved a rental car, and a short drive brought them to the beachfront high rise where DunMar Carpets maintained an apartment for the use of clients and employees.

Alex was overjoyed with her first glimpse of the blue-green waters, the breaking waves and the sun-dappled sand. Like children, she and Ty paused only long enough to open their bags and pull on swimsuits before racing outside to the water's edge.

"I love it!" she squealed as the first wave broke over her head. She came up sputtering, but her face was a study in delight. "I've missed the ocean."

Watching her scamper happily through the waves, Ty experienced a surge of well-being so complete he wondered how anything could destroy it. Nothing, he vowed silently, nothing would keep them apart again.

Their few short days at the beach seemed to pass too quickly. They walked through the sand to the boardwalk and rode a dozen dizzying amusement attractions. They played on the beach, building sand castles and riding the waves on canvas rafts. Ty even tried windsurfing, gliding across the white-capped peaks of water like a sun-bronzed god.

The resort offered a fascinating variety of restaurants. They dined on Mexican fare the first night at a place called Garcia's, and braved the lines of tourists to sample delicious seafood at Outrigger's.

But it was music this town was famous for—beach music. Ty took Alex to a dimly lit hotel lounge where they listened to a local band. Then, still wide awake despite the late hour, they wound up at Cowboy's, a country-music club, where a female singer was crooning songs of lost love and heartbreak.

They danced, swaying together on the tightly packed floor, reminiscing about the nights they'd spent at Nick's bar. When the singer's husky voice began the first verse of

Nick's favorite song, "Crazy," Ty's arms tightened around Alex, and they seemed to move in a world all their own.

"Maybe I'm crazy, just like the song," he said against her ear. "But I want you to know how much this week has meant to me, Alex—how much I love you."

Alex stumbled slightly, staring up at him, trying to read his expression through the smoky haze of the club. "You love me?" she repeated, raising her voice to make it heard above the music.

"Of course."

Grasping his arm, she drew him through the crowd to a darkened corner near the door. "Now say that again. Slowly."

Ty grinned and repeated, "I love you."

Her tears of happiness spilled over. "You don't know how much I've been hoping to hear that from you."

"And what about you?"

"Me?"

"Do you love me?"

"Oh, yes," she murmured breathlessly as her arms wound round his neck. "I never stopped."

They kissed in the velvet darkness of that corner until Ty broke the embrace and drew her behind him out the door. "Let's get out of here."

They hurried back to the condominium, but once there they were reluctant to go inside. Instead, they walked in the moonlight on the beach, content in being together, saying over and over the words each had longed to hear.

When finally they did go inside, they made love in a new way—without urgency. Only now, as Alex responded to Ty's gentle, loving touch, did she realize that every time they'd come together she'd been afraid it was the last time. Tonight, as her body trembled under his, she allowed herself to savor the taste of his skin, the hard, eager muscles of his body and his deep cry of pleasure as he spilled his seed into her.

Ty slept, but Alex couldn't. Wrapping herself in his heavy velour robe, she crept outside to the balcony, which faced the water. Dawn was breaking, turning the eastern sky a soft pink. As she watched, the sun spread gold-and-russet fingers across the water. The early-morning breeze was cool, and she nestled into the robe, which smelled of Ty, his musky after-shave and the fresh scent that was his alone. Never had she felt so content.

"Aren't you tired?" Ty's voice, husky with sleep, came from just behind her. Alex turned and saw that he'd draped his nude form with a sheet from the bed.

"I'm too happy to sleep." She pointed out across the ocean. "Anyway, how can you sleep with something this gorgeous happening just outside the window?"

Ty's arms slipped around her, drawing her into the folds of the sheet and against his body. "I have a request to make of you."

"Anything."

"Marry me."

Alex breathed a small, thankful prayer, but she kept her voice steady in answering. "Of course."

"Then you might want this." Ty held his fist out in front of her and opened it to reveal a glittering ring, its central pear-shaped diamond flanked by a quartet of smaller ones.

Turning in his arms, Alex let her tears fall unchecked. To her surprise, there was moisture on Ty's cheeks as well.

"I wasn't going to tell you I loved you for a while," he said in a voice thick with emotion. "I had this crazy idea that we had to take it real slow."

"I know. I did, too."

"But I've been carrying this ring around with me for a while, waiting...waiting for something...a bolt of lightning or something. Then, when it happened last night, I forgot about the ring!"

Their shaky laughter mingled until Ty said, "Don't you want to put it on?"

"I guess I forgot about that."

The sheet slipped from his shoulders and pooled at their feet as Ty drew her hand up and put the ring on her finger. His silver-touched eyes looked deep into hers. "I love you, Alexa Thorpe. I always have; I always will. Believe me?"

Her smiled rivaled the diamonds in brilliance as she answered, "Would I argue with a naked man on a balcony at dawn? This has to be love."

"Good. Come inside and show me." Gently Ty led her indoors and slipped the robe from her shoulders. As she stood there naked, silhouetted against the rising sun, he knew he'd never forget her beauty or the love that shone from her eyes.

Chapter Ten

The expression "walking on air" had never held any special significance for Ty. Until now. Until Alex had said she loved him, accepted his ring and his proposal of marriage. With those promises, he could honestly say his feet left the ground and he skimmed along somewhere at least a hundred feet from reality.

"I want a wedding," he told her on the way from the Atlanta airport to his condominium Sunday morning. "A big wedding, with everyone looking on as we promise to love, honor and cherish."

"Thank goodness you're not going to insist on me 'obeying' you," Alex teased.

"Honey, you can do almost anything you want as long as you just love me forever. That's all I want from you." His grin lit his gray eyes with teasing lights. "Except maybe two or three kids, that is."

"You don't ask for much, do you?"

Suddenly serious, Ty's voice deepened. "Only everything you have to give. Is that too much?"

"No, I want the same from you."

Lifting her hand, he kissed the finger that held his ring. "You've got it. You always have."

They drove back to Grayson that afternoon, going straight to Ty's mother's house. Rose Duncan greeted their news with tears of happiness.

"I've been waiting for this," she said, hugging her son. She turned to Alex and held her arms open wide. "I've always believed in happy endings. Welcome to the family."

Listening to his mother and Alex chatter about wedding plans, Ty had to blink away the moisture from his eyes. He'd never dreamed he'd love anyone as much as he loved Alex at this moment.

"Well, what does your family think?" Rose asked Alex.

"We haven't told them."

"Haven't told them?" Rose turned a reproving glance on her son. "Don't you think you should?"

"I was thinking about sending them a telegram, or maybe just an invitation to the wedding," Ty replied sheepishly.

"Coward."

"I don't deny it."

"Maybe I should tell them alone," Alex ventured.

"No," Rose said firmly. "This is something you should do together. I bet it won't be so hard once you get started." She pointed toward the door. "Now get going. I'm going to call Sally and Keith and give them the news."

Surprisingly, Rose was right. Telling the Thorpes was easier than Ty had anticipated. Carrie was ecstatic. Grady seemed pleased, and Gina kept whatever negative thoughts she might have to herself. Lucia accepted the news calmly.

Alex knelt beside her mother's wheelchair, covering the older woman's fragile hand with her own. "Please be happy for me, Mother. Be happy for us."

Ty didn't see how Lucia could resist the happiness in her daughter's face, but she was silent, gazing at Alex thoughtfully. Then she smiled, her striking cornflower-blue eyes full of love. And for the first time ever, Ty could see the resemblance between mother and daughter.

In a hushed tone, Lucia said, "If you're really happy, Alexa, if you're absolutely sure this is what you want, then I'll be happy, too."

"I'm absolutely, positively sure, Mother," Alex whispered.

Lucia cleared her throat and looked up at Ty. "And what about you, Tyler? Do you really love her?"

"I always have." His reply was strong, steady.

"And what about the past?" Lucia pressed, her eyes narrowing. "Is it truly behind you?"

It seemed to Ty there was a warning beneath her words, perhaps an entreaty not to tell Alex the complete truth about why he'd left twelve years before. He had no doubt Lucia knew about the beating, the warning and the threats. He'd even lay odds the entire setup had been her idea. For all her gentility, there was iron in this woman, a much harder core than her husband had ever possessed.

Ty didn't need the warning, however. He had no desire to rob Alex of her illusions about Sam Thorpe. Part of him knew there was no room for secrets between them now, but he ignored that tiny voice of reason and answered Lucia truthfully. "The past is over and done with. I've got no scores to settle. I only want Alex to be happy."

"Then we're in complete agreement." Lucia looked back at her daughter. "We have to have a party."

"I don't think—" Alex began.

Ty interrupted her. "That sounds like a terrific idea. We have to celebrate." Perhaps it was primitive of him, but the idea of announcing their engagement to a gathering of Sam and Lucia's friends was appealing. Maybe he'd just lied to Alex's mother. Maybe there still was a score to settle between the millworker's son and the owner's family. If so, being accepted by that family and by this town would surely appease the lingering trace of bitterness. He hoped so. He was tired of living with the hate. All he wanted was Alex in his life.

So they planned an engagement party, a wedding—and a life together.

Alex found herself caught in a never-ending swirl of activity. She prepared for another school year, spending most of every day in her classroom. The rest of the hot August days were taken up with addressing party invitations and selecting a wedding gown and dresses for Carrie and Suzie, her only attendants. Then there were wedding invitations for the planned late-September ceremony, meetings with the caterer and decisions about flowers, decorations and a place to live.

They'd be staying on in Grayson for at least the next year, probably in the house at the lake. After the mill was up and running, there was a good chance they'd move back to Atlanta. In the meantime, Alex would continue working, a plan Ty supported although he was anxious to start a family. Alex didn't care where they lived or where she worked; she only wanted a future shared with Ty.

The school year began, and Alex was busier than ever. However, she was full of energy for all the tasks and decisions demanding her attention. She hadn't been terribly keen on the idea of a big wedding at first, but now she just wanted it to be perfect—the right start to a perfect new life.

"What do you think?" she asked, turning from the bridal shop's full-length mirror to face her sister-in-law. "I really want your opinion, Gina. Do you think the dress is too young-looking for a thirty-year-old bride?" She was surprised to see tears glistening on the other woman's cheeks. "Gina?"

Hastily wiping her tears away, Gina smiled tremulously. "I'm sorry, Alex, I'm just so happy for you."

Alex felt her own eyes fill. "It seems like all we do these days is cry."

"Yes, well, that's what weddings are for—laughing and crying." Gina stepped forward and straightened the net veil that fell about Alex's shoulders. "And the dress is perfect. It suits you. Thirty is not too old for white lace and pearls."

"That's good, because I love it." Alex looked back into the mirror and studied her reflection with approval.

The dress was simple—white satin covered in lace, a flattering off-the-shoulder neckline, three-quarter-length sleeves, a dropped waist and a full, flowing skirt. The train was short, just a bit longer than the lace-edged veil that cascaded to the floor from a pearl-encrusted glittering circle. Sparkling highlights scattered throughout the veil haloed her face in brilliance. With the white silk flower bouquet she planned to carry, the effect would be dazzling.

Catching Gina's eyes in the mirror, Alex said, "I'm glad you think it's right. I always trust your judgment on clothes."

Gina smiled slightly as she knelt to shake out a fold of the satin skirt. "I think you could wear sackcloth and no one would notice anything but your smile, Alex. You're radiant."

"I feel radiant." Alex glanced down at the diamonds glittering on her hand. "Are you really happy for me?"

"Of course." The two women's eyes met again in the mirror.

"But you totally disapproved of me seeing Ty again. What happened?" Alex stepped down from the little pedestal in front of the mirror.

Gina hesitated a moment before speaking. "I was wrong. I was afraid he'd hurt you again."

"Ty told me all about why he left." Alex took off her veil and laid it across a chair.

Pausing only slightly, Gina undid the tiny buttons at the back of the wedding gown and slowly let down the zipper.

She turned away and picked up the veil, smoothing its folds. "Your mother said he got panicky about becoming a husband and father. Is that right?"

"Yes." In the mirror, Alex could see the troubled frown that came to Gina's face. Why did the woman always act so strangely when they discussed what happened that summer? "Don't you think that kind of feeling was understandable for a twenty-year-old?" she asked as she slipped out of her dress.

Gina took the garment and slipped it onto a hanger, busying herself by making sure the delicate material draped smoothly. She didn't answer Alex's question.

Alex stepped out of her full-length slip and reached for the cream-colored slacks and cotton sweater she'd worn into the shop. Gina's behavior was more and more puzzling, and she was determined to get to the bottom of it. "What do you know about that summer, Gina? You and Grady were in Birmingham."

"Your parents told us, and then of course when you ran away to Florida we were all very worried," Gina said, avoiding Alex's eyes as she zipped a protective plastic cover over the dress.

"But you've been acting weird about it ever since Ty came back."

"Have I?" Gina picked up her handbag from the dressing-room chair, drew out a lipstick and freshened the rosy color on her mouth. "I suppose the entire subject made me uncomfortable, Alex. But I was determined your mother wouldn't be upset. And I didn't want you hurt," she repeated.

Alex was silent, and the other woman continued. "I'm sorry I upset you. I'm just glad you and Ty are getting married, that you love each other and that you're really happy. I see now that everyone was wrong to keep you apart in the past."

The apology came straight from the woman's heart. Of that Alex was sure. Perhaps Alex needed to stop worrying about any information, real or imagined, that Gina had about the past. It was best forgotten. She linked her arm through Gina's and said, "Let's go over to the Taylor Inn and have something fattening. I think it's about time you and I got a little better acquainted. After all, you've been in the family seventeen years, and we've lived under the same roof for over three."

"I think you're right," Gina agreed easily. "It's about time we stopped acting like strangers."

The new feeling of closeness with her sister-in-law was only part of the changes taking place within Alex's family—her mother and Ty seemed to actually be getting along. The night before the engagement party she found them sitting on the back veranda, and Lucia was laughing. Pausing in the doorway, Alex stared at the two figures, blank with shock. Wonders will never cease, she thought, backing silently into the house. If Ty and her mother were having a civilized discussion, she didn't want to interrupt.

The day of the party dawned sunny and clear, a perfect September Saturday. Alex spent most of the day helping Clarissa, Gina and Carrie put the house in order. Lucia rolled from room to room, supervising everyone and getting in the way. Finally, by midafternoon, she pronounced the house ready and retired to her room for a nap.

"I'm going to rest before the caterers arrive with the food," Gina said just before answering the telephone. She held out the receiver. "It's for you, Alex."

The call was from Sally. She sounded frantic. "Alex, my shoes don't look right with the dress we picked out. You've got to help me find some others."

Alex sighed in resignation, agreeing to meet Sally at the mall. From the moment this party had been mentioned to Ty's sister, Sally had been a nervous wreck.

"These are *your* friends, Alex," she'd said. "Keith and I won't fit in."

"Nonsense," Alex replied. "There are lots of people you know coming, people you went to high school with."

"But I'm no good at these kinds of things, Alex. I'm strictly a pizza-and-beer-party person. I never know what to say or do."

"Don't be silly." Alex patted Sally reassuringly on the arm. "We'll find you a gorgeous dress, and all you'll have to do is smile and say hello to the people you don't know and really talk to those you do."

"You're sure?" Sally said doubtfully.

"I'm sure."

However, Sally's nervousness about the occasion had grown out of all proportion. She had permitted Alex to pick out a becoming dress, had even allowed Ty to pay for it and a new suit for Keith. Her husband was taking all the fuss in stride. He was busy these days, having finally given in and accepted a supervisory job from Ty at the mill. A full work force had been hired and was now being trained. The first product would roll off the line in about two weeks, just before the wedding.

Alex thought about how well everything was going for both her and Ty's families as she parked her car and hurried into the shopping mall to meet Sally. Maybe everything's going too well, she thought, but she quickly subdued the tiny prick of apprehension.

By the time the party began, Alex was too caught up in her roles as hostess and guest of honor to offer more than a passing thought to Sally's nerves. The evening began well, and Alex felt as beautiful as Ty told her she was in an ivory lace cocktail dress. At her side, he was handsome in a conservative gray suit as they positioned themselves with Lucia near the front door to greet the arriving guests. Soon the house was filled.

During a faint lull in conversation, Ty bent forward and whispered in Alex's ear, "Later, let's sneak away from this circus and go upstairs. You look entirely too prim and proper in your silk and lace. What have you got on under this thing, anyway?"

The promise in his deep, caressing tone sent a shiver of arousal through Alex, but she merely smiled and nodded to a newly arrived couple. "Stop trying to pretend you're not enjoying this, Tyler Duncan."

"You think I am?"

"I know you are. You can't fool me."

Of course, she was right. Ty was having a great time. The woman he loved was at his side, and there was acceptance in the faces of the people who greeted and congratulated him. He tried to tell himself the approval didn't mean anything, but failed. It was important to him. He'd come full circle from the troublemaking millworker, and he was damn proud of it.

He happily watched the aplomb with which his mother blended in with the other party guests. She had that rare ability to make herself at home in any situation. She talked easily with the cream of the town's social group and moved just as confidently to joke with a crowd of Ty's old high-school friends.

In fact, most everyone seemed to be getting along fine. Alex and Ty's two worlds seemed to be meshing at last. Moving through the press of people, which filled every room and spilled out onto the verandas, Ty felt happier and more at ease than ever in his life.

Ty did notice, though, that Sally didn't seem to be herself. Every time he spied her in the crowd she was laughing a little too loudly, and her champagne glass was always full. At a party that behavior was normally forgiven. But it was totally out of character for his sister at any time, and Ty worried that her nervousness had gotten the best of her.

He hadn't understood Sally's trepidation about this party. She and Alex had become friends, and Sally said she was pleased about the coming marriage. But somehow she couldn't seem to work through the differences in background between the Duncans and Alex and her family. For Sally, the stigma of being from the south side of the railroad tracks had left a mark.

Ty could identify with her feelings to a degree. After all, most of his adult life had been spent trying to overcome those same hang-ups. But to get so upset about a party? He couldn't see it.

The party was in full swing when, around ten o'clock, Lucia had a little bell rung and everyone crowded into the front sitting room and the foyer. Alex and Ty stood with Rose a little way up the stairs while Grady and Gina joined Lucia at the bottom of the stairs. With the melodrama she could always be counted on to inject, Lucia offered a toast: "To my daughter, Alexa, and to her intended, Tyler. May they be happy." A ripple of agreement ran through the crowd as glasses were lifted and champagne was drunk. In the little hush that followed the toast, Lucia added, "I only wish Alexa's father could be here to see how very, very happy she is."

Like a bomb, Sally's giggle split the poignant silence. "Oh, God, why? He'd only have Ty thrown out of town again."

"Sally!" Rose said sharply.

Sally's champagne glass slipped from her fingers and shattered on the floor, and with a stifled sob she fought her way through the crowd to the front door.

Lucia gasped and Gina blanched, holding on to the back of the wheelchair as if it was a lifeline.

Alex felt only a curious numbness, a feeling of dread that spread throughout her body.

Trailed by Keith, Ty took off after his sister, turning just once to meet Alex's eyes, his expression a mixture of guilt and pain.

A wave of questions spread through the guests. Many of them hadn't heard what Sally had said, and those who had didn't appear to understand. Suzie came to the rescue of the awkward situation, saying brightly, "I think Sally's had a little too much celebrating. She'll be fine in a moment, I'm sure."

"You're right," Grady added smoothly, moving out among the guests. "Let's get back to the party."

The explanation was accepted handily and repeated as everyone went back to the business of enjoying themselves.

Only Alex and Lucia were motionless. Rose patted Alex's arm, telling her Sally had indeed had too much to drink and was confused. But Alex stared at her mother, then stared hard at Gina, who now fluttered about the older woman, casting nervous, anxious looks up the stairs.

Sally's words kept echoing in Alex's head. What did she mean, Alex's father would have Ty thrown out of town *again*? Ty had left of his own accord.

Ty soon reappeared without Sally or Keith. Alex sent him a desperate, questioning look, but he turned away from her eyes, made his way to the bar and ordered a whiskey, neat. He downed it, ordered another and, thus fortified, made it through what little remained of the party. But every time he saw Alex approaching he went in the other direction. How was he going to explain his sister's impulsive, explosive statement?

He'd wanted to strangle Sally when he'd caught up with her in the driveway. But his fury had been matched by the angry words that had tumbled out of her.

"I'm sorry I spoiled your big night, Ty. I know how much you were enjoying playing the big shot."

Ty winced at the sharp edge of truth in Sally's statement. "That doesn't have anything to do with this. I don't want Alex hurt. She loved her father. She doesn't know—"

"Well, maybe it's time she did. She's had it pretty easy..."

"No, she hasn't," Ty ground out through clenched teeth. "You don't know half of what you think you do, Sally."

"Come on, let's go home," Keith urged, taking his wife's arm.

But Sally was not to be deterred. Pointing her finger in Ty's face, she said bitterly, "You're a coward, Ty. You hide behind your nice clothes and your big success, but you've forgotten that you let him drive you away. You're ashamed to admit to her that you let her father get the better of you twelve years ago...."

"But you said yourself there was nothing else I could do!" Ty protested.

"Yeah, well, if that's so, why not tell Alex? You're not worried about her feelings. You're worried about yours. You're afraid you're still not good enough for her."

"Stop, Sally, please," Keith begged. "She's had too much champagne, Ty. She's not thinking clearly. She got too keyed up about the party."

"Yeah, sure, take her home," Ty told him, but in the dimness of the outdoor lights he could see the challenge burning in his sister's eyes.

"Tell her the truth," Sally tossed at him. "Tell her now. You can't start a marriage on a lie." Keith pulled her away down the driveway, leaving Ty to return to a party that had suddenly lost its appeal.

But Ty couldn't avoid Alex's questions forever. The door had barely closed on his mother, who was the last to depart, when Alex demanded, "What did Sally mean?"

"It was nothing." Ty turned and headed back to the sitting room. He poured himself another whiskey and gulped it down in one swallow. He was reaching for the bottle again when Alex's hand stopped him.

"I want you to tell me. Now."

Ty licked his lips nervously and set down the glass. Looking up, he saw Lucia in the doorway.

"I thought we all had agreed the past was behind us," she said, touching the mechanism that sent her chair forward. The excitement and heightened emotions of the evening had taken their toll; she looked worn and haggard.

"I thought I knew everything about the past, Mother." Alex moved to a point midway between Ty and Lucia, looking from one to the other. Neither would quite meet her gaze. "But obviously I was wrong."

"Alexa, let it go—" Lucia began.

"No!" Ty interrupted loudly.

"Tyler, it won't do any good...." Lucia's blue eyes were wide with fear.

"No, it probably won't," he agreed in a low, bitter voice. "But I'm tired of keeping a secret, any secret, from Alex."

Alex stared at him, feeling the ache of fear begin in her stomach. Why, oh, why had Sally started this?

Ty continued speaking, his gray eyes intent on hers. "Your father forced me to leave town twelve years ago."

Instinctively denials sprang to Alex's lips. "That's a lie—"

"No, it isn't," he insisted. "I was at Nick's the night before we were supposed to leave together. Your father sent a messenger with a note for me. He said he was beginning to see things my way. He wanted to meet me at the mill. But he indicated he didn't want you upset, that I shouldn't tell you." Ty laughed sarcastically. "I was stupid. I thought he was sincere, and I went to see just what he had in mind without telling you about it."

"He didn't send you that note," Alex protested in a faint voice.

"Oh, yes, he did. But he didn't meet me. He had a couple of good ol' boys waiting for me instead. They worked me over pretty good and told me to get out of town and leave you alone, or my father would lose his job.''

"My father wouldn't stoop to that!" Alex shouted, trembling with anger. Why was Ty lying like this? Her gentle, peace-loving father would never, never have resorted to such brutality.

"Well, he did, Alex, and I couldn't fight him. My dad was fifty-five years old. He'd never worked anywhere but in that mill. He couldn't start over, and how could I help? If we ran away, I knew it was going to be a helluva struggle just to support you and a baby. What was I supposed to do?" His voice was hoarse with appeal.

Alex put her hand to her throat as if to still the crazy fluttering of her pulse. Her eyes burned with heavy tears of disappointment. It wasn't true. It couldn't be true. Her father had been the only one who had understood about her feelings for Ty. "Why are you lying like this, Ty? What can you possibly have to gain by attacking a dead man? I knew my father. He wouldn't do this. He was good and decent and—"

"He was a conniving bastard!" Ty bit out. He poured himself another shot of whiskey and swallowed it quickly, then looked at Alex with beseeching eyes. "Look, I know how much you loved him. That's why I didn't tell you the truth earlier. I don't enjoy hurting you. But your father was a weak and pitiful man. That's why he resorted to those kinds of tactics to get me out of your life."

"No!" Alex screamed. She groped in her mind, searching frantically for some plausible reason for Ty's wild accusations—and finally arrived at the only possible conclusion. "You're the coward, Ty. You made this story up for your family so you could save face—"

"That's ridiculous!"

"Is it?" Alex choked back her tears. "It all makes perfect sense now. You were so full of yourself then, spouting off about your plans and what you were going to do. A wife and baby didn't fit into those plans too well, did they?"

"Alex, you know that's not true—"

"Yes, it is! You wanted to go chasing your dreams, but you didn't want your family to think you were too scared to accept responsibility for me and the baby. So you lied to them."

Her accusations were wildly illogical, but Ty could see she actually believed them. "Alex, I swear that's not how it happened. I'm telling you the truth about your father."

"No, you're not. You lied all those years ago, and tonight Sally spilled the beans on you and now you're too ashamed to tell the truth. You'd rather blame it on a dead man, someone who can't defend himself."

"If you don't believe me, why don't you ask your mother?" Ty said, nodding coldly toward where Lucia sat, seemingly paralyzed by the drama unfolding before her.

"I don't need to ask her," Alex said hotly. She jerked the diamond ring off her finger. "And I don't need this. I can't marry you, Ty. You're not the person I thought you were." Her chin lifted slightly. "You're not good enough for me."

Her words slapped Ty like a physical blow. She'd never said that to him before, never hinted she might feel that way. "Not good enough?" he echoed, feeling fury sweep through his body. Right now Alex looked every inch the snob his sister had accused her of being. "It always comes back to that, doesn't it?"

Alex said nothing, but her eyes blazed with scorn.

Ty's laugh was short and mirthless. "You Thorpes certainly have an exaggerated opinion of yourselves. Once upon a time, you owned the mill and most of this town. But that power's all gone. I have the mill; I've earned attention and respect. And I got it all without you, Alex, or your family."

"So I was just going to be the icing on your cake, wasn't I?" Alex returned.

"A rather unnecessary adornment, I think now," Ty said coldly. "I'm not some millworker daring to touch the boss's daughter. I don't need you to bestow upon me some mystical feeling of self-worth or to prove anything to anybody." In his anger, Ty neglected to add that he'd never needed her for that.

Alex listened to his angry shouts with a frightening sense of déjà vu. It was just like when Ty had left town twelve years ago. It was just as her mother had said; Ty had been using her to improve his own position here in Grayson. The trappings of success and the acceptance by the town's upper class were really more important to him than she was. He didn't even understand what she meant by saying he wasn't good enough for her.

She couldn't help but try to explain. "It takes more than money to have class, Ty. It takes honor and loyalty—"

"The kind of honor your father had?" Ty said sarcastically. "Oh, yes, Alex, it takes a real gentleman to intimidate a twenty-year-old."

"Get out!" Alex held out her engagement ring. "And take this." She couldn't stand to listen to Ty's lies any longer, to be reminded of how he had used her.

Ty walked to the door, ignoring the proffered ring with deadly calm. "You keep the ring. I certainly don't need it or your ideas about who and what are good enough for you. I should have forgotten you twelve years ago when you didn't answer the note I sent you."

Alex frowned. "Note? What note?"

"Now who's lying?" In the doorway, Ty turned and saluted Alex and Lucia with a rakish gesture. "It hasn't been a pleasure. See you around." And then he was gone.

The front door slammed, rattling the front windows with its force. Grady and Gina came into the room, their eyes wide, questions on their lips. Thank goodness, Alex thought distractedly, Carrie had gone upstairs. Hopefully neither she nor Clarissa had heard any of the bitter argument.

"Did you hear him?" Alex asked in a high, strained voice. "Did you hear the lies he told about Father? Oh, God, how could I ever have thought I loved him? How could I have thought of marrying him? Mother, you were right—"

"No, I was wrong." Lucia's low, even tone snapped Alex out of her rising hysteria.

"What?"

Her mother's blue eyes were focused on a point high above Alex's head. "He was telling you the truth, Alexa. Or at least the truth as he knows it."

"Don't—" Gina choked out, stepping forward to lay a hand on Lucia's shoulder.

The older woman put her own hand over Gina's and patted it soothingly. "No, it's time the truth was known. I should have said this while Tyler was still here, but it all sounded so awful the way he told it, so ugly. I just couldn't think of how to put it...." Her rambling words broke off, and she sighed sadly. "God, I wish Sam were here."

"What are you talking about?" Grady demanded.

"It's about forcing Tyler out of town twelve years ago, son. I did it."

Alex gasped, but it was Gina who spoke. "Please, try to understand."

"What do you have to do with this?" Grady demanded.

Gina gulped, but met his eyes squarely. "It was my idea."

"Yours?" Alex said, feeling as if all the breath had been knocked from her lungs. She sank into a nearby chair.

Lucia nodded, a faraway look on her face. "It was Gina's idea to trick Ty into going to the mill, to have him beaten up and threaten him with his father's job if he didn't leave."

"My God!" Grady exclaimed, groping for the back of the couch for support. He stared at his wife. "You did that? How?"

"Now, don't go blaming Gina completely," Lucia said. "I asked her to help me. I called her and told her everything about Alexa and Ty. I knew I had to do something drastic. I knew Alexa was going to marry him if I didn't. Even her father was beginning to accept it. So Gina helped me plan the whole thing."

"You had someone beat Ty up? How did you even know such people?" Alex asked, her voice sounding faint and far away even to herself.

"I'm not proud of it," Gina exclaimed tearfully. "A thousand times I've wondered what in the world possessed me. I called my cousin in Jackson. I told him a man had been...well...bothering you, Alex. I said we didn't want the police involved because we didn't want it in the papers...."

"And so, like a good southern gentleman, he came up here and helped out," Grady finished for her, shaking his head in amazement. His voice was a sarcastic snarl. "And here I thought chivalry was dead."

"Oh, God, Grady, I wanted to tell so many times. I felt so guilty. What if they had really hurt Ty? I kept seeing him lying dead in some ditch...."

"Shut up, Gina. Just shut up," Alex snapped, closing her eyes against the horror such an image brought to mind.

"It was her cousin who found Ty at the bar and delivered the note he said was from Sam," Lucia continued. "We paid him and each of his two friends two hundred dollars to keep their mouths shut."

"So Father knew nothing about it?" Grady asked.

Lucia shut her eyes and shook her head. "Nothing."

"What about the note Ty said he left for me?" Alex demanded, getting to her feet. "Was that something else you took care of, Mother?"

"No." Lucia looked at her daughter, tears sliding unchecked down her faded cheeks. "I don't know anything about any note. I promise you that."

"Please forgive me," Gina said, sobbing. "Please, Alex, I did an awful thing. I know that. But I'm so, so sorry."

Alex shook off the woman's clutching hands and walked to the bar, pouring herself a drink just as Ty had done. Perhaps the alcohol would give her the distance she needed to accept all she'd learned tonight.

"My God, Gina," Grady said. "Do you think saying you're sorry is going to make it all right? Who gave you or Mother the right to play God with someone else's life?"

"You have to understand," Lucia began in a broken voice. "Everything was falling apart that summer. The mill was sinking further and further. And your father just couldn't get ahold of it. He'd just shake his head and tell me it would work out. We'd sold everything we could. The mill was already mortgaged to the hilt. Everywhere I looked, the things I'd always thought were important were slipping away. And then Alexa, my beautiful, perfect daughter, waltzes in and announces she's pregnant. That she's going to marry a millworker. I thought my world was caving in."

Sobbing openly now, Lucia covered her face with her hand. "And later, when I saw how destroyed you were, I couldn't make it right. I couldn't bring him back. I prayed you'd never find out, Alexa. I thought he'd never tell you, wouldn't want you to know the truth. I should have known we can't run from the past. I've been trying to do that almost all my life. I should have known better."

The words rang true to Alex, and she studied her mother, perhaps seeing her for the first time, understanding her at last.

Lucia Nelson Thorpe's life certainly hadn't turned out as she'd planned. First she'd been a spoiled, pampered debutante. Then she'd married a man of whom her father had disapproved, a man who had belonged more to his books and his dreams than to this world. As she had watched, her family's business had slipped through his fingers. The life she'd known had been crashing around her when she'd come between Alex and Ty. She'd been desperate to save a little piece of her genteel southern pride, finding it impossible to stand by while her daughter married a millworker's son.

Misplaced pride and mistaken prejudices had caused Lucia to make a terrible mistake. In the process she'd shattered several lives. But Alex couldn't find it in her heart to hate her mother, or even to condemn her. Perhaps she'd never quite forgive her, but she couldn't let it stand between them.

So Alex took her mother's hand and said softly, "It's okay, Mother. You made a mistake. I don't think you or Gina should have to suffer for doing what you thought was best. I think Grady and I can both live with that."

"But what about Ty?" Gina burst out.

"Yes," Lucia said quickly. "You have to go after him and tell him the truth."

"Maybe we ought to just leave it." Alex turned away from her family and walked to the windows.

Grady protested. "You're not going to just let him walk away, are you?"

"Yes, I think I will."

"No!" Gina came and stood beside Alex, grasping her forearm urgently. "You have to talk to him. You two can work it out. You said some things in anger, but—"

Alex interrupted her. "This is really for the best, Gina."

What she couldn't say was what she'd learned about Ty tonight. He didn't really love her. He loved all the things she represented: a respected family, a privileged background, a big house on the right side of town. It didn't matter now if Ty thought her father had driven him out of town. It wouldn't matter if Alex apologized for calling him a liar, if she explained what had really happened. For the relationship Alex had thought was based on love was rooted instead in ambition—at least on Ty's part.

After all, Alex thought, Ty couldn't have ever really cared. Even with what he thought were her father's threats, he could have tried to get in touch with her. But he hadn't. He had turned his back on her and their child twelve years ago. And tonight? Well, he seemed to have realized this time that he didn't even need her for acceptance by the town. He'd won that on his own.

There was nothing, absolutely nothing, left between them. Even loving him as she did, Alex could not begin to think of going after him, of trying yet again to make her impossible dream a reality.

Squaring her shoulders, she turned back to her family. "Tonight I realized what everyone tried to tell me all along. Ty and I come from different worlds. We want different things from life."

"Now, Alex," her mother said. "You can't hold the things Tyler said tonight against him. He was upset and hurt—"

"And isn't that when we often really speak our minds?" Alex sighed.

"I think you should—" Lucia continued stubbornly.

"Mother, please don't tell me what I should do," Alex interrupted. "That's what you've always tried to do, but this is my life and my decision. And believe me, I know breaking my engagement is the right thing to do."

"But doesn't Ty deserve to know what really happened—that it wasn't Father who drove him away?" Grady said quietly.

"No." Alex gave a firm shake of her head. "I think what Ty and I both really deserve is to finally, at long last, forget everything that happened and each other. Maybe now we can both get on with our lives." Her tone brooked no argument, but even as Alex said the words she knew she was lying. She would never forget Ty.

Ty brought his car to a stop in front of his mother's house and sat staring at its small, neat lines. He didn't want to go to the lake house. It was full of Alex—her scent, her things,

her love. Love that was now destroyed. Reaching into the
paper bag beside him on the floorboard, he drew out a bottle of beer and unscrewed the top. "Can't even buy something to get decently drunk on in this damn town," he
muttered angrily.

Alex hated him now, hated him just as he'd known she
would. He'd known she wouldn't be able to accept the truth
about her father. Ty only hoped Lucia would tell her it had
really happened. He'd rather Alex went on believing him to
be a coward than that she think him a coward *and* a liar. He
drained the last of the beer and reached for another.

He'd never forget her face when he'd told her. Now that
was something to remember. He could file that shocked and
disbelieving expression in his memory under *X* for exit. And
then, when he was old and alone, he could run through the
entire book of Alex memories. He could start with *L* for the
love he'd seen in her eyes that morning at the ocean when
she'd accepted his ring....

Shaking his head to dispel that particular memory, Ty
watched as his mother came down the front steps from the
porch, her pink party dress a pastel blur in the moonlight.
He rolled down the window and said, "Got any room for an
unengaged bachelor?"

"Oh, Tyler, no!"

"Oh, but yes, Mother. Once again, Miss Alexa Thorpe
and I are *not* to be married."

"You're drunk," Rose said accusingly.

"And proud of it," Ty proclaimed. "Let's go in the
house, and I'll tell you the whole sordid tale."

Rose led the way inside, and Ty sprawled at the kitchen
table while she started a pot of coffee. "What happened?"
she demanded. "Surely this is just a misunderstanding. Was
it because of Sally?"

"My dear sister didn't help matters. You should have
taught her either how to hold her champagne or how to keep
her mouth shut." Ty rubbed at his temples, his shoulders

slumping in defeat. "Actually, Sally only sped things up a bit. This would have happened eventually." He told his mother the entire story.

"And Alex didn't believe you?" Rose exclaimed. "Why would she think you'd lie?"

"Because I'm a low-down piece of worthless millworker scum."

"Ty!"

"Oh, for God's sake, Mother, face it. She never really loved me. It was just like Dad said it was. I was a little bit of excitement, a taste of forbidden fruit. I guess she counts on me to come around every twelve years or so to liven up her life."

Rose interrupted him with a firm shake of her head. "No, I don't believe that. I think she really loves you."

"I think she was fed up with living in this backwater, and I once again represented a little adventure. If she loved me now, she would have believed me tonight. If she'd loved me then, she would have answered my note and come to Atlanta. She didn't even remember the note when I asked her about it tonight."

Rose got up suddenly and went to get the coffeepot. Silently she poured the steaming brew into two mugs and carried them back to the table. She sat down, took a sip, then burst out, "She doesn't know about the note, son."

Ty's head jerked up. "What?"

"Your father never gave it to her."

"But Dad said—"

"He lied." Rose got up, crossed the room and returned with her treasured book of family recipes. She flipped through the pages hurriedly, withdrew an envelope and laid it on the table. There, on the front, in Ty's irregular scrawl, was Alex's name.

Mechanically Ty picked up the envelope and pulled out the folded sheet of paper. He read aloud the words he'd written so long ago:

"Dear Alex,

I know you think I've abandoned you. It isn't true.
Something happened which I can't explain now, and I
had to leave. Please trust me. Meet me in Atlanta at
Peachtree Plaza in two weeks, on Saturday at two. It's
important to my family that you not tell your father
about this note. I love you. We can work this out, I
promise.

Love, Ty."

Ty sat staring at the note for long moments. All these
years he'd thought she'd given up on him, and she'd never
even gotten this message. "Why?" he asked his mother.

"I was against it, Ty. I thought your father was wrong.
But he felt he was doing the right thing. You see, if he'd
really thought Alex loved you and that you would be happy
with her, he'd never have let you leave town. He'd have
marched right back to Sam Thorpe's house and told him
what he could do with his threats and his job."

Rose's eyes were burning with emotion as she continued,
"Sam Thorpe tried to give your father a raise after you left
town. Your father cashed his check and threw the raise in
one-dollar bills back in the man's face. Harris said Sam kept
saying, 'Why are you doing this?' It was the last time the
two of them ever spoke to each other. Alex's father acted
like he didn't understand, but he kept his distance."

"But Dad shouldn't have interfered," Ty shouted,
pounding the table in rage and frustration. "He lied to me.
He told me he'd given Alex that note."

Rose plucked at his arm, trying to explain. "He did it because he thought it was the right thing, Ty. He knew when
Alex didn't show up in Atlanta that you'd think she didn't
care and you'd get on with your life."

"But neither of you let on, even when I called asking what
had happened to the note. How could you do that?"

"I don't know, son. Now it all seems so silly. Your father and I argued about it for weeks, but he held steady, and by the time I'd made up my mind to give Alex the note anyway, she was gone."

"Sally told me you argued. Now I understand why." Ty stared at his mother, feeling a fresh wave of fury sweep over him. "So what happened? Why didn't you go ahead and give it to her?"

"I went to her house. The housekeeper said she was gone, her parents weren't home, and I didn't know what to do. After a while I just let it be."

Ty stood, paced a little distance from the table, placed his hands on his hips and wheeled around. "You had no right, Mama. Neither of you did."

"No, we didn't," she agreed in a small voice. "But we loved you and thought we were doing the right thing." She spread her hands wide. "How could you support a wife and child, especially someone like Alex who was used to the best things in life? Tell me how."

Ty looked down at the floor. "Alex lost the baby."

"I know. I figured she'd lost it or had an abortion when I saw her in town that Christmas."

He jerked his head up. "You never told me that."

"You didn't ask, and anyway, I was glad about it."

"Mama!"

"Don't shout at me, Ty. I was thankful there wasn't an innocent child to suffer from everyone's mistakes. You should be happy about that, too."

Ty's voice was tight with barely suppressed anger. "Oh, I'm happy, Mama. I'm damned ecstatic about the whole damn evening. First the woman I love calls me a liar and a coward and says she doesn't want to marry me—that I'm 'not good enough for her.' Then I find out my mother and father invested a lot of time and energy in lying to me." He swung out of the room, shouting over his shoulder, "I'm so happy about all of this that I think I'll go somewhere and get so drunk I'll forget how happy I am."

Rose trailed him through the house, trying to make him listen. "Ty, don't do this. Go back to Alex. Explain things to her. Or I will. I'll take her the note." She held up the undelivered letter.

Ty swore a violent oath and snatched the envelope out of her hand, ripping it into tiny bits and tossing them aside. "You stay away from Alex, Mother. Don't you tell her a damned thing. We never had a chance in the first place, what with interference from our well-meaning families. From the first time I saw her, right up to Sally's little performance tonight, all of you have done your best to ruin us. Well, you've finally succeeded. We're so far apart tonight it'd take a miracle to get us back together. And there won't be a miracle. We'll stay apart. Everyone will be better off!"

He stormed out of the house to his car, ignoring his mother's tearful pleas. Then, driving as if the demons of hell pursued him, Ty went to the mill.

Taking the beer with him, he strode through the darkened building to his office. There he drank the remaining bottles of beer and sat in the darkness, replaying the evening's events, searching for ways he could have prevented the disaster, but the black silence of the empty mill offered no answers.

At last, filled with the hopelessness of broken dreams, Ty laid his head on his desk and cried, his sobs echoing off the newly painted walls.

Chapter Eleven

The last semblance of summer had disappeared from the mountains surrounding Grayson. The humid heat was gone, replaced by the cool mornings and warm afternoons of late October. Green leaves had turned to the fiery hues of autumn.

Alex loved this time of year, loved the cool rush of air in the gentle twilights and the scent of smoke on the breeze. She enjoyed the loud, boisterous evenings of high-school football and the warm feel of sweaters against her skin. This autumn, for all her sadness, was no different; she loved it just the same.

She rose early in the mornings now, in the small apartment she was sharing with Janie Kilgore, a fellow teacher. Janie taught physical education, and she'd convinced Alex a swift walk was the cure for most any malady. Alex welcomed her early-morning hikes, but she wasn't sure they were doing anything for her broken heart.

After the revelations of the night of the engagement party, it had been impossible to remain in the house. Lucia, anxious not to sever the fragile bond remaining between them, hadn't argued with Alex's decision to move out.

So far, the arrangement had worked well. Janie was the ideal roommate—so immersed in her own activities that she spared little thought to Alex's long evenings alone. If Alex sometimes cried long into the night and rose with red-rimmed eyes, there was no one to ask why.

She visited her family often. Carrie had been told everything, even the ancient history of Alex's pregnancy, Ty's departure and the miscarriage and misunderstandings. The teenager, who loved Ty and believed in happy endings, had urged her aunt to go to him and explain. Alex had declined.

She'd seen Ty. In a town the size of Grayson, that was probably unavoidable. They'd passed each other on the street, caught a glimpse of each other across a crowded mall corridor. She turned her head; he walked away.

Alex didn't want to see him. She wanted him to finish his business at the mill, appoint a manager and move back to Atlanta. She wanted him to find happiness, but perversely she hoped no one else would share that sinfully sexy tub with him or help him bring life to his sterile, barren condominium.

After the hoopla of the party, it had been difficult to spread the news of their breakup. Grady had taken the ring to Ty's mother with a message asking her to make sure he got it. Alex's brother said Rose had cried, sat right down in the rocker on her front porch and sobbed. She'd mumbled something about it all being her fault. Alex had felt new sorrow upon hearing of Rose's tears, remembering the nice times they'd shared, the talk of future grandchildren, the plans for family holidays. But then, what was one more sorrow? It seemed that was all she had—now.

Alex worried most about her brother and Gina. Their relationship was another reason she had moved out. Gina's part in Lucia's treachery had not been taken lightly by her husband. After that night there had been storms between Grady and his wife. Even now, Grady was often tense and out of sorts. Gina had lost weight. They needed time and space. They certainly didn't need Alex's constant presence to remind them of their problems.

She was thinking of her brother and sister-in-law as she walked briskly through the town park on this early Sunday morning. It was just seven o'clock, and there wasn't a soul in sight. Alex had risen at six, thinking if she got up early enough she'd be able to sleep at night. The day lay ahead of her, devoid of plans to fill it. Deciding suddenly to surprise her family by having breakfast with them, she quickened her pace and headed for her car.

Her family had gathered as usual in the kitchen, and Grady was scrambling eggs and frying bacon. He blew his sister a kiss when she walked in the back door.

"Alexa!" her mother said with pleasure. "What a wonderful surprise."

"Yes, it is," Gina added. "I hope you'll go to church with us."

"In these?" Alex pointed to her faded gray jogging clothes. "Reverend Mitchel would faint."

"You could go home and change," Carrie said, placing glasses of juice on the table."

"I'm too lazy." Alex looked her niece over from head to toe, noting the crisp navy plaid dress. "You certainly look nice today. Some kind of special occasion?"

"Nope. But supposedly Paul Dixon is coming to our church."

"Paul Dixon?" Alex echoed. "What about Billy? I saw you two together at school on Friday."

"I broke up with him last night."

"Kind of sudden, isn't it?"

"Not really," the teenager returned airily. "We were really kind of tired of each other." Carrie took her seat and spooned eggs and bacon out of the platter her father placed on the table.

"But you said Billy was the miracle of your life," Alex pressed, filling her own plate with food.

"He was. Now it's over. I'm counting on Paul asking me to the homecoming dance. Mom, will you pass the toast, please?" Apparently unaffected by her shifting romantic interests, Carrie began to eat.

"Oh," Alex said, amazed as always by the resilience of youth.

Grady, Gina and Carrie left for church soon after breakfast, and Alex stayed to straighten the kitchen while her mother looked over the Sunday paper. The silence between them was companionable. When she'd finished the dishes, Alex poured them both another cup of coffee and sat down to share the paper.

"You look tired," Lucia ventured.

"I got up early and went for a walk."

"You walk a lot."

"I'm trying to get in shape."

"Oh." Lucia turned another newspaper page. "How is Janie?" She seemed to like Alex's pert, active roommate.

"She's fine. She went into Chattanooga to visit her folks this weekend."

"Did you do anything special yesterday?"

"No. I read a book."

Lucia hesitated only slightly. "Are you all right, Alexa?"

Taking a sip of her coffee, Alex considered the question for a moment. "Am I all right as opposed to before Ty came back, or am I all right as opposed to when we were together? Which one? There's a difference, you know."

Perhaps Lucia hadn't expected her daughter's candor, for she drew away as if stung. In a small voice, she said, "I didn't mean to pry. I'm just concerned."

Instantly contrite, Alex patted her arm. "I know, Mother. I'm sorry, too. I didn't mean to snap at you."

"Perhaps now you should talk to him."

"No."

"Maybe I could."

"No!" Alex leaned back in her chair with a weary sigh. "Please, just let it alone, Mother."

"All right, all right." Lucia returned to her newspaper, but several times during the morning Alex looked up to find her mother's blue eyes studying her thoughtfully.

She left when the others returned from church, declining their invitation to lunch to return to her empty apartment.

Weekends were hardest. The rest of the time Alex was so busy with school and preparing for classes that, except for late at night, she had little time to dwell on her unhappiness. She'd volunteered as sponsor for several school clubs, filling her evenings and most Saturdays. Sundays were always empty.

Drawing some papers from a manila envelope, Alex leafed through the application to her old school system in Florida. Surely there'd be no problem in getting a job back there. It was an idea she'd been toying with for a couple of weeks. She'd written for the application soon after her engagement had ended, eager to put distance between her and Ty. Of course, she couldn't leave until the end of the school year, but she'd wanted to make plans, to take the first step quickly.

Now she wasn't so sure. She'd miss the changing of the seasons if she moved back to Florida. And here she'd be assistant department head after old Miss MacGruder retired next year. In Florida she'd be starting over.

Still, the thought of being near the ocean was tempting. Unbidden, pictures of her and Ty romping in the surf sprang to her mind, and for a moment Alex gave in to the memories. Ty had chased her in the sun-warmed sand, following her into the waves, holding her tight against his strength as the water cascaded over them, kissing her with lips that tasted of salt and desire....

"Stop it!" she said aloud, getting abruptly to her feet. It was so easy to remember, so hard to forget. Alex knew she could go to Florida, go to the ends of the earth, and she'd carry these memories with her. They'd spring to her mind when she least expected it; they'd torture her sleep and color her reactions for years to come.

Looking around the empty apartment, Alex sought some relief, a balm for her shattered dreams. As usual, there was only silence. She wondered bleakly if that was all there'd ever be. How many Sunday afternoons would she spend with the silence, counting the minutes until Monday when she could lose herself again in her work? The prospect was grim, but as Alex sat again at the small table, she really could see no alternative.

Ty shuffled the same stack of papers for the third time in as many minutes, then pushed them aside, sighing. He couldn't concentrate. He didn't know if it was the bright, beckoning autumn sunshine outside or the problems spread across his desk, but he didn't want to be in this office.

The mill was going well. There'd been a few bugs in a couple of pieces of machinery, but those had been quickly solved. They were turning out beautiful commercial carpeting, filling orders as quickly as the sales team could write them. Of course, Linda and her crew had only been peddling the designs and samples for two months, but it was a sure bet this new commercial venture wasn't going the way of their earlier attempt. Success seemed assured.

Ty had worked hard these last six weeks. There'd been little else to do. He hadn't realized how completely Alex had filled his life until she was gone. At first the days had stretched blankly ahead. His long summer vacation had put him out of touch with the extended workdays he'd always undertaken. Getting back into the rhythm had been difficult, but he'd done it.

But still there were days like today—days when all he could think of were the hours he'd had with Alex. During these periods he'd imagine he smelled her sweet perfume or heard her voice. He'd actually gone to the door of his office and looked for her, and awakened in the middle of the night, thinking she was near.

She never was.

The few times they'd seen each other in town had been painful. Ty wanted desperately to leave Grayson, to go back to his life before their reunion. He couldn't, however; he and Chuck had made an agreement about getting the mill operational. It would be the first of the year or later before he could even think of spending most of the week in Atlanta or on the road instead of here.

Sighing, he turned back to the report on his desk. Sales were up three percent across the board. It was a healthy sign; the company was growing. When all else fails, Ty told himself, I'll have this company. Maybe Sally's kids will be interested in carrying on the tradition. Now that's a reason to stay in town, he thought.

When Ty was being honest with himself, he admitted he didn't really want to leave Grayson again. He'd grown accustomed to being closer to his family, had finally gotten used to the slower pace.

He'd made peace with his mother over her deceptions. She'd been so sorry, as was Sally. He'd dismissed their apologies and had even thanked his sister for forcing the issue with Alex. It had all been a delusion, he thought now, a grand delusion. What he and Alex had shared as teenagers had been broken beyond repair. He had been foolish to think the delicate pieces could ever be mended.

"Mr. Duncan?" His secretary's voice came over the office intercom.

"Yes?"

"Mrs. Thorpe is here to see you."

Ty's heart jumped with hope. "*Mrs.* Thorpe?"

"Mrs. Lucia Thorpe," the girl explained.

Alex's mother was here. What does she want? Ty thought. Surely it was too late for her to be trying to rub salt on the wound. "Send her in," he said.

The door opened, and Lucia's wheelchair glided inside. As always, she looked lovely, her white hair brushed into soft curls, her soft purple suit immaculately pressed. Those strikingly blue eyes were calm and clear.

Ty stood behind his desk. "This is a surprise, Mrs. Thorpe."

"Yes, I suppose it is." The door shut behind her.

Circling the desk, Ty pulled one of the armchairs out of her way and helped maneuver her chair into position in front of the big desk.

"You've certainly changed the looks of this room," she commented, looking around with interest. "I like it."

Ty raised his eyebrows and took his seat. As he'd promised, there was little in the office to remind him of Alex's father. The walls were a pale blue, the furniture sleekly modern, the carpet a geometric design of blues and grays. The contemporary room bore little resemblance to the antique-filled office of its last occupant.

"I also like the way you've got the place moving," she added, gesturing toward the outer office. "It reminds me of when my father ran the mill. Business was always booming. Men were running here and there. Clerks were typing. Orders were being filled. I used to love to come up here and visit him." Lucia chuckled. "My mother said it wasn't ladylike."

"Perhaps you should have been the one who ran the mill, not your husband," Ty ventured boldly, watching the pleasure these memories brought to her face.

"That's what my granddaughter says," Lucia returned. "I'm glad she'll be able to make choices like that. It was almost unheard-of when I was young."

The room was quiet for a moment, filled only with the muted sound of Ty's secretary's typewriter and the rumble of a truck pulling into the parking lot.

"I guess you're wondering what I'm doing here." Lucia touched the pearls at her throat with a hand that shook ever so slightly, betraying the only sign of nervousness Ty had ever seen in her.

"The thought had crossed my mind, yes."

"It's about Alexa."

He shifted in his seat. "Yes?"

"I think the two of you need to talk."

"I'm afraid that's not going to happen, Mrs. Thorpe."

"But you don't understand. Alexa knows the truth now."

"Of course she does. I told her the truth. She simply chose not to believe me." Ty couldn't help the note of anger that crept into his voice.

"No. *I* told her the truth," Lucia said. "Now I want to tell you." Slowly, deliberately, she recounted the fantastic tale of her and Gina's deception.

Ty greeted the story with a swift intake of breath and a curious loosening in his chest. Strange how knowing the whole truth eased the burden of bitterness inside him.

"So it was you, not Mr. Thorpe, who sent those three men up here to meet me."

"Yes." Her bright blue gaze faltered a bit under his. "You and Alexa have every reason to hate me. But I'm sorry, Tyler. I was wrong."

Ty got up, crossed to the window and stood, hands in pockets, staring sightlessly at the distant mountains. There were so many misunderstandings, so many deceptions, big and small. He and Alex hadn't stood a chance.

"I wanted you to know this, Tyler," Lucia said softly. "I hoped it would make a difference in how you felt. Alexa has some stupid notion that your relationship would never work anyway."

"I know how she feels," Ty muttered.

"I think you're both wrong."

"Do you?" Ty turned from the window. "Has it ever occurred to you that what you think isn't really worth a tinker's damn?"

Lucia seemed a bit taken aback, but her chin lifted and she forged ahead. "Maybe I have interfered too much. I know I'm to blame for this whole mess. That's why I'm here. I just want you and Alex to talk."

"Why didn't you go to her?"

"She won't listen."

"Smart girl!"

"Oh, damn you!" Lucia cried out, then covered her mouth with her hand, as if astounded at having spoken those words. Ty grinned slightly. One thing for sure, the old lady was still full of fight. "You children have always been the most obstinate, hardheaded couple of know-it-alls ever born," she added.

"No, I'd say that distinction belongs to our parents," Ty replied. "You see, you weren't the only person out to thwart the course of young love." He proceeded to tell Lucia about the fatefully undelivered note.

"Then I don't understand the problem!" Lucia exclaimed. "Go to Alex. Tell her. I know you can work it out."

Studying the older woman's determined face, Ty felt his first stirrings of hope since the night he'd stormed out after the party. "Do you think she'll talk to me?" he asked doubtfully.

"Good heavens, make her! I'm tired of seeing her mope around. She moved out of the house. I don't think she eats decently. You've got to do something!"

The tempo of his heart increasing dramatically, Ty stared at Alex's mother. "What should I do?"

Lucia snorted in disgust. "Do you love Alexa?"

"You know I do," he answered fiercely.

"Then follow your heart," Lucia told him, her face softening. "I followed mine, you know—to Sam. And even though it wasn't always perfect and the road was sometimes rocky, I never regretted my choice." Her voice broke, and she whispered, "Just follow your heart, Tyler. It knows exactly what you should do."

"I'm going to find her right now," he decided abruptly, striding toward the door. He turned back to Lucia, grasped one thin, frail hand and leaned down to kiss her cheek. "Thank you."

Momentarily startled, Lucia glanced sharply up at him before regaining her poise. "I'd like to stay here for a few minutes if that's okay, Tyler."

"Certainly," he said, backing toward the door.

"It sort of feels like I'm home, you know," she murmured, smiling brightly as he left the room

Grayson's high school hadn't changed much in the fourteen years since Ty had left it. The halls were still painted light green, the floors covered in the checkerboard tile that was buffed to a high gloss on Monday mornings and revealed every impatient scuff mark by Friday afternoon.

He followed his memory to the second floor, through the swinging door marked English Department and down the wide foyer. Peering through the strips of glass in the closed doors, he searched frantically for Alex, finding her at last in the fourth room on the right. The door was open.

Her back was to the class as she wrote something on the board. Standing there in front of those young people, she looked different somehow, like a teacher. Ty grinned at his foolishness. She *was* a teacher. Moving as silently as possible, Ty entered the room. Students swiveled around, but he silenced them by holding a finger to his lips and slipped into an empty desk.

While Alex finished writing on the board, she talked. "The play we're going to read next is one I'm sure you're all familiar with: *Romeo and Juliet*. It's quite possibly Shakespeare's best-known play, about two young lovers who are kept apart by their families—the Capulets and the Montagues."

"It's quite a tragic story, isn't it, Miss Thorpe?" Ty asked.

Alex jerked around at the sound of his voice, her startled brown eyes locking with his gray ones. What was Ty doing here, disrupting her class? She glanced nervously at the students, whose speculative gazes went quickly from her to him.

"Isn't it tragic?" Ty pressed, unfolding himself from the desk and strolling casually toward her.

"Why...yes...it is," she stammered. The shock of seeing him nearly robbed her of speech.

"Romeo and Juliet were the victims of their families' hatred for each other, their parents' prejudices. I wonder if anyone has ever explored what might have happened to them if their families had simply let them alone?"

Alex swallowed. "I don't think that's relevant. Shakespeare wrote the play. It stands on its own."

Ty turned to face the students. "But can't we explore the possibilities?" He selected a young man in the back of the class whose slightly bored, knowing expression reminded him of himself at the same age. "What about you? Wouldn't you like to know what would have happened to Romeo and Juliet if their parents had stayed out of the way?"

"Yeah, parents are always messing somethin' up." The boy sat up a little straighter, seemingly as intrigued by the strange turn of events in the classroom as by the question Ty posed. Alex stood behind her desk, mesmerized by the scene.

"Well, I have my own theory about what would have happened." Ty turned to Alex, his eyes bright with an emotion she couldn't read. "I think Shakespeare made a big mistake killing them off at the end. It would have been much more interesting to follow their lives and watch them get married, have kids, struggle to pay the rent."

A trickle of laughter fanned out across the room, but Ty's eyes never strayed from hers. "Oh, it would have been a struggle. I bet Romeo would have come home late from the salt mines or wherever he found a job, and Juliet would have nagged him, and the baby would have cried, and the plumbing would have broken down and their chariot would have had a flat tire—"

"I don't think they had chariots," a girl in the front row said suddenly, then blushed when Ty turned his brilliant smile on her.

"Maybe not," he agreed. "But my point is, Romeo and Juliet would have had problems and they would have solved them. Because they loved each other." He stepped closer to Alex, and she wondered if the students could hear the loud, erratic pounding of her heart. What was Ty trying to tell her?

"It takes more than love," someone said from the back row.

"Yeah," Ty answered softly, not bothering this time to take his eyes from Alex's. "It takes trust and hope and plain old hard work. But it's the love that makes all those other things possible. If Romeo and Juliet's families had just stayed out of the way, I think they would have lived to be a very old married couple. And I think *that* would have been a great love story."

"Ty, what are you saying?" Alex whispered, forgetting the twenty-five young pupils watching from their desks. All she saw was the intensity in his gray eyes. All she wanted to know was if, as she suspected, he was trying to ask for another chance.

"I'm saying let's forget our families and their annoying habit of interfering and let's get on with our lives, Alex. Together." Closing the distance between them with one last step, Ty caught her lips under his, kissing her soundly while the third-period freshman-literature class cheered.

"Ty!" Alex pulled away, protesting, as her face flamed red. Scribbling a hasty note, she handed it to a student in the front row and announced, "I want you all to go very quietly to the library. Give this note to Mrs. Harris."

Amid protests, grumblings and amused glances, the class finally filed out. Ty barely waited until the last student was out the door before he sat down in Alex's desk chair, pulling her into his lap and kissing her again. He drew away at last and whispered, "I meant what I said. I think we can make it if they'll just let us alone."

"Oh, Ty." Brushing her fingers across his cheek, Alex said, "I was so wrong. It was Mother who—"

"I know," he interrupted gently.

"How?"

He told her of Lucia's unexpected visit and of his own parents' deception about the note.

"So that's what happened to it," Alex murmured. "I didn't know what you were talking about that night, and Mother denied knowing about it, either. I suspected she'd done something with it, though. God, Ty, it's been such a terrible, stupid mess. I thought the only reason you really wanted me was to show everyone in town that Ty Duncan could get a rich girl. I thought that twelve years ago, I thought that this year."

"The only reason I want you is that I love you. I've always loved you." The look in Ty's gray eyes left Alex no room for doubt.

"I didn't think this could happen," she said breathlessly.

"Believe it. Believe in me." From his pocket Ty withdrew her diamond engagement ring and slipped it on her finger. "We're getting married as soon as possible. Today, tomorrow or this weekend. Do you still have your dress?"

"Oh, yes," Alex murmured, staring down at the glittering circle of diamonds on her hand. For the first time in weeks, her finger didn't feel bare.

"Then we're not wasting any more time. We're not going to give anyone the chance to ruin it again."

"Absolutely," she promised, offering her lips to him yet again.

The loud clearing of a throat tore them apart. Miss MacGruder, the straitlaced wearer of orthopedic sandals who had terrorized Ty's tenure in English, stood in the doorway. Her bristling eyebrows were drawn together in a disapproving glare. "Miss Thorpe, what in the world is going on?"

"Miss MacGruder!" Ty called cheerfully, holding Alex firmly on his lap. "It's me, Tyler Duncan. Remember?"

The woman's face blanched. "Tyler Duncan! What are you doing here? Still disrupting English classes, I see!"

"Actually, I was asking this beautiful lady to marry me."

"Oh."

Alex thought she saw the ghost of a smile soften the woman's stern, uncompromising mouth, so she started to explain, "Miss MacGruder, there are extenuating circumstances—"

"Miss Thorpe!" the woman barked.

"Yes, ma'am?"

"I would suggest that you and Mr. Duncan get this matter resolved quickly. The bell will be ringing for fourth period in exactly fifteen minutes, and if I recall correctly, Mr. Duncan has been known to disrupt entire days. Please see to it that that doesn't happen today."

"Yes, ma'am!"

"Fine then, get on with your business."

Ty gave the woman an impudent wink before the door closed behind her ample backside.

Alex and Ty smiled deep into each other's eyes. "Do you think you could get the rest of the day off?" he asked.

"I don't think her understanding will stretch quite that far."

"Then I'd better make the most of these fifteen minutes."

"Right, because when the bell rings this Cinderella turns back into a teacher." Alex's giggle was smothered beneath his eager, questing lips. They kissed and made promises, oblivious of the smell of chalk dust, the creaking of the old wooden chair and the plump, grinning woman who stood guard at the door.

* * * * *

COMING NEXT MONTH

Silhouette Classics

**The best books from the past by
your favorite authors.**

The first two stories of a delightful collection...

#1 DREAMS OF EVENING by Kristin James

As a teenager, Erica had given Tonio Cruz all her love, body and soul, but he betrayed and left her anyway. Ten years later, he was back in her life, and she quickly discovered that she still wanted him. But the situation had changed—now she had a son. A son who was very much like his father, Tonio, the man she didn't know whether to hate—or love.

#2 INTIMATE STRANGERS by Brooke Hastings

Rachel Grant had worked hard to put the past behind her, but Jason Wilder's novel about her shattered her veneer of confidence. When they met, he turned her life upside down again. Rachel was shocked to discover that Jason wasn't the unfeeling man she had imagined. Haunted by the past, she was afraid to trust him, but he was determined to write a new story about her—one that had to do with passion and tenderness and love.

Take 4 Silhouette Desire novels
and a surprise gift

Then preview 6 brand-new Silhouette Desire novels—delivered to your door as soon as they come off the presses! If you decide to keep them, you pay just $2.24 each*—a 10% saving off the retail price, *with no additional charges for postage and handling!*

Silhouette Desire novels are not for everyone. They are written especially for the woman who wants a more satisfying, more deeply involving reading experience. Silhouette Desire novels take you beyond the others.

Start with 4 Silhouette Desire novels and a surprise gift absolutely FREE. They're yours to keep without obligation. You can always return a shipment and cancel at any time.

Simply fill out and return the coupon today!

* Plus 69¢ postage and handling per shipment in Canada.

ATTRACTIVE, SPACE SAVING BOOK RACK

Display your most prized novels on this handsome and sturdy book rack. The hand-rubbed walnut finish will blend into your library decor with quiet elegance, providing a practical organizer for your favorite hard-or soft-covered books.

Only $9.95

Approximately 16" x 8" when assembled

Assembles in seconds!

To order, rush your name, address and zip code, along with a check or money order for $10.70* ($9.95 plus 75¢ postage and handling) payable to *Silhouette Books*.

Silhouette Books
Book Rack Offer
901 Fuhrmann Blvd.
P.O. Box 1396
Buffalo, NY 14269-1396

Offer not available in Canada.

BKR-2A

*New York and Iowa residents add appropriate sales tax.

Silhouette Special Edition

COMING NEXT MONTH

#421 NO ROOM FOR DOUBT—Tracy Sinclair
No job too small or too difficult, Stacey Marlowe's ad boasted. But then she hadn't considered the demands her first customer would make. Shady Sean Garrison wanted—of all things!—her trust.

#422 INTREPID HEART—Anne Lacey
Trent Davidson would forever be a hero to Vanessa Hamilton. After all, he'd twice saved her life. But how could Trent settle for Vanessa's childlike adoration when he needed her womanly love?

#423 HIGH BID—Carole Halston
Katie Gamble was thrilled when fellow building contractor Louis McIntyre reentered her life. But Louis's gentle deception—and uneasy memories of a night long ago—threatened their bid for a future together.

#424 LOVE LYRICS—Mary Curtis
Ambitious lyricist Ashley Grainger lived and breathed Broadway, while her former fiancé, conservative lawyer Zachary Jordan, was Boston born and bred. Despite their renewed duet of passion, could they possibly find a lasting harmony?

#425 SAFE HARBOR—Sherryl Woods
When sexy neighbor Drew Landry filed a complaint about Tina Harrington's unorthodox household, they battled it out in the boardroom . . . and the bedroom . . . even as they longed for sweet compromise.

#426 LAST CHANCE CAFE—Curtiss Ann Matlock
Rancher Wade Wolcott wanted no part of Ellie McGrew's struggle to build a new life for her daughters. But the lovely, unassuming widow bought the farm next door, waited tables in his diner—and somehow crept into his heart.

AVAILABLE THIS MONTH: